Joel Fox

Lincoln's Hand

To Aunt Mary –
Thank you for your love
and support and many
years of wonderful memories

Joel Fox

Echelon Press
Publishing

LINCOLN'S HAND
An Echelon Press Book

First Echelon Press paperback printing August 2010

Cover Art © Nathalie Moore
Award winning Graphic Artist

Echelon Press
9055 G Thamesmeade Road
Laurel, MD 20723
www.echelonpress.com

ISBN: 978-1-59080-674-6
1-59080-674-3
eBook: 1-59080-675-1

PRINTED IN THE UNITED STATES OF AMERICA

10 9 8 7 6 5 4 3 2 1

For Cydney.

Finally!

Thank you for all your support, encouragement and for
never giving up on me.

Prologue

November 7, 1876

The screech of a heavy object pulled against marble penetrated the wall. Percy English knew what that meant– the wooden coffin was being freed from its marble sarcophagus. These ghouls were stealing his body!

Where the devil was Tyrrell? English had heard the faint but distinct cutting of a saw through metal removing the lock on the outer door of the catacomb. He held his post on the backside of the brick wall at the rear of the catacomb as some instrument–an axe, perhaps, or a mallet–pounded against the sarcophagus.

Now they were into the sarcophagus, moving the coffin. English put an ear against the bricks and squeezed his eyes closed, as if that action allowed him to hear better. Still no Tyrrell, nor his men. English had to report. Bootless to prevent unnecessary noise, he pushed away from the brick wall and picked his way through the labyrinth created by the tomb's foundation. He followed the lamps the tomb's custodian had placed earlier to allow him to maneuver in what would otherwise be a pitch-black corridor.

English found Tyrrell in the dark outer chamber. He was peeking past the white cloth screen he had put over the glass window of the chamber door to hide his officers. Tyrrell had recruited a couple of Pinkerton detectives for the mission along with an Illinois detective, a former federal agent, and John Power, the tomb's custodian. All stood in the chamber with Tyrrell.

English approached Tyrrell and whispered, "The time is now, Captain. They're moving the coffin."

Tyrrell maintained his position, looking out to the cemetery beyond the tomb. English could see the full moon bathing the landscape in a milky light.

"We need the all clear from Swegles," Tyrrell said softly.

English knew there was an informant working with the grave robbers. However, he did not know all the details of the raid. He was not a government agent like Tyrrell; he was a reporter known to one of the men on the team and recruited to help thwart the abomination revealed by the undercover man.

"You must spring the trap," English said, the pitch of his voice forced high by excitement and tension. "They'll get away."

One of the Pinkerton detectives said, "The gentleman may be right, Captain."

Tyrrell set his jaw tightly. He knew the danger of acting at the wrong time. He wanted to catch the criminals in the act, but could not let them proceed too far with their awful scheme. Where the hell was Swegles?

Suddenly, a brilliant lantern light came through the window and brightened the white cloth. Tyrrell moved back against the wall where he could still peer outside. English fell in behind him. Was one of the grave robbers on guard?

The man outside holding the lantern placed it on the ground, fired up a match, and lit a cigar.

Tyrrell relaxed. He moved toward the window and listened.

The man with the cigar said, "Wash."

Tyrrell stepped back and opened the door. English understood the password had been accepted. Outside the door the man crushed the lit cigar under his foot.

"Swegles, where–" Tyrrell said.

"They had me holding the lamp inside the catacomb," Swegles muttered. "I couldn't come. They got the coffin pulled partway out the sarcophagus now, so they sent me after the team and wagon."

Tyrell nodded. "All right then. Go get the wagon. By the time you get back we'll use it to haul away our prisoners."

Swegles walked away from the tomb. Tyrrell turned to his officers and motioned them to follow him. Before exiting the chamber Tyrrell reached into his coat pocket and pulled out a revolver. English had no weapon, but he needed to see the game played out. He followed behind the posse, noting that, like him, they had all removed their boots to maintain quiet.

The company of men slipped out of the chamber into the cool night air. The moonlight cast a shadow of the tomb's obelisk across their path. They followed Tyrrell around the stone foundation, headed for the catacomb entrance at the opposite end of the monument, and the unwary grave robbers.

Tyrrell reached the open doorway and pushed his back against the stone wall, his gun at the ready.

"You. Inside there. Surrender."

No response from inside the catacomb.

"This is Captain P. D. Tyrrell of the United States Secret Service. Come out. You can't escape."

No one responded. No sound emanated from inside the tomb.

Tyrrell lit a match and edged around the doorframe. In a moment his body relaxed. The room was empty. The flickering match passed enough light to see the sarcophagus lid was leaning against the rear brick wall and the marble front plate of the sarcophagus had been dislodged. The coffin was there, jutting out from the front end of the sarcophagus where the nameplate had been.

Tyrrell flicked out the match, which had burned down

toward his fingers. "McGinn, Hay," he called out to the Pinkerton detectives. "Check the bluff and see if you find them. Power, get those lanterns from inside the foundation, and put some light on this place. I'm going back for my boots."

The party scattered in different directions. Tyrrell found his boots and pulled them on. He stepped back outside the monument and waited for Power to retrieve the lamps from the labyrinth.

Something moved on the terrace of the monument. Tyrrell spotted two shadowy figures. He had them. He raised his revolver and squeezed off a shot.

Crack!

From the terrace a gun flashed and a return bullet flew by Tyrrell's head. Tyrrell ducked and ran for cover, but not before he sent another shot at the terrace.

"There, up on the terrace, boys," Tyrrell yelled as another bullet flew at him. "Surround them."

From the terrace of the monument a voice called out, "Is that you shooting us, Tyrrell?"

The Secret Service man recognized the voice: McGinn, the Pinkerton man.

Tyrrell stood up. McGinn and Hay held up their hands and came into the moonlight on the terrace.

"We thought we'd see better from up here," McGinn said. "Can't find them nowheres."

Tyrrell cursed. The conspirators had fled. Had they succeeded? He could imagine the awful deed. This was more than grave robbing. These men were defiling America.

Power emerged from the tomb holding two lanterns.

"Bring those lights," Tyrrell said, waving Power forward. With a tremble in his voice he went on: "We must see if they got what they came for. God forbid."

Chapter 1

Rigby and his men ran from the rooftop. Inside the building and down a flight of stairs the five FBI agents scrambled as if responding to a fire bell. If only there had been a fire pole in the three-story old city library building for them to use. The tip was good. They had been watching, and there he was. Just as described. In a red windbreaker and khaki pants with a blue Boston Red Sox cap pulled low over his eyes. Most ominously, an orange backpack slung over one shoulder.

They had him. The Monument Bomber.

At the bottom of the stairs they ran through a doorway into the museum entrance area. The old library was a museum dedicated to the battle that occurred here so long ago. Rigby noticed the displays and open gift area to his right as they sprinted across the entrance, past the elevator to the street stairs. Rigby saw the agent next to him had pulled his gun. There would be plenty of guns. Rigby left his holstered. Running with the gun was awkward. He needed every advantage to keep up with these younger agents.

Out the building and across the street they charged, up the steps and onto the monument grounds. No need for surprise. The Bomber was inside the exhibit lodge that served as an entrance to the monument. He wouldn't see them coming. They had him now.

This was hallowed ground. American blood had been spilled here in the name of freedom. The Battle of Bunker Hill had actually been an American defeat, but showed the Americans could take on the best army in the world. Rigby knew there would be another battle on this spot today against a foreign attacker and this time the Americans would win.

The FBI agents sprinted past the one statue on the hill dedicated to William Prescott, the American commander.

"Don't shoot till you see the whites of his eyes," Rigby blurted to his men between breaths. Prescott said something like that to his troops so they would hold their fire until the last moment. Rigby didn't want to miss this chance to take down the Bomber.

They moved past the base of the obelisk enclosed inside a wrought iron fence and stopped their run at the door of the stone building exhibit lodge. Deep breaths all around, even from the younger agents. Only maybe not as deep as his, Rigby guessed. He felt the sweat dampen his back and neck.

Rigby surveyed Monument Square. The green grass on top of the hill where the Americans fought off charge after charge of British soldiers in the first major battle of the American Revolution was the only area left that remotely looked like a battlefield. Even that was a stretch. If it were not for the 221-foot obelisk sitting in the center of the hill, the square would look like any number of city square parks.

The square was quiet this workday. Labor Day had come and gone and with it the summer tourist season.

Rigby steadied himself and pulled his gun from the shoulder holster underneath his jacket.

He nodded to the agent with a hand on the door handle. The agent opened the door and Rigby charged in, followed by his team.

The man in the red windbreaker was nowhere to be seen.

At the side door of the building leading to the monument, the tall FBI agent dressed as a park ranger stood with a walkie-talkie in hand looking out at the monument. When the agent saw Rigby he indicated with a jerk of his head the suspect had gone into the monument.

Rigby quickly stepped over to the tall agent. "You're supposed to keep him here!"

The agent's face reflected resignation. "I tried. Asked him questions... 'Where you from?' He ignored me. Went right for the monument. You didn't want me to use force to hold him, did you?"

I didn't want him inside the damn monument with a bomb, Rigby thought. No need for an outburst now. Straightening out this young agent could come later. Now they had to get the Bomber before he set off the explosive device.

Rigby led the way. They walked quickly, did not run. They tried to keep the noise to a minimum. Across the short open space from the entrance building to the monument Rigby led his team. He hesitated a moment at the doorway to the obelisk. Cautiously, he peeked inside. An ancient monument, the first to commemorate the battle, was on display in the base of the obelisk. It was almost twenty feet tall with an urn on the top. No Bomber.

Rigby walked deliberately inside the monument. Not many places to hide. The stairway spiraled toward the top. An opening in the middle of the obelisk was secured by padlocked iron bars both down here and at the top of the monument. Rigby signaled to one of his agents to make sure the padlocks were still in place, and then he began the climb.

One step, then two at a time, then one again. Rigby used to be a runner, then a jogger, now a walker. He did his exercise walks hard; he felt he was in pretty good shape, but he was over fifty now. Attacking such a steep climb would have him sucking air at the end. He didn't move slowly because of his concern for physical difficulties. He did not want to cause a stir and alert the Bomber.

Rigby felt time was on his side. The Bomber would set his explosion then run for cover. This man was not a suicide

11

bomber, and there was only one way down. Into the waiting arms of the FBI. Rigby wanted to grab the bomber before he could set the timer.

Rigby's men lined up behind him, moving at his pace. The number 25 was stenciled on one of the steps. Rigby knew there were 294 steps to the small viewing area at the top.

Up they went. Rigby kept his back to the outer wall, his eyes fixed to the curve of the stairs above him, his right hand gripping the gun and keeping the barrel pointed up the stairs.

He passed a small covered opening in the wall. It was too generous to call it a window. To Rigby, it looked like those arrow loopholes built into a castle wall. Nesting inside the opening cut between the granite blocks were two pigeons. Feathers from the birds clung to the window, obscuring a clean view.

Rigby listened closely for any sounds coming from above. A distant echo rolled down the stairs. A steady footstep, Rigby concluded. The Bomber was still climbing.

Waving his men forward, Rigby considered his options. He wanted to take the man alive, of course. Take him to justice, but he would also protect his men from any harm. That was paramount.

Past step 100.

He would protect the monument as well. That, too, was of great importance to him. America gained strength and courage from its history and its myths. He would not let this Bomber tear down what America was all about. By tearing down the monuments, the Bomber was intending to tear at the spirit of the country. Rigby knew this. He would not let it happen.

Step 150. More than halfway.

The information about the Monument Bomber's new target had come in anonymously. The description of the bomber matched the man who was now inside this building.

The Bomber's first attack on the Statue of Liberty had torn a hole through the robes of the sacred lady.

Enough. They would take him down.

As Rigby led his team up the stairs, the agent behind him tapped Rigby on the shoulder. Rigby didn't stop, but turned his head so he could hear what the agent whispered.

"Everyone's in place outside. In case he's tries to rappel down."

Rigby nodded. He picked up the pace.

Step 200.

Rigby felt he could keep the increased pace up to past step 250. If the Bomber heard them, he might dismiss the sound as tourists climbing the stairs. If he heard a rushing forward of many feet he might act differently.

At step 250, Rigby had a change of heart. It had taken too long to reach this point. He would not slow down. However, he signaled for the last two men in this FBI train to drop back. He figured three men were enough to take down the Bomber. The others could come in as reinforcements, but dropping them back would reduce the sound in the stairwell.

On they went. Rigby feeling confident the mission would be a success. The Monument Bomber was enjoying his last moments of freedom and his reign of terror would come to a sudden stop. This was why he had become an FBI agent, Rigby thought–stopping the bad guys. This, and that night...

Rigby broke away from his thoughts. *Concentrate. Don't get cocky. Nail this bastard.*

Step 275.

The confrontation was a minute away. Rigby steeled himself. He pulled up just shy of the landing. Sun coming through the observation windows splashed gently down the stairs, making the dark interior lighter as he approached the top. Rigby wanted to see if the man knew they were coming. He had no intention of running into a blazing handgun. He looked back to make sure his man with the tear gas and gas masks strapped in a pack on his back was still with him. When Rigby made eye contact with the man, he nodded. The man nodded as well. He was ready.

Rigby started moving again. He moved slowly. He crouched a bit, making himself a smaller target.

The landing was just above. The muscles in Rigby's arms and back tensed. He was prepared for anything; prepared to drop down, or to sprint forward; or to pull the trigger. He felt the sweat sneak out from his hairline at his forehead.

The red windbreaker was the first he saw of the Bomber. He could see the edge of the back panel of the windbreaker. He knew the man had his back to him. The Bomber had not heard their approach. What a break. There was no gun barrel waiting for them.

Don't give the bastard a chance to recover, Rigby told himself. His feet pushed off the fourth step from the top. He exploded to the landing, his legs churning hard, his muscles driving like pistons from a standing start.

The Bomber turned suddenly at the sound of the rushing man.

Rigby saw the man had a moustache, then he was on top of him, banging into the man like a blitzing linebacker hitting the quarterback. The man crashed to the ground with a thud and a clang. Rigby realized the metallic sound was made when the man hit the iron grate in the center of the landing. Rigby landed on top of the Bomber. His eyes looked past the shoulder of the man's red windbreaker down into the well, below the grate, that dropped all the way to the bottom of the obelisk over 200 feet below.

"Get the hell off me," the man grunted.

Rigby got up as soon as he saw other agents taking up their places around him. The landing was not large, and the three agents and the man on the floor seemingly filled the place. Soon the other two agents squeezed onto the landing as well.

The man looked frightened as he stared at the five guns pointed down at him.

"You're under arrest," Rigby said between gasps of breath.

"You crazy?"

Rigby told one of his agents to read the man his rights. He watched the man's expression. No resignation, no defiance, Rigby had expected to see one or the other, but the man's face showed bewilderment. The man was older than Rigby expected. Maybe forty-five. He was dirty. His mustache and two- or three-day growth was covered in a fine thickness of dirt. Soot streaked his face. The man's shirt, visible under the open windbreaker, was torn in a number of places. Rigby noticed an unpleasant odor came from the man. The smell of someone who lived on the street and seldom if ever bathed. Under that mask of facial dirt appeared a very white complexion. Expecting a foreign terrorist from some Middle Eastern country, Rigby was surprised.

The man was protesting his arrest. Even as the agent was going on about his rights, the man wasn't listening. He was yelling something unintelligible at the agents.

Rigby looked around for the orange backpack. It was on the one metal bench in the landing, sitting under a small cannon from the battle displayed on the wall. One of Rigby's agents was opening up the backpack.

Another agent helped the man to his feet. Rigby knew they would make this guy confess. He felt a wave of satisfaction sweep through his tired muscles. They had saved the Bunker Hill Monument and brought the Monument Bomber to heel. Mission accomplished.

An explosion ripped through the air. The agents and their prisoner all ducked reflectively.

Looking through the window to the east, Rigby could see a cloud of smoke billowing up from the Charlestown

Navy Yard less than half a mile away.

Rigby turned to the prisoner and screamed, "Did you set another bomb?"

"What the hell you talkin' about, man?"

"We know you're the Monument Bomber," Rigby said. "Don't play games with me."

"Monument… Man, you *are* crazy."

He had no accent beyond what you'd hear from any native Bostonian. Rigby looked at him closer. Had they made a mistake?

"What are you doing here?"

"Makin' money," the man said. He started to reach for his pocket as if he was going to show Rigby the money, but another agent slapped the man's hand away from his pocket. They had frisked the man as soon as they could, but no one was taking chances.

"Guy gave me two hundred bucks to deliver this here bag up the top of the stairs. Said a friend was coming to pick it up."

"And he told you what to wear?" A note of resignation floated in Rigby's words.

"He gave me what to wear," the man said. "Said I could keep these here things as a bonus. The BoSox cap and everything."

"Old Ironsides," one of the agents said, pointing in the direction of the explosion.

Rigby stepped toward the window. Underneath the cloud of smoke caused by the explosion, the masts of the *U.S.S. Constitution* could be seen clearly, like a small forest above the water. The ship was listing to the starboard.

Rigby understood the awful truth. No wonder the tip about the Bomber had been so good. The Bomber had sent it in himself. He had not only pulled the FBI away from his intended target, America's oldest warship, he had set the FBI up with a box-seat to watch the show.

"Damn," Rigby said softly.

The agent who was examining the orange backpack called, "Chief."

Rigby turned toward him.

"No bomb, Chief. Just a note."

The agent walked past the surrounded prisoner, still standing on the grate in the center of the landing, and handed Rigby the note. He read it.

More MONUMENTal destruction to come

Chapter 2

The first thing Rigby saw when he entered the FBI Director's cavernous office was the hand. It was in a big jar encased in a clear plastic bag. A long hand: maybe a foot from the tip of the middle finger to where it had been severed from the arm. The hand was mummified, not much flesh left on the bone, it was a sick brownish color with streaks of yellow, like a rotting orange that had been left on the ground for a month and had lost all its juice. The texture of the skin reminded him of papyrus once inscribed with the wisdom of the ages.

Who the hand belonged to, and why the head of the FBI had it on her desk, Rigby had no idea. He didn't care. The hand was not why he'd been called there. He'd failed at Bunker Hill. Now Old Ironsides listed in Boston Harbor and he was sure he was listing in the eyes of the Director. He knew it wasn't going to be pretty.

The Director had a phone pressed against her ear. In the brief time she had been on the job, Rigby had never met her. The Judge, they called her, because she was one—once upon a time. A fairytale life: rich daddy, Harvard, Yale Law, assistant D.A., elected D.A., federal judge, head of the FBI, and not even forty-five. Must have eaten her Wheaties. Do people still say that? Or only old people?

The Judge finally said to the person on the phone, "Keep me posted," and hung up.

Rigby extended his hand.

She didn't even look at him. "You're Agent Rigby?" she said as she picked a sheet of paper off her desk.

"Right."

"Sit down."

He withdrew his proffered hand and sat down in a chair opposite the desk.

"What happened in Boston?"

"We were set up. He wanted us to watch his handiwork."

"And now they're laughing at us." The Judge looked up at Rigby for a moment and said emphatically, "Now they're laughing at me!"

Full of ego, Rigby thought. Not a surprising trait for someone in the Judge's position. Not a terrible trait, either, he knew, if it didn't blind you.

"We'll get the Bomber," Rigby said calmly. He had years of experience dealing with the higher-ups and the holier-than-thous that populated D.C. and environs.

"You had your chance," the Judge shot back, reading from the paper on her desk. "We can't afford another failure with the Bomber threatening another attack."

"A Red Alert posted. Did the Bomber give up more since we took his note from the backpack?"

She did not respond.

The silence crushed Rigby. He was sitting across from the Judge and she was ignoring him. Okay, he got the message. He failed. The hole in Old Ironsides was on his hands. He would make up for it. He'd pound nails into replacement planks of the old ship himself if he could. One thing he would do, bring in the bastard who was bombing America's monuments. First, a hole in the base of the Statue of Liberty. Then Old Ironsides. What's next? Destruction of another monument, Rigby knew; he'd read the note. He would be ready this time.

Tapping the lid of the jar the Judge said, "You have to investigate the hand." She continued to read over the sheet of paper.

"What's the hand's connection to the Red Alert?"

Her eyes moved from the page and finally looked at

Rigby for more than a fleeting moment.

"Nothing."

An uncomfortable silence followed. Rigby felt sure the Judge was calling him in to help with the newly issued Red Alert. Not the first mistake he'd made at the Bureau. She brushed her long brown hair off her shoulder. Finally she said, "Your wires are crossed. You're off the Bomber."

Rigby was stunned. He never expected this. A scolding, yes. Maybe even a reprimand, but not getting kicked down the stairs.

"But, I'm one of your most experienced agents," he said firmly.

"Then you know how to take orders."

"Look," Rigby started, then stopped. Bring it down a notch, old boy, he told himself. Of course she's disappointed. You're disappointed, too. When he spoke up again his voice dripped with sympathy.

"I know you didn't need this screw-up starting out as Director. I got plenty of motivation to get this guy. And, it's about more than him tricking me. It's about what his actions are saying about my country."

She responded without hesitation, "You will investigate the hand."

Okay, Rigby thought, I can take a hint. He didn't want to get off to a bad start with the new Director. He could work his way back into the Monument Bomber investigation. He'd been around a long time. He knew how to work the system and avoid the traps. He took a breath and pointed to the hand in the jar. "What's the lab say?"

"It's old and it's real. The hand's here because of the note found with it." The Judge picked up a thin file from her desk and handed it to him.

Rigby opened it. The top page was a photocopy of a note written on smaller paper than the photocopy sheet. The edge of the original notepaper was seen in clear silhouette a few inches in from the edge of the photocopy paper. The words on the page had been written with a broad writing tool, probably some kind of pencil with a thick, dull edge. The lines of the letters were wide, the handwriting clean and clear. The note was dated October 20, 1901. It was not addressed to anyone and bore no signature.

You have before you the great Lincoln's Hand. You want the rest of Lincoln I demand 500-000. You stopped me once when trying to help Boyd but not again. I snatched the body before reburial. The Hand's my say-so. You want Lincoln back it will cost 500-000. You want him piece by piece? We can negotiate. Ha! Get the money. I will write again and give instructions on how we trade.

Rigby looked up at the Judge and said, "A hoax."

"Perhaps. But we have to know."

"Why do we have to know?"

The Judge spat out her reply. "Congress!"

"What did they do this time?"

"The McClavity Bill?"

She stared at him, awaiting some acknowledgement. He had none to give.

"What do you do with your days, Rigby? Don't you read the memos?"

Actually, he didn't. Rigby thought how so many meaningless memos numbed the brain. This place should be called the Federal Bureau of Paperwork.

She tossed her hair. "McClavity Bill. Any important historical investigation has to have federal involvement."

He remembered. "The digging up dead presidents law."

"Digging up dead anything," she said, her hawk nose pecking up and down as she nodded in agreement. "New science. So some historian has a theory that President Zachary Taylor was poisoned. He died unexpectedly after eating fruit. Had political enemies, said the historian."

21

"Who doesn't in this town?"

"But the historian makes a case, teams up with a distant relative of the president and they get permission to raise the old guy's bones from the dust."

"I read about it. No poison found."

"Then there's Jesse James. Was it really him in the grave? Was his shooting death staged so he could get away and live quietly till the Grim Reaper flagged him down? Dug up the bones. DNA proved Jesse James was…"

"Jesse James."

The Judge nodded. "All you need is a curious historian, or authority figure, and permission from a relative and you can start digging. Congress didn't like it. McClavity didn't like it."

"You would think they have more important matters to deal with," Rigby said. He hoped the Judge would understand that *he* wanted more important matters to deal with, too.

The Judge scowled and nodded. "I've had a few drinks with McClavity. He wanted me to understand his bill. Any time a case involving historical significance is being investigated, he wants the feds to be part of it. That means us. Terrorism threatens Americans living and breathing today, an Al-Qaeda agent or some nutcase is on the loose striking at our heart, blowing up our treasured monuments, and I have to assign an agent to look after dead people!" She slapped the sheet of paper to the desk.

"I'm with you," Rigby said with all the empathy he could muster from his college acting classes. "We both want the same thing–to catch the Monument Bomber. Put me on that case."

"I'm ordering you on this one." *Tap, tap, tap*. She treated the specimen bottle lid like a drum.

"History wasn't my favorite subject in school," Rigby said with a crooked smile, hoping that humor would soften her resolve.

"Let's say you've lived more history than my other available agents."

If Rigby were a betting man he'd wager that the curl on her lips was actually a smile. He resented the way he was being treated, second-class agent, and the boss making no bones about it. Pardon the pun. Especially, with a Red Alert issued over the Monument Bomber threatening a new attack.

"As to your hoax theory," the Judge continued, "the lab compared the DNA from a bone fragment from the hand with bone retained by the government after the assassination. It matches."

That shut Rigby up. He stared at the hand. How could this be true?

"Wouldn't it be better for some young up-and-comer in a field office to handle this?"

"I want to use your talents. I am counting on your maturity. This is McClavity's district where I'm sending you. He'll be watching us. Besides, your file says you were a Private Investigator before you went to law school and joined the Bureau."

"For a short time," he responded, trying to figure out why the Judge brought up his history.

"Looking for a missing person is right up your alley."

Missing person. Good one. Apparently the Judge had a sense of humor after all. He looked down at the photocopied note. "Who's Boyd?"

"That's your job to find out. You have the file with the *What* and the *Where*. You figure out the *Who* and the *Why*."

"How far along is this business?" Rigby shook the thin file.

"Far enough. That's why I have to deal with it even with the Red Alert on. We got a weird piece of evidence." *Tap, tap, tap* on the jar. "We got a historian, and we got a willing relative. Now we have the final piece, FBI Special Agent Zane Rigby. Do your job."

So she could get back to more important matters, he thought, as he pushed out of his chair. Rigby asked, "Exactly what is my job?"

"Confirm that Abraham Lincoln is in his grave. If not…find him."

Chapter 3

He watched the television and clenched his fists in anger. The damage inflicted wasn't enough. The monuments were already being patched. Pictures from New York showed welders affixing new pieces of iron into the foot and lower robes of Lady Liberty.

Lady Liberty. Bah! *American* liberty for *Americans* only. Americans liked to lord it over others. He had seen that from the very beginning. The Americans were better than everyone else. They spoke loudly, drawing attention to themselves in foreign lands. 'Look at us, we're Americans.'

He'd felt this way when he first came to these shores. He wanted to be treated as one of them, to belong, but he was always the outsider; always not as good as they were.

He *was* better than they were, and he would make them see that. He would tear down their pride. Destroy their heroes.

The view cut to the Charlestown Navy Yard and the dock where Old Ironsides was berthed. Wooden planks were piled up on the dock. Men in Navy uniforms and workers' clothes were watching equipment arrive to begin the repairs on the old ship.

With his next action, the Americans would wail so loud, they would be heard back in the mountains of his homeland. This time there would be nothing to repair.

Maybe–*finally*–these Americans would look inward to see what kind of people they really are. Arrogant. Detested around the world. Dictating to peoples who have no respect for the Americans' culture. Isn't that the way to measure if you are doing right? Be aware what others think of you and act righteously? That's the way he was taught. He knew his teachers and his family would understand what he was doing now, would believe that he was doing right. America lived by its myths. He understood that from watching so much American television. America commemorated its myths. If he attacked their myths, he would get Americans to think.

Maybe he would even get them to change their ways.

Chapter 4

Zane Rigby liked to fly when the sky was like ice and the plane slid along like a hockey puck. Today, the plane felt more like a basketball being dribbled on an asphalt driveway. The prairie wind bounced the commuter plane up and down as it approached the Abraham Lincoln Capitol City Airport in Springfield, Illinois. He held tight as the plane hit another air pocket. The plane dipped and fell a few feet to a mixed chorus of 'oohs', gasps, and screams from the twenty passengers making up the manifest of the twin-engine commuter plane. Rigby let out a yelp. At least his shout was shorter than the teenage girl sitting next to him. He told her through gritted teeth that everything would be all right.

He gripped the seat's armrests as if by sheer muscle he could hold the plane aloft. Rigby wasn't superstitious. He didn't believe he had to continue pulling up on them to keep the plane flying. He realized his iron grip on the armrests was a way to ground the tension coursing through his body. He thought about taking his mind off the nerve-wracking flight by reading up on his assignment. Usually, Rigby didn't like working on planes; found it hard to concentrate. Besides, he didn't want to worry that the dude next to him was looking over his shoulder. Wouldn't do for a foreign agent to know Rigby was on a top-secret mission for the country to protect the president–who'd been dead 145 years.

To take his mind off the bumpy ride, he decided to take a quick look into the *What* and *Where* file the Judge had given him. He released his grip on the armrests and pulled his briefcase from below the seat in front of him. Removing the single file in the case, he looked at the teenager next to him. Pigtails. When's the last time he saw those? No, he'd never dunked a girl's pigtails in the inkwell on his school desk, but when he was in the first and second grade he sat at desks that *had* inkwells, holes cut into the top of the desk to hold bottles of ink. The girl was probably thirteen. One pigtail appeared longer than the other. She didn't look like a foreign agent but you never knew. He opened the file, keeping the back side of it perpendicular to the tray so the girl couldn't see the paperwork.

These fools really intended to go through with it–they planned to open up Lincoln's grave to see if the body was missing. A note indicated an excavation company had been contracted and was ready to dig. How did such a major thing move so fast with no press leak? Springfield, Illinois obviously wasn't Washington, D.C.

Why were they doing this? What if the body wasn't there? Are they going to tell anybody? If the body is missing it's not going to be recovered after all these years. They'll just have the hand to rebury. Better just to assume the body's there and let everyone go on living their lives.

Rigby closed the file and thought of the Monument Bomber. If the Bomber had not been successful, if Rigby had done his job, he wouldn't be bouncing along on this plane bound for the middle of nowhere. He didn't mean Springfield, Illinois was the middle of nowhere. Although he was sure some snooty coast dwellers had that attitude about Springfield and anywhere else in what they called the *flyover* states when traveling from coast to coast. Rigby wasn't one of those people. He was proud of that fact. He thought his career was headed for the middle of nowhere after he had been removed from the Bomber case. At his age there was no time to turn things around. Rigby felt like the Old Soldier that General Douglas MacArthur said would just fade away. He understood what MacArthur meant now.

The plane made its descent. Rigby looked out the

28

window to see how close they were to the ground. Poking out from amid a clump of green trees was a white obelisk. He recognized it immediately. His destination. Lincoln's monument, which housed his grave. The tomb seemed out of place amid the bucolic landscape below. It stood like a giant in the wilderness. The symbolism was inescapable. Lincoln, the giant, had returned to the wilderness once his mission on Earth was done. In the nineteenth century when the obelisk was built, the tomb must have seemed even more imposing and otherworldly. Rigby would be at the tomb soon, although he doubted he would stay for long.

Once the plane touched down Rigby reminded Ms. Pigtails that he had told her everything would be all right. She said, "I wasn't scared till you screamed."

"Fair enough," he said. He headed for the baggage claim. He retrieved his bags and picked up a rental car. The drive to the center of Illinois' capitol city was quick, less than twenty minutes. He tried to imagine the place when Lincoln lived there: open spaces, dirt roads, few people. It's the conveniences he'd miss, Rigby decided. No fan at night when the air gets heavy and stuffy. No light switch. No Monday Night Football.

Springfield was a thriving place. The state capitol and surrounding buildings were in good shape. Rigby noticed that in seats of government there is always money on display. Some Illinois cow town, or even a manufacturing center on the plains, did not have the smell of money that Springfield provided with modern buildings to house papers and government officials and those who would lobby government officials.

Springfield, of course, didn't forget its historical side, the thing that put it on the map. Yes, it was the state capitol, but it was—as every automobile license plate reminded you— the *Land of Lincoln*. Rigby took note of the Lincoln Motel, the Lincoln Laundry, the Lincoln Pizza Parlor, and all sorts of road signs directing visitors to Lincoln historical sites.

Rigby's destination: the Lincoln Presidential Library and Museum, the newest presidential library. Smitty had told him the modern presidential libraries began with FDR. It was actually his idea to have a library for his papers and memorabilia. There's a library built to FDR's predecessor, Herbert Hoover, and from Hoover on the libraries are mostly maintained on government dollars. The Lincoln Presidential Library was run by the state of Illinois and Rigby guessed it was probably the brainstorm of the local chamber of commerce.

Thinking of Smitty, Rigby made a mental note to call her. Smitty was his shortcut past the bureaucratic research arm of the FBI. She was a crack researcher at the Smithsonian. More importantly, she was a good kid, still in her twenties, and a pretty fair drinking partner for someone who was maybe one hundred pounds when she dressed like an Eskimo, which she did even when the Washington weather dipped no lower than 45°. He'd call her if he needed any quick information on this weird expedition.

Considering what was in store for him over the next twenty-four hours or so, he concluded he wouldn't be talking to Smitty again until he was back in D. C. What would he need to know from her? Lincoln was either in his coffin or he wasn't. Either way, that would be the end of the story. There would be no finding the body after all these years if it wasn't where it was supposed to be.

The Library and Museum on Sixth Street was a new and exciting building full of curved architecture and glass entryways. A note in the file said Dr. Henry Crease, the Library's director, had been told Rigby was coming.

The white-haired old lady behind the desk in the administration area had surely ignored the Social Security retirement age. Rigby nodded at her and pleasantly asked to see the director.

"Do you have an appointment?" The nameplate at the

edge of the desk identified her as Mildred Huffington.

"He's expecting me. Name's Rigby."

"And what's your business, Mr. Rigby?" She asked the question like a police sergeant to the driver of a beat-up motor vehicle stopped in a swank part of town.

Rigby didn't respond. Since there had been no leak about opening up the presidential grave that he was aware of, Rigby wondered how widespread the story was. If they had somehow managed to keep it quiet, he didn't want to be the one to spill the beans.

The receptionist read the non-response as a rebuke. "Oh, I'm sorry," the lady said and blushed. "I didn't mean to offend. It's that we're so new and draw some of the most interesting people. Professors, writers, Lincolnphiles. It's so exciting to hear them speak. I just thought you might be an expert that I'd be interested in."

"I'm not interesting," he said.

"We're all interesting in some way, Mr. Rigby. We all have a story to tell. You should work on yours."

Mildred Huffington picked up a telephone receiver and punched in a number. In a moment she informed Dr. Crease that "a Mr. Rigby is here to see you."

She nodded and hung up the phone while instructing Rigby to enter the office door behind her desk.

On the other side of the door a man standing about five-foot-five in a skinny frame greeted Rigby. The little man had rounded shoulders and a bald head with a band of gray hair circling around the back from ear to ear like an ancient Olympic victory wreath.

He took Rigby's hand and said, "I'm Henry Crease, the museum director. Agent Rigby, is it?"

The FBI man nodded.

"Tell me, Mr. Rigby, is everybody mad?"

Rigby thought this guy was on to something. He thought the Judge was mad for pulling him from the Monument Bomber case and sending him to Illinois. He thought the people digging up Lincoln were mad for wasting their time and his when no good result could come of the dig. He thought the Monument Bomber was mad for trying to destroy some of America's iconic memorials. Rigby looked at the museum director and answered, "Yes."

"Then we're in agreement," Crease said with a satisfying smile.

"Is it true?"

"What? That someone robbed the body a century ago? I don't see how."

"I don't understand. I thought your institution was behind this..." Rigby couldn't find the right word. "...project."

"No. You should have better information at the FBI. I find no historical record. A grave robber returned twenty-five years after the first attempt and spirited the body away? Really! Preposterous, don't you think?"

"But my file says your historian found the hand and the note that went with it."

"And she believes it could be true. I don't. The coffin was opened after the robbery attempt. Twice. In the 1880s and again in 1901, right before the last reburial. September 1901. The anniversary is this month. Eyewitnesses saw the body each time. Every one of them agreed. You see why I think this is folly?"

He didn't have to sell Rigby too hard.

Crease paced a moment in silence and then turned back to Rigby. "Our new Lincoln Library and Museum got a lot of people digging into corners...going up into dusty attics looking for memorabilia that might be put on display. They want to sell the stuff to us."

"The hand was sold to you?"

"No. That's not what I meant to say. Our historian, Dr. Claire Orange, did her own digging. Found the hand and the note in some remote area of an old state storage facility."

"And you still don't think it's real? The DNA matched."

He sighed. "Yes, the DNA. The only thing I can think of is that someone made a mistake. There was no police record from the time. No record of this...what would you call it, a ransom note? But Claire thinks it should be checked out. We have a family member..." He lowered his voice. "A benefactor." Then he raised it again. "She believes too, or maybe *believes* is not the word. She demands to *know* if her renowned relative is resting peacefully."

He won't be when all these people were through with him. It all came clearly to Rigby now. Back to basics, the key ingredient in many a story: follow the money. A nervous director who objected to the search was willing to move ahead because there was a benefactor involved. Still he was surprised at Crease's attitude, given his position here.

"Why aren't you curious?"

"Because I know better. Here, let me show you this." Crease walked to his desk, opened a drawer and gently extracted a flat piece of paper covered in a plastic protector. He placed it tenderly on the desktop and motioned for Rigby to join him at the desk.

"We're in the process of acquiring this correspondence for our collection," he said with reverence. Wrapped in the protective covering was a handwritten letter on yellowing paper, addressed to a Mr. Phillip Sturbridge of Springfield, Illinois and dated August 11, 1901. The letter was short and concluded its message on the front of the page. The signature scrawl was clear enough: *Robert Lincoln*.

"See here," Crease said, pointing halfway down the page, "Mr. Lincoln was instructing the people of Illinois how to make his father's grave theft-proof. 'A steel cage around the casket... Ten feet below the ground... Covered with cement'."

"Who was Sturbridge?"

"A banker. Member of the Lincoln Guard of Honor. They were a group of Springfield's leading citizens who

33

banded together after the grave-robbing attempt to make sure the body was protected. Sturbridge and Robert Lincoln were friends. They hunted together, competed in games of chess. See here at the bottom of the letter; they even played poker against each other via the U.S. mail."

Below Lincoln's signature was a series of playing card symbols, each suit symbol followed by a card number. Being one who enjoyed the art of the game, Rigby said, "Could be a winner if he gets a good draw."

The museum director pursed his lips. This was serious business and he clearly wanted the FBI agent to take it that way.

"The FBI could put an end to these shenanigans," he suggested.

"I'm here to do my job, Dr. Crease. And the way I see it, that job is to do nothing. Just watch. The people who want to do this got all the permit papers, so to speak. They got the historical uncertainty. They got the relative. They got the Board who oversees the tomb for the state."

"This is all McClavity's doing," Crease said. "Why do you think he wanted to pass that bill? Lincoln. And the digging's going on right now. It's so hard to accept."

"And where's..." Rigby lowered his voice and whispered, "...the benefactor?"

"Out at the tomb with Dr. Orange. They're watching the...dig!"

He spat out the last word as if it were a spoiled peach pit.

"Then I should go out there and look around."

"You should go out there," Dr. Crease snapped, "and stop them all from desecrating a national treasure."

Rigby grimaced. Apparently, he was not too good at stopping people who were desecrating national treasures. That's why he was put on this crazy assignment.

Chapter 5

Henry Crease drove like he talked. Quick acceleration for short bursts followed by slammed brakes. He screeched to a halt at a stop sign on a tree-lined street of modest homes, bouncing Rigby gently against the seat. On the short ride from the library to the tomb, Crease continued to talk about the abominable decision to dig up Lincoln. Rigby finally figured out he was just encouraging him by filling in the few silent moments with an "uh-huh."

The car turned onto Monument Avenue. A souvenir shop housed in a faux log cabin building stood ahead on the left. Beyond were the cemetery headquarters, a building of stone-block construction, and the entrance to the Oak Ridge Cemetery.

"This was a fairly new burial ground when Lincoln was murdered," Crease said. "It took us only about ten minutes to get here from downtown Springfield, but back in 1865 this was the outskirts of town. Big shot city officials built a crypt in Springfield proper. But when Mrs. Lincoln arrived with the body she wanted none of it. When the big shots resisted, she threatened to bury her husband in Washington, so they acquiesced."

"Uh-huh."

A short hop through gravestones on both sides of the road opened to an expansive field of grass and the huge obelisk-topped monument at the far end of the field. Lincoln's Tomb. Temporary signs on the field and across the road informed the public that the monument was closed for restoration.

"They wouldn't have to fix anything if they didn't rip it

apart in the first place." Crease practically shouted at the subterfuge.

A uniformed private security officer recognized Crease and waved. He pulled a sawhorse across the road so Crease could drive through.

As the car followed the road to the parking area, Rigby marveled at the granite structure and bronze statuary standing in the four corners at the base of the obelisk, which rose from the terrace above the entrance to the tomb. Lincoln himself stood before the obelisk on the terrace level, an imposing figure in bronze. The statues at the corners represented Civil War scenes. Rigby thought they were interesting and wanted a closer look.

Crease parked the car in the lot and they headed toward the monument, past a home identified by a sign as the old custodian's place. The house stood a couple of stories tall, built of stone blocks of varying sizes with a small tower in the center beginning midway up the building and exceeding the roof line. The stones on top of the tower and the top of the house walls were cut like a castle turret. Maybe they expected an attack from the Goths and Huns. The place wasn't totally old fashioned. A bag of recycled soft drink cans sat on the wooden porch.

"Ran an alarm from the tomb to this place after the grave robbing attempt," Crease said. "Gave the Lincoln Guard of Honor a sense of security."

"Too little, too late, I'd say."

"Robert Lincoln agreed. When he came to visit after his father was reburied in the spring of 1901, he said security wasn't good enough. He'd been a lawyer for Mr. Pullman–you know, the railroad car man. Pullman had been buried in an underground metal vault covered with concrete. That's what Robert wanted for his father. So they dug deeper. Reburied the president again a few months later."

"Old Abe needs a travel agent. He sure moved around a lot after dying."

"Seventeen times the coffin was moved," Crease said. "Don't you think that's enough?"

They continued past an extremely tall flagpole and headed to the entrance of the tomb. As they approached, Rigby looked up at the Lincoln statue and obelisk and decided they were more impressive up close. The statuary at the southwest corner of the obelisk was a group of infantry soldiers. They looked ready for battle, although not yet engaged. Even the drummer boy was prepared to fight. He'd lost his cap and haversack, but he'd drawn a revolver.

A few workmen in hardhats sat on the edge of the grass before the tomb, smoking cigarettes. Some tools, heavy-duty equipment, and dump trucks were scattered about. Rigby spotted more equipment on the backside of the tomb and assumed there was another entrance more convenient for the workers to do their job.

Rigby told Crease he wanted to walk around to the back of the monument. Crease protested, but Rigby ignored him, and set out for the back of the tomb. Crease quickly followed.

The rear chamber wall had been opened wide, stones removed so workmen and equipment could easily be moved in and out of the burial chamber. Crease said that when the monument was originally built, visitors to the tomb entered from this end to view the sarcophagus, which no longer existed, but the entrance had been long closed.

Marble from the floor had been broken up and removed, and jackhammers and a small machine with a blunt pounding tool had already done some damage to the concrete below the marble floor. It had to get quite noisy when all those instruments were banging away in the small chamber. Rigby was glad he'd arrived during a break in the work.

With Crease's encouragement they moved around the outside of the tomb to the opposite side. Another statue of Lincoln greeted them at the visitor's entrance. This was a large sculpture of Lincoln's head, about three feet tall.

"No beard," Rigby said to Crease.

"He grew the beard after he was elected president. The first bearded president."

Gutzon Borglum had carved the sculpture, but it was not the original. That was in the U.S. Capitol Hall of Fame. Rigby read the plaque on the rear of the bust. The Lincoln head did look familiar and he wondered if he had seen it at the Capitol. The bronze nose had been rubbed shiny by many visitors, so he continued the tradition. Maybe it would bring luck and this assignment would end quickly.

Two stone stairways on each side of the front of the tomb ascended to the terrace above, where he could get a closer look at the statuary. For now, Rigby followed Crease into what the museum director called Memorial Hall.

"This is where they viewed Lincoln's body before they buried him for what should have been the last time."

The room was stunning, especially its red-brown marble floor. Of course, there was another statue of Lincoln. This one Rigby recognized with certainty. It was a bronze of the famous statue in the Lincoln Memorial in Washington, D.C., except on a much smaller scale. The bronze stood on a pedestal in the center of the room.

"Red marble," Crease said, indicating the floor. "From Arkansas. It's the same marble used on the monument stone over the grave. But you won't see that. It's been removed for the dig."

"Stop with the tour, Doctor." It was a female's voice. "Let the man do what he's supposed to do."

Rigby turned to see a woman emerge from the hallway to the left. She looked to be in her early sixties but quite expensively preserved. An Egyptian mummy would be proud, although the mummy would probably be wearing less jewelry. The woman's hair was a colorful brown with an orange tinge, with a diamond-studded comb in it. The diamonds matched those in her earrings and on three of her five rings. Her skin was stretched tight over the facial bones. A knife probably did the sculpting, or maybe she used that Botox stuff. Rigby pulled at his own jowls and wondered how much younger he'd look if he went under a knife.

The lady wore a red leather jacket over a black and white pantsuit. Over a zippered left breast pocket on the jacket, the name *Lincoln* was stitched in black script. Rows of pearls looked like they strangled her neck. As the woman stepped around the Lincoln bronze he caught a glimpse of the rear of her jacket–and wished he hadn't. Lincoln's head, all in leather, covered the back: brown leather face, black leather hair and beard with dyed blue leather for the eyes. The lady's own eyes were green and they twinkled with excitement.

"I'm Abby Lamont. It's about time McPherson sent you."

Rigby looked to Crease for help. He said, "The excavation company. Mrs. Lamont, this is Zane Rigby. He's not with McPherson, he's with the FBI. Agent Rigby, Mrs. Abigail Lamont, distant relative, though not direct descendant, to Abraham Lincoln."

Rigby noticed the two exchange hard stares. The *direct descendant* shot had clearly been bounced back and forth between them before like a tennis ball. Rigby noticed a charm bracelet on her wrist decorated with tiny Abraham Lincoln heads–all in gold. He wondered if there was an official website that sold this stuff but concluded the leather jacket and the woman wearing it had to be one of a kind.

Lamont turned her attention to Rigby. "Congressman McClavity told me an FBI agent would join us. You will solve this mystery." It was an order.

"There really is no mystery, Mrs. Lamont," Crease said gently.

Lamont patted Crease on the shoulder. "Mr. Lincoln was a great man. The greatest the world has known. He wasn't just a man for his times. If he were here today he'd fix the things that need fixing. Wouldn't it be wonderful if he were here to fix our problems?"

Maybe she was not a direct descendant, but Mrs. Lamont had acquired some of the debating skills of her distant relative. At least the hard-nosed Henry Crease backed off for the moment. Then again, she was a *benefactor*.

"I understand you donate to the Library and Museum," Rigby said.

"I've done well in this life, Agent Rigby. I have many charity works. My late husband, Daniel, and I owned a number of car dealerships. We even named one after me—well, in a sort of way. We called it *Mrs. Lincoln's Lincolns*."

"Clever," Rigby said, although he really didn't think so.

"My middle name is Lincoln after my great relative. I was born Abigail Lincoln Carson."

"And, they called you Abby Lincoln as a child."

"They called me Gail. I called me Abby. As I grew older, I realized what a great gift to the world Mr. Lincoln was. I had the ability to help promote his story, so I often came here to Springfield and got behind the idea of building a Library and Museum to honor him."

"And now you want to see him. In the flesh, so to speak."

She stared at Rigby a long moment, probably trying to determine how she should take his comment. He figured the sarcasm was obvious, but maybe she couldn't believe anyone would perform the disrespectful act of sarcasm in referring to Mr. Lincoln. Rigby wasn't quite sure, but wasn't Mr. Lincoln a champion at sarcasm?

"Don't let Dr. Crease fill your head with doubts. It's important to know the truth about Mr. Lincoln. I'm funding this dig myself. And I'm put out with McPherson and his shoddy equipment. The drill bit broke today and there's no replacement on hand."

"I understand Dr. Orange is with you," Rigby said.

"I can hear her approaching now," she said dramatically, cupping her hand to her ear, the little Lincoln heads on the bracelet dancing a jig.

They turned their attention to clicking footsteps coming from the same corridor from which Abby Lamont had recently appeared. The woman walking into the hall was fairly tall, with shoulder-length brunette hair containing a touch of gray, and soft appealing features that would make a man take notice.

Rigby drew his breath in, took three quick strides across the hall and wrapped Claire Orange in a bear hug.

Chapter 6

His next attack would be at the heart of America. He would destroy a monument in the nation's capitol. There were many choices. America liked to build monuments.

Not for a moment did he believe he made this decision because Washington was where he came to reside when he immigrated to this land. He was willing to travel to a target. He had already done so. In fact, it was his belief there was more danger to him choosing a monument where he lived. The authorities would be close to him, tracking him, and he would always be under their magnifying glass.

This town was full of monuments, however. It was like a fruit basket and he would simply pluck the most juicy fruit from the basket. Immediately, he pictured a target in his mind. Of course. This was a revered place. It would bring Americans to tears when it was destroyed. Would it bring them to their senses?

Destroyed. Yes, the word was important. That was the key. Destroyed. Not to just blow open a hole, but to destroy the monument. His approach must be different this time. His weapon must be different. Suddenly, he knew which weapon, for he had used that weapon before.

The perfect weapon. The perfect monument to destroy.

Chapter 7

"How dare…how dare you!"

The challenge came from Henry Crease. Claire Orange's reaction to Rigby's hug was not nearly as sharp. Her expression was a mix of surprise and inquiry. Once Rigby released her, she stared up at his face studying his eyes, taking in his features. Familiar appearance, familiar smells.

Rigby wondered how much his looks had changed in her eyes. He knew what the mirror, mirror on the wall told him. He wasn't the fairest of them all. At least not anymore.

Claire was still lovely. Still Claire.

"Is-is it…you?" Her voice was barely a whisper. She reached up and gently touched her fingertips to his cheek. "Zane?"

Rigby nodded and put his hand over the one touching his cheek.

She pulled her hand away abruptly, as if his touch burned her skin, and she intertwined the fingers of both hands, pressing the palms together over and over as if pumping up a basketball. As she did this she took a couple of deep breaths.

Rigby understood. He wondered if her heart raced as his did. Memories cascaded in his mind, one overtaking another. He wanted to choose just one wonderful moment with Claire and enjoy it to the fullest, but why bother with memories when Claire herself was standing before him? Lovely Claire. Sexy Claire. Still lovely and still sexy Claire after all these years.

"You look wonderful, Claire," Rigby said, aware a

wide smile split his face.

"What…a surprise," she said before blowing out a breath. "So much time…"

"Too much time," he agreed. "But here you are."

"What are you doing…" Claire looked past Rigby to Crease and Lamont.

Henry Crease said, "Mr. Rigby is the FBI agent assigned to this…" and he didn't finish the thought. He didn't have to.

Rigby couldn't keep his eyes off her. The memories of Claire continued to rush at him. He could feel fireworks exploding inside, the fireworks that always seemed to be there when he was around her.

"FBI? Well, what do you know?"

Claire seemed stunned to see him, which was understandable after so many years. He saw something else in her eyes. Was it fear? Rigby didn't understand. Maybe it was the awkward situation, two ex-lovers meeting in the tomb of the great man with curious observers looking on. That had to be it, he thought. How could she not have the same feelings he was now experiencing? He wanted to reach out and hug her again, not let her go this time.

Claire stepped back. "So nice to see you," she said, as if greeting a business associate she might see once a year.

"It's *great* to see you," he responded with enthusiasm.

"I've got to go. Work to do. Perhaps, later…" Claire walked swiftly past him, nodded to Abby Lamont and Henry Crease and exited the tomb.

"An old friend?" Mrs. Lamont said with a curious grin.

"An old *best* friend," he replied with no hesitation, staring at the chamber door. Claire had been much more than that, but she did not act like she'd just found her long lost best friend.

"Well, time passes, things change," Lamont went on, as if reading his thoughts.

Lamont could see what he had seen. Claire was

running from him. After all these years, she did not want to remain in his presence.

Rigby looked at Lamont and the jiggling Lincoln heads on her bracelet and the leather Lincoln face on her jacket, and knew he didn't want to take life lessons from this woman. He hurried for the chamber door.

Outside the tomb, Rigby looked around to see which way Claire went. He soon saw her at the wheel of a car making its way down the cemetery road toward the exit. He stopped, watching as the car went out of sight. Give her time to compose herself, he thought. Seeing Claire again was a miracle. He couldn't believe he'd found her. She'll come around, just give her time–

The ground shook under his feet.

Rigby sensed something wrong an instant before the shockwave pounded his eardrums and tossed him onto the grass.

Smoke filled his nostrils–the scent of burning rubber. Rigby hugged the ground, but slowly lifted his head, squinting under the thick, billowy strips of smoke as they floated into the air and vanished. Pieces of metal and rubber strafed the ground around him.

He waited for a moment–would there be another blast? –then rolled over on his back and sat up. A wounded dump truck sat across the walkway on the grass field. The truck's empty bed lay flat on the ground behind the rear wheels, one of which burned with a small flame. Pieces of the hydraulic mechanism that raised the dump truck's bed were scattered across the field: bolts, pistons, fragments of the metal arms. The truck's rear tires were chewed up by the blast, chunks of rubber left a trail from the truck across the field and beyond Rigby.

Then he saw a man's body lying on the ground at the front of the truck.

Rigby jumped up and ran to the man, who wore workman's clothes. Probably the truck driver. The man was alive. He whimpered while making small, jerky movements with his legs against the ground as he struggled with the pain. When Rigby reached him, he saw the man clutching his right side, blood pouring from two wounds. Shrapnel from the explosion had ripped open his right arm and penetrated the trunk of his body at the abdomen.

The FBI agent pulled off his belt, tightened it around the man's bicep to form a tourniquet, and closed off the blood flow. There was little Rigby could do to the abdomen wound except apply pressure to slow the bleeding. He pulled off his jacket and used it to press down on the wound.

Workmen rushed to the site of the explosion.

"You okay, fella?"

Rigby nodded. "But your man here needs help. Call an ambulance."

Another workman rushed up and said, "Medic training in the Corps. Let me help." Rigby nodded again and backed away.

The first man said, "Gas tank...must be."

Maybe. The FBI agent picked up a baseball-sized piece of rubber sitting on the grass and tossed it gently into the air, caught it and tossed it again. *Maybe.* He guessed if it was the gas tank that exploded, it had been *helped* to explode.

Rigby looked back over his shoulder at the Lincoln Tomb. Excitement built inside him. *The Monument Bomber!* Here. Right where he was.

Abby Lamont and Henry Crease ran up. "Oh, my God. What happened?" Crease exclaimed.

Lamont saw the blood on Rigby's shirt and trousers and asked if he had been hurt. Rigby shook his head and explained about the injured driver. Crease looked around, and Rigby guessed he was searching for Claire.

"She drove away."

"I'll call the police," Crease announced.

46

Lamont protested. "No, it was an accident. We don't need the police. They'll only slow things up. It's taken too long already. Besides, we have the FBI here."

"He's not here to investigate violence," Crease said. "Isn't that right, Agent Rigby?"

"I'm here to protect old bones." *And maybe catch a terrorist.* His fingers twitched over the prospect.

"But this was an accident," Lamont said again.

Rigby looked over the busted truck from closer range. The engine had been off. No signs of a gas leak on the ground. His nostrils sniffed the air. Smoke, no gas. The explosion was deliberate, he felt certain. If the wounded workman didn't pull through it would be murder.

Soon, Crease announced he had called the police. Rigby immediately pulled out his own cell phone and a scrap of paper he carried with the number for the Bureau's field office in Springfield. If the Monument Bomber was behind the explosion, he wanted the FBI to smother the place before the locals could mess things up. He identified himself and asked for the Special Agent in Charge. "Emergency."

He made his way through two guardians to the SAC, a guy named Crosby. Rigby explained he was on a special assignment at the Lincoln Tomb from the director herself.

Crosby repeated: "The director herself."

"That's right," Rigby said with an air of authority.

"We know all about your *assignment,* Rigby." The emphasis told him all he needed to know about Crosby's opinion of the job.

Rigby took note of the condescending tone and prepared to give the SAC an attitude correction. He walked away from Crease, Lamont, and the knot of workmen and said, "There was just an explosion at the Lincoln Tomb. I'm thinking Monument Bomber."

"In the tomb?"

"Outside. A dump truck."

Crosby was silent a moment. "Doesn't quite fit the M.O. The guy bombs monuments. He's not the Dump Truck Bomber."

"Lots of people around the tomb because of the dig," Rigby said. "The dump truck was as close as the bomber could get."

Crosby was quiet for a moment then said in a thoughtful tone, "Maybe. Best to see. Okay, I'll send my bomb guy. But ten to one it's not what you think. Drop in and see me when you're clear of there."

The first police officer on the scene was a rookie patrolman who had been driving nearby. He cordoned off the area and was soon joined by a couple more cops with stripes on their sleeves, arriving in different patrol cars, one with siren blaring. Other sirens announced the arrival of a fire truck and an ambulance.

Finally, a superior officer arrived in an unmarked car. The car may have been unmarked, but the officer was decked out in her finest uniform, polished buttons, and shiny bars on her shirt collar. Her cap was pulled down low on her forehead, probably to allow for her ponytail, which fell to her shoulders. Rigby wasn't fond of uptight cops who liked to show authority and he thought he had a prime example here. She spent a moment talking to the workmen and checking on the injured man, then noticed the small knot of onlookers and made her way over.

"Dr. Crease, good to see you." She offered her hand.

"Detective." He shook it. "I've never seen you in a uniform before."

"The chief suggested...I was testifying before the council. But I hate this rig." She removed her cap, undid her tie and loosened the button at her collar. Rigby wondered if he had to re-evaluate his first impression of her.

"Detective Lisa Hunt, please say hello to Mrs. Abigail Lamont and to Mr. Zane Rigby."

"Special Agent Zane Rigby, you mean," Abigail

Lamont said.

"Special Agent Rigby?" Hunt cocked an eyebrow.

"I'm here to protect the tomb's restoration. Make sure nothing's stolen or destroyed during the work."

Hunt looked at him suspiciously. "But, this place is run by the state of Illinois. It's not under federal authority. Isn't that right, Dr. Crease?"

Crease nodded. "Turned over to the state in 1895 by the Lincoln Monument Association."

A slight smile danced on Hunt's lips. "You're here to see if Mr. Lincoln is where he's supposed to be."

Since he had not heard of the dig previously, Rigby assumed it was a secret. He turned to Crease. "This been in the papers?"

"No, Agent Rigby. We'd prefer to keep what's going on here as quiet as possible. But Detective Hunt knows. She's a member of the LGH."

Rigby shrugged. "You got me…"

"Oh, of course," Crease continued. "You wouldn't know… LGH, the Lincoln Guard of Honor. Remember, I told you about the Guard when you were in my office. The modern version's been recently constituted."

"Just in case the grave's empty?"

"It will not be empty," Crease said firmly.

"I suppose I'm standing in the presence of members of the Guard." Rigby pointed at all the other people in the small circle.

"Care to join?" Hunt asked.

"It may be too late depending what they find in there," he said, indicating the tomb with a nod of his head.

"Bite your tongue," Abby Lamont scolded.

"I'm more concerned with what happened out here." Hunt looked over the exploded dump truck.

"Frankly, so am I," Rigby told her.

"How's the injured man?" She looked at the blood on his clothes.

Rigby shook his head. He didn't know, but the paramedics had his wounds wrapped, the man on a stretcher, and were wheeling him toward the ambulance, the ex-medic at his side.

A van arrived on the scene. A man wearing a suit and carrying a satchel emerged. He looked like a country doctor off a Norman Rockwell painting, but he flashed a badge and moved toward the crippled dump truck. Rigby assumed it was Crosby's bomb guy.

Hunt stared hard at Rigby for a moment as he tried to read her thoughts through the movements of her appealing brown eyes. Claire had brown eyes, too. He needed to connect with her again. *Connect.* What did that mean? Touch? Kiss? More? Or simply connect by looking deeply into those eyes. Suddenly, he realized the eyes he was staring into were not Claire's, but those of an attractive police detective. Younger than Claire. Pretty like Claire, but not Claire.

"Agent Rigby?" Hunt said, snapping him back to the present. "Any thoughts on what we're facing here?"

"Just got into town myself," he said. "This is your home field." Until it's proven that the Monument Bomber was at work here, he thought. Then, the pretty young detective would get shoved hard out of the way by Washington.

The country doctor arrived at the little gathering and excused himself for interrupting. "I'm looking for Special Agent Rigby."

"Me."

"Special Agent Partosian. Explosives. Crosby sent me. A bomb of some kind. Got some samples, do some tests, get the report to Crosby ASAP. You can pick it up at the Bureau office." He nodded to the group and left.

Hunt turned to Rigby and said, "Why did you send for the bomb squad?"

He had no intention of telling this police detective

about his suspicions of the Monument Bomber. He said, "I wanted to help."

"Thank you," she said in a way that said she didn't mean it. "The bomber could be someone who wants to stop the dig."

They all looked at Crease.

"Not me! I don't believe in this dig, but I don't believe in violence, either."

"No one's accusing you, Dr. Crease," the detective said in a somewhat accusatory tone. "But you would probably know others who don't want this to happen, who would resort to violence to try and stop it."

"No. No one I know would do such a thing."

Rigby sensed some concern pulling at Crease. Was he worried he could be accused of a crime and ruin his status and reputation, or did he have a suspect in mind he didn't want to share with the police?

If this bomb was the work of the Monument Bomber, then it wasn't someone who wanted to stop the dig. On the surface, Rigby couldn't see any connection to the Monument Bomber. Still, if almost twenty years in the FBI taught him anything it was not to hold your intuition too tightly. It had been overruled by bizarre facts more than once.

"Well, we'll be asking the workmen if they saw anything." To Rigby, Hunt said, "I trust the FBI will share its findings with us."

Rigby bowed to her, but said nothing, which was his way of making no commitment at all. He didn't know how Crosby ran his outpost. If the Monument Bomber were involved, Hunt would have no need for the information except in a tangential way.

Lamont touched the detective on the arm, "Could you keep what's happening here a secret?"

"A man has been badly injured. He could die. That's pretty public. You three will be questioned by my officers,"

Hunt replied as a way of saying goodbye. She turned and headed back to the truck where her officers, pads and pencils in hand, were questioning some of the workmen.

Rigby turned and walked toward the tomb, thinking about Claire. He thought, wistfully, had they stayed together he would not have gone through the horrible night of nights that had scarred and changed his life.

Here she was. Claire. He'd found her. He marveled at the thought. Was this some kind of reprieve? Of course, it wouldn't be that simple, he knew. They'd both changed. A lot of years have gone by, different experiences. She must be married, or was at one time. She was Claire Orange now, not Claire Spencer.

Rigby shifted his thoughts to the Monument Bomber. He thought if he could track the Bomber down... If he could end the Bomber's reign of terror, he would be restored.

Within a span of fifteen minutes Claire had re-entered his life and Rigby found himself on the edge of cracking an important investigation. He felt as though he'd drunk a powerful potion giving him strength and invincibility.

Rigby reached the bust of Lincoln in front of the tomb and, for the second time that day, rubbed Lincoln's nose, hoping this assignment would last a lot longer.

Joel Fox

Chapter 8

The knock on the hotel room door came early the next morning. Rigby had already showered, shaved, and dressed. His plan was to meet Claire when she arrived at the Museum and Library, catch her going through the door. No secretaries to interfere. She had the night to get over the shock of seeing him, and this time he wouldn't let her run away.

The knock on the door was a bit early for housekeeping. The young man in his twenties who stood there was not associated with housekeeping. He wore a well-tailored dark blue suit with a yellow tie.

"Special Agent Rigby?"

"Who's asking?"

"Oh, I'm sorry." The young man blushed, and held out his hand. "My name is Lenny Poler. I work for Congressman McClavity. He sent me to get you. He wants to see you."

His plan to see Claire was just ruined. "Now?"

"The Congressman insisted. He's home from Washington. I'll take you to his office. It's in the old town."

Reconnecting with Claire was like *staying* with Claire: obstacles at every turn. Still, he knew what he had to do. Make the congressman happy. He grabbed his coat.

Lenny's old town was very old. This was the real old town, a couple of blocks set aside as a historical park, Springfield as it was in the time of Lincoln. Abraham Lincoln's house stood at 8th and Jackson Streets. The main part of the house was two stories high and narrow, with chimneys extending from the roof on each end and plenty of windows looking out onto 8th street. The front yard, up a couple of steps from the sidewalk, was also narrow. Someone of average height could lie down on the grass, stretch out and touch the house with his hands and the fence at the edge of the yard with his feet.

Many houses from the same time period stood along the two blocks, supposedly looking as they had in the 1860s. There were some vacant lots. Some houses had fallen into disrepair and had been cleared away. The place had too much of a museum feel to it. For one thing, all the lawns were neat and trimmed. Whatever grass there might have been all those years ago must have been in clumps.

Congressman McClavity's office occupied the lower floor of one of the restored houses. A sign called the place the Henson Robinson House. Painted mustard yellow, it had a porch with four pillars. The sign said Henson Robinson lived in the house in the 1860s, that he built stoves and tin ware, and during the Civil War he held a contract to supply tin cups to the Union Army. *Life doesn't change much. It's still who you know that counts.*

Lenny led the way into the parlor, which now served as a reception area. A middle-aged lady sat at the reception desk. Lenny greeted her with, "Can he see us?"

The lady nodded; Lenny went to a closed door and opened it while Rigby took a moment to greet the lady with a nod and smile, and got a smile back in return.

Inside the congressman's office there was Abraham Lincoln—everywhere. Busts, photographs, paintings, political posters. The man standing in the middle of this mini-museum was thin, stood less than six feet tall, and wore a black suit.

"Good of you to come, Agent Rigby. Please sit down," Congressman McClavity said with a forced smile.

"I'm only here because of you," Rigby said as he sat down in an ornate wood carved chair with wide arms.

"Really?"

"Your bill. That's why I'm here instead of out chasing terrorists." Actually, Rigby thought he'd be pushing papers across a desk, but McClavity ought to feel guilty for creating his bill.

"The bill was written so someone like you is present at these important events," the Congressman said proudly.

McClavity sat in a chair across from Rigby. Lenny disappeared out of the line of sight, quietly making himself inconspicuous.

"I've been informed about the sabotage at the tomb," the congressman said in a sympathetic voice, an affectation for any respectable politician.

"Yeah, somebody had a beef with a dump truck." Rigby knew the Judge would want him to treat the congressman with kid gloves, but he wasn't in the mood. He was still upset he could not search out Claire.

"They tell me the driver injured in the explosion is touch and go, but they think he'll pull through. You might have saved his life with your heroics."

"I was just the first one to him, that's all."

"I'm glad you're here. They want to stop this important historical research and we can't let them," McClavity said.

"What's your interest in the dig, Congressman? Besides your obvious fascination with Lincoln."

"The truth, Agent, the truth. And I feel a special obligation to protect all my constituents. The living and the dead."

Rigby thought: Now, that was an interesting theory, but not all that far-fetched. After all, some graveyard votes have been known to decide elections.

"You realize, Congressman, that if we dig up the grave and there's no body, we won't find it. It's a very cold trail and there are no clues as to who wrote that note."

"I have every faith in the FBI. It'd be a historic tragedy if President Lincoln's grave is empty. Pennies from Americans young and old built that memorial. Modern

55

Americans will do all they can to see his remains recovered. I'll lead any effort necessary; do what it takes, to find those sacred bones. But we're getting ahead of ourselves. Perhaps the note was phony. Maybe one of those long ago body-nappers got soused one night, decided to fake the note, make a quick gold strike. We'll soon see. But, your own laboratory says the DNA from the hand matches the DNA from Lincoln's skull fragments that are kept on the grounds at Walter Reed Hospital. So if I were you I'd prepare myself for the investigation."

The idea of chasing a missing corpse was not appealing. However, with Claire on the scene, searching for the old bones would have its bright side.

"Tell me, Agent Rigby, who do you think exploded that bomb? And why?"

"I haven't seen any police report, Congressman, but the why part is easy. Someone wants the grave to remain undisturbed." He thought it best not to mention the Monument Bomber, especially to a congressman.

McClavity rose and shuffled over to a table with a large wooden box. He lifted the lid and took out a cigar, not offering one to Rigby. McClavity absently prepared the cigar with a small tool, cutting off the tip of the cigar and poking a hole into the core of the tobacco. He lit the cigar with a brass lighter sitting next to the box. Rigby wondered if a congressman's inner office was covered by no smoking ordinances for public buildings. Maybe he should arrest the guy. Wouldn't that get the Judge's goat? Of course, congress members notoriously exempted themselves from many of the laws they placed on everyone else.

"Do you believe a descendent of the culprit may actually know where the body is?"

No idle question coming out of the blue like that. "Do you have some information you want to share?"

McClavity turned to Rigby and let a cloud of smoke escape from his shallow cheeks. "I have something to show you."

The congressman walked to his office door. Opening the door he turned and said, "Well, come now. Shake a leg."

Rigby got up and followed. They went out of the office down the wooden sidewalk in the Lincoln Disney-like Park, passing Lincoln's house on the way. The congressman put his hand close to his forehead and gave a half-hearted salute to the home. A block to the north they emerged into the Springfield civic center. McClavity led without a word, nodding or saying hello to the occasional passers-by, some of whom appeared to recognize him. At the Lincoln Library, Springfield's own municipal library, the congressman put out his cigar in an outside ashtray.

Inside the library McClavity led the way up a couple of flights of stairs to a door marked, *Sangamon Valley Collection.*

"An excellent collection of documents here," McClavity explained. "Covers the history of Springfield and the surrounding area for a radius of fifteen miles or so."

McClavity nodded to the young woman sitting behind a desk at the entrance to the room. "Good morning, my dear. Have you put all those pieces together?"

"Yes sir, I have it here." She opened a desk drawer, pulled out an ordinary manila folder and handed it to the congressman. He waved Rigby over to a research table next to the file cabinets. Inside the folder were photocopies of old newspaper and magazine articles. He shuffled through them, found what he wanted, and pushed the page over to Rigby.

The photocopy was from a newspaper containing an old photograph. The newspaper was published in 1967, but the photograph was much older. It was printed under a headline, "Remember Way Back When."

The photograph was of men and women, maybe fifteen, though only two were women, standing on the bottom stairs of a stone stairway. This was one of the

57

stairways to the terrace of the Lincoln Memorial in the Oak Ridge Cemetery Rigby had noticed the day before. The people in the picture were dressed formally, the usual dress of the time when photographers were present. Nearly all the men wore bowler derbies, although one wore a straw hat, all were in ties, and jackets, pocket watch chains were clipped to some vests, the women were in ruffled blouses and flowery hats. As normal for such old-time pictures, no one seemed happy posing for the photographer. There wasn't a smile among the bunch.

Rigby scanned the photo and couldn't figure out what McClavity was trying to show him. "Who are these people?"

"The ones who looked upon Lincoln's face before the reburial. Most of them, anyway. The photo was taken outside the tomb. Each person testified that Lincoln's body was in the coffin. The caption under the photograph in the original says: 'They Viewed Lincoln's Body on September 26, 1901 before the final reburial.' This photocopy cut off the caption."

"Pretty solid evidence that the body's in the grave."

"Robert Lincoln did not want the grave opened before the reburial. But he wasn't here and those present decided they should look into the coffin. Do you know why?"

"Curiosity, I guess. A last chance to see the great man."

"Some of those things, perhaps, Agent Rigby. But this little group of Lincoln devotees and members of the Lincoln Honor Guard decided to take the highly unusual step of opening up the great one's coffin because they wanted to put an end to *rumors* that the body was not there. Rumors, mind you, that were running rampant. Remember, there was a nearly successful grave-robbing attempt. Or was it successful? Some people said so. That rumor had currency. These individuals felt honor bound, I repeat, *honor bound*, to discover if the body was in fact in the coffin. For the same reason these individuals decided to look into the coffin, some today insist we look in the coffin. To end rumors that the body is not there."

"I haven't heard those rumors, Congressman. I've heard Elvis isn't dead, but no one's going around questioning if Lincoln's in his grave."

"Until the hand showed up, eh?"

Rigby wondered why McClavity brought him to the library to see a photograph of the last people to see Lincoln's corpse. Time to get to the bottom of things. "Why else are we digging up the grave, Congressman?"

McClavity fidgeted a bit, running through the documents in the file then said, "Look at the photograph again. Closely."

He looked. Closely. He looked at the background to see if some telltale object was unnoticed with a quick perusal; at the clothes for insignias or patches; at the facial expressions for some sign of guilt. Then he looked at the young man on the right side of the group standing on the highest step and wondered if he had seen that face before.

The young man must have been in his late twenties. His derby was pushed back and he had a thin mustache and slightly sunken checks. Rigby tried to imagine what this man looked like when he got older. Rigby looked up at McClavity, then back at the picture and pointed to the young man at the end of the row.

"Very good detective work, Agent Rigby. My grandfather, Samuel McClavity, was present for the viewing of Lincoln's body."

"Uh-huh. Don't you trust your own grandfather's eyes? Didn't he tell you Lincoln was where he was supposed to be?"

Looking over to the young woman at the reception desk he said in a louder voice, "Could you please leave us, my dear? Go outside for a moment and close the door."

The young woman looked perplexed. "But, Congressman McClavity, the room is open to the public. I can't abandon my post. No one else is on duty this morning."

"Yes, very conscientious of you, I'm sure. Do you realize this library receives federal funds? Probably helps pay your salary."

The young lady seemed shocked, but she gathered up her purse.

Working in Washington for the government you learned your place when it came to a congressman, but Rigby would be damned if he would stay in that place and let McClavity get away with that kind of intimidation.

"The federal government pays my salary, too," he said, an edge to his voice.

McClavity looked surprised at Rigby's tone, but quickly backed off. "Yes, of course," he whispered. "I must be careful around big ears."

In a louder voice, McClavity told the librarian to never mind and asked her to collect the items on the research desk and replace the file. With a wave of his hand he indicated Rigby should follow him.

McClavity exited the research room, but didn't go far. He walked down a side corridor with a copying machine in the hall. On one wall was a series of pictures of Lincoln during different stages of his life from his Illinois days. They were much like the heroic pictures in a grade school text published in the 1950s. There was Lincoln the lawyer, Lincoln the postmaster, Lincoln the candidate.

Rigby noticed there were three pictures of Lincoln and Ann Rutledge. Curiously, there were no pictures of Lincoln and his wife. The first love can be very strong. He thought of Claire again and knew he must get away from McClavity and see her.

McClavity put a hand on Rigby's arm and pulled him closer. Rigby smelled the cigar smoke on his breath. The congressman was back to whispering.

"The world must know these witnesses were correct.

60

But if the body is not there, the world must understand the witnesses were not responsible for this atrocious crime. They were not inattentive to their duty after viewing the body."

Especially if a descendant of one of the witnesses was running for re-election. Rigby had had enough of this guy.

Chapter 9

The plan to find Claire in the presidential library parking lot or greeting her as she entered the building had been derailed by McClavity so Rigby headed for the executive suites of the library.

His cell phone vibrated in his sports coat's vest pocket. Vest pockets on suits and sports coats seemed doomed to go out of fashion since few men wore a handkerchief in that pocket. The pockets became useful again when someone invented pocket sized cell phones.

"Rigby."

"I thought you were going to call."

"Smitty," he said with a smile. "Got busy, sorry."

"After what I did for you on short notice, how about calling me Veronica for once. The name's Veronica Wong. And the number's in the phone book."

"For me it's the Wong number." He couldn't help himself.

"Like I haven't ever heard that before. You're such a dolt."

"You know you'll always be Smitty to me. That's how I remembered you at first."

"That's where I work, at the Smithsonian, that's not who I am." She paused a moment. "It's the glasses, right?"

He could picture Smitty in his mind. She was in her late twenties with dirty blonde hair tied behind her neck capping a China doll face. The blonde hair was startling over her Asian features, but that's the way she always colored it. The hair was not her most notable feature. She wore thick, black-rimmed glasses.

It wasn't the glasses; it was her age. Smitty was young enough to be his daughter. He said, "Your glasses are just your secret identity. You're like Clark Kent. Supergirl."

Smitty said, "You're cute, somehow. That's how you get away with it."

It was long past steering this conversation in a new direction. "Did you find out anything for me?"

"The coffin was opened in 1901..."

"Yeah," he said quickly before she could get started with a full analysis. "I know about that. What else?"

"Then why did you ask? Honestly, Zane, you got a whole FBI working for you and I got my job to do."

"No one does it better and quicker than you, Smitty."

"Apparently, someone was quicker than me."

"Local historian," he said, deciding not to tell Smitty about finding his college sweetheart. "What did you find out from federal records?"

"Nothing. I mean, a little historical research told me what I gave you when you were boarding the plane. Boyd was a counterfeiter. That old movie called *The Abductors*."

He forgot she had mentioned that movie. Interesting stuff.

Smitty continued: "But there was no government record I could find that indicated another attempt at stealing Lincoln's body after 1876."

If the ransom note were real there had to be a record of the grave robbery. If not, how did the DNA sample of the hand match that of the fragments of Lincoln's remains stored by the federal government?

"Okay, Smitty, thanks. Maybe you can do a quick check on a group called the Lincoln Guard of Honor. They were formed after the grave-robbing attempt and they're still around."

"Why should I?"

"Cause, I'll owe you."

"I'm keeping count," she said. "You owe me twenty!"

She laughed and hung up.

During the conversation with Smitty, Rigby had entered the library and walked through the exhibits to the administration offices. He approached Dr. Crease's secretary, Mildred Huffington, who was opening and closing drawers in her desk.

"Lose something?"

"Keys," she said. "They should be here. I'm so absentminded sometimes. You don't think its age, do you?"

"Age is not a problem."

"That's easy for a young fellow like you to say."

He liked this lady. "I came to see Claire Orange. Does she have a secretary?"

"That would be me," Mildred said. "One moment."

Claire had time to get over the shock of seeing him the day before. Certainly, she would want to visit with an old college friend.

Apparently not.

When Mrs. Huffington informed Claire that Rigby was waiting to see her, the word came back that she was busy and not available at this time.

Rigby sighed, deflated. Why? He was going to find out.

Reaching into a pocket, Rigby removed his wallet and opened it to show Mrs. Huffington his badge and identification.

"Tell Dr. Orange that I'm here on official business."

Mrs. Huffington picked up the phone and repeated his message. Claire came down a hallway a short time later. She was not smiling and her arms were folded across her chest. Yeah, she could be stubborn, but so could he.

"Please follow me, Agent Rigby," she said. "I can only spare a moment."

He followed her back down the hallway and into a small office. The office had books and papers scattered all around in an order that only Claire could understand. A poster of the statue in the Lincoln Memorial occupied the wall behind her desk. After closing the office door, Claire sat behind the desk. She did not offer Rigby the chair opposite her desk and he decided not to take it. He would stand.

"It's wonderful to see you, Claire."

She remained like a statue herself. Two seated statues, one in the poster, the other behind the desk, coldly staring at him with serious expressions.

Indicating the poster, he said, "Strange world. He's been dead over a century but I expected to see him yesterday, not you."

Claire didn't move, although maybe Lincoln blinked.

"It's wonderful to see you," he repeated. "How are you?"

"Married," she said.

He wondered if this statement was meant as a warning to him or a reminder for her. A flicker of desire mixed with hope sparked in his chest. He wanted to ask, *Happily?* but held his tongue.

"Great," he said. "How could you not be?"

"Are you?"

"No."

"Never?"

An odd question. She must have taken his silence as an affirmative. She said, "I'm not surprised."

Good for you, he thought. The timbre of her voice indicated pride and self-confidence. If he did not marry her then there was no one in the world worth marrying. Claire was still strong, still prideful, and still beautiful despite the years. He wondered if in her marriage she'd settled for second best.

"You're an FBI agent. I'm surprised. How come?"

"Melanie."

"Who?"

"A victim."

"The noble hero riding to the rescue. You always had that in you, Zane. There's no one to rescue in this case. No one alive, anyway."

"I'm older now. My clientele's changed. Now I also rescue the dead."

Claire studied his face.

"Why are you here, Zane?"

"It's my job."

"No, I mean *here*. You told Mildred your visit was official business."

He did, didn't he? He thought of the info Smitty was able to come up with on short notice. Checking the historical facts with the museum's historian made business sense.

"This Boyd guy mentioned in the ransom note..."

"A counterfeiter. He was imprisoned in Illinois. His partners in crime wanted him out. They decided to trade for something the folks in Illinois would want. They were businessmen, too. The hero's remains in exchange for Boyd and $200,000 in cash."

"The non-counterfeit kind, I assume."

She didn't respond.

"So what happened?"

"The Secret Service got wind of the plot. Shots fired, scrambling in the dark. Grave robbers got away. At least for a time. They were tracked down in Chicago ten days later and arrested. Ended up serving a year in jail."

"Only a year?"

"There were no laws against grave robbing in Illinois at the time. This was 1876, only eleven years after the assassination. That was the best they could do."

"So one of the grave robbers could go back and try again," Rigby said. He recited a line from the ransom note, "*'You stopped me once when trying to help Boyd but not again. I snatched the body before reburial.'*"

"Yes, I suppose that's what it means," Claire said. "The

66

grave will be opened tomorrow and you'll be leaving Springfield."

"If the bones are there. If not, I may be here a while. You found the hand and the note. You must believe the body's missing."

"I supported this dig because I thought it was the right thing to do…for history's sake. What I found was probably a hoax. We'll know tomorrow, then we all go back to living our normal lives and that will be a relief."

"You seem as certain as your boss, Crease. Well, maybe I'll get lucky and the body will be missing."

"Don't say that!" Her voice sparked and her eyes flared. "That would be terrible. And it won't happen. Believe me. Zane, you've got a vacation day. Go see the sights of Springfield. Tomorrow everything will go smoothly. You'll have the privilege of looking at the great man's remains and then its over."

He had no intention of being a sightseer. He wanted to break down Claire's resistance to him. Maybe they couldn't recapture the spirit between them of thirty years ago, but he was determined to rekindle some of that warmth. Despite the lost years he still cared for her.

"I've already seen the sights," he said. "Your local congressman showed me around. He took me by the city library. All those pictures of Lincoln and Ann Rutledge. The first girlfriend he kept loving."

Claire looked at him. Her eyes stared right through the mask he created. She could always read him. "The Ann Rutledge-Abe Lincoln love story is greatly exaggerated." Her voice was softer. Not convincing.

"All love stories are exaggerated," he said, "unless you play a principal part."

Claire rose. "It was nice of you to drop by. So many years. I'm glad you did well."

So formal and so reserved, not the Claire he remembered.

"Let's go to dinner tonight," Rigby said quickly. "Lot's of catching up to do."

"No, Zane. We just caught up. Our past lives are just that, past. Let's leave it that way."

"Strange statement coming from a historian."

The reserve weakened. She said, "Zane, life's changed for both of us."

"I'm not trying to disrupt the universe." He stopped and watched her face for a reaction. "I'm just talking dinner. We could share some information. You can tell me more about the grave robbing and what happened after."

"And what information do you have for me?" Claire asked. He could hear the skepticism in her voice.

He thought of the oddball fact that Smitty dug up. "Well, I could talk about the movie."

"Movie?"

"*The Abductors,* starring Victor McLaglen. Remember him?"

Claire had no idea what he was talking about.

"McLaglen won an Oscar in the '30s. But this film was at the end of his career in the late '50s. It was based on the Lincoln grave-robbing attempt. Bad flick. Maybe it ended his career."

Finally, a slight smile touched Claire's lips. Thanks, Smitty, he thought, I owe you another one.

Claire looked down at her desk, picked up a pencil and jotted something on a notepad. She tore off the top sheet and reached it across the desk.

"All right, Zane. For old time's sake. Dinner. But we'll do it at my house. This is the address. I want you to meet my husband and my son."

The vision of a dark, candlelit corner vanished from his mind. Dinner with Claire and her family. How romantic. Still, she would see him. Maybe he was disrupting the universe after all.

Chapter 10

In the field, he was able to tear down the weapon and put it back together. He was not troubled that he had to assemble the weapon from many pieces. He'd collected each piece from different places. One piece delivered to a mailbox store in Northern Virginia, where, under an assumed name, he rented a box he would never use again. Another piece handed to him by a boy on the street, the son of a great friend and patriot, who put his family first so he stayed away from the battle, but helped with resources.

He had collected all the pieces now, but he needed the grenade. That's why he was in this section of Washington known as Chinatown. Chinatown only consisted of a few blocks now, a gentrified area east of the center of town. Its most notable feature, a Chinese Gate on H Street, was made up of thousands of tiles and decorated with hundreds of painted dragons.

He, too, would soon be a dragon breathing fire.

He walked past the gate and spotted the place he was looking for. Lee's Chinese Laundry was an unassuming shop with a purple awning that came out over the sidewalk, a couple of white bird droppings staining the awning. He entered the shop and waited patiently for a young woman in a red warm-up suit to collect her dry cleaning and pay the bill.

The man behind the counter was old. Over seventy-five he guessed, with nicotine stained teeth and nicotine stained fingertips. His wispy beard was the only hair on his head. He probably had witnessed China's great revolution. He may still be fighting for it, which could explain why he was the contact.

When the young woman left the store, the old man turned his way and waited for him to speak. He said nothing. He pulled the blue ticket stub his friend had given him out of his pocket and handed it over to the old man.

The old man studied the ticket for a moment. Without looking back at his customer he waddled slowly into the back of the laundry.

Could it be a trap? Alone in the front of the shop, he began to sweat. He knew nothing of this place, of this old man. He had been sent here by his friend to secure the ammunition. His friend did not fight. He supplied resources. Could he have been turned by government agents? The friend's family came first, he knew. Had the agents threatened the friend's family?

His fears dissolved when he heard the old man returning. The old man was carrying a shirt box. The box could easily fit a missile grenade. Probably two.

The old man held the box over the counter. He took it with steady hands. The box weighed more than a bunch of shirts, but he didn't want any passersby to know that. He thanked the old man who looked back at him passively. No sign of recognition of what might be in the box.

He knew what was in the box. He would assemble the weapon and affix the grenade. He was just about ready for his attack, to send another shock wave through America. He wanted the FBI to know he was coming.

Chapter 11

Claire's house was west of downtown Springfield. The directions Rigby received at the hotel were simple enough. She lived on Washington Street, which cut through the city a couple of blocks north of the hotel. However, Washington Street through downtown was a one-way street going east. Once he maneuvered to a point where Washington Street allowed travel both east and west, it was straight sailing past Veterans Parkway and through the cornfields west of the city.

The home lots in this part of the world were large, measured by the acre, with plenty of trees. Real country, no sidewalks and little rolling hills on the roadway. He found the street number attached to a roadside mailbox, turned in on a gravel road, crossed a wooden bridge and drove up to a large two-story washed-out red-and-white brick house with a wooden porch supported by carved wooden columns. A stand-alone garage was made to look like a barn. The Oranges were doing quite well. Rigby wondered if he could afford something like this on his government salary. Maybe in Springfield, certainly not in Washington. He didn't know home prices hereabouts, but somehow he tended to doubt he could even buy this house.

Claire would not be the type to marry just for money. At least not the Claire he remembered. He wondered how Mr. Orange achieved his success.

Rigby's guessed Mr. Orange was a lawyer. He'd spent a few moments in the hotel room looking through the local phone book. Not many with the surname Orange, but there was a lawyer.

What might the nationality of the name Orange be? English? There was an English king once, somebody of Orange. Or was this one of those kings England imported from someplace else? An attorney descended from royalty. Tough competition.

Competition for what? He'd just seen the woman for the first time after thirty years and she'd run away. What was he expecting to happen? That she would be waiting for him all this time? Of course she was married. She found someone else. He found someone else, too. He thought of Melanie again, and wondered how she was doing, if she too had nightmares.

He was a lawyer, too. Lawyer trained, at least, before joining the Bureau. The hell with royalty. He liked being the common man. It was the American thing. Abraham Lincoln was the epitome of the common man who made good. Rigby laughed out loud. Abraham Lincoln. What could possibly make him think of that?

Rigby exited the car, pulled out the table flowers and California wine he had purchased earlier in the day, hipped the car door shut, and headed for the house.

Claire must have been on the lookout for him. The front door opened before he reached the porch.

"I see you found us all right."

She smiled that glorious smile he often thought of to seek warmth on the coldest day in some foreign land after he left college. He handed her the flowers and wine.

"You improved with age. Last time you came for dinner you brought a six pack."

"Half a six pack," he said. "Had a few on the walk over to your place."

Rigby felt the urge to hug her, and he sensed she knew this. She held the flowers and wine away from her body in such a way that made it impossible for him to get his arms around her.

"Come inside."

The entry parlor was spacious, an open floor plan with high ceilings and a staircase reminding him of Tara in *Gone with the Wind.* Descending that staircase was the lord of the manor. The short, fat, bald, ugly guy of Rigby's imaginings exploded into a thousand pieces. This regal man was tall and in good shape. Rigby thought he looked younger than him, rugged and tanned, just a touch of gray at the temples.

Claire said, "Zane, I'd like you to meet my husband, Peter Orange. Peter, Zane Rigby."

Sir Peter had a firm handshake. "Heard a lot about you."

"But not all, I hope." Rigby looked at Claire and saw she blushed. He frowned. *Bad move, idiot. Hold thy tongue.*

Sir Peter gracefully ignored both reactions. "It's extraordinary that you two should run into each other after all these years. Must be predestined."

"Thank the gods," Rigby responded with a laugh. "I regretted losing touch with Claire."

"As would I," he said with a laugh of his own as he slipped an arm around her waist and pulled her close for a kiss on the lips.

Rigby felt a sharp pang in his gut and knew it wasn't hunger. Jealousy would be his appetizer for the evening. When they broke, Claire handed the wine bottle and flowers to Sir Peter and instructed him to take care of them. He obeyed like a good boy. Rigby followed Claire, also as instructed. Through the spacious living room they walked past a sofa covered with assorted pillows, then through the dining room, where the table had been already set up for the evening, finally toward a closed door that could not hold back the sounds coming from a TV.

Claire walked through the door first and she ordered a reduction in the volume. As Rigby entered the room the noise did go down and he saw a boy of about ten with a remote control in his hand pointing it toward a big-screen television that would never get up the stairs to his apartment. The boy sat in a wheelchair. The push handles were colored red with red and blue plastic streamers affixed to them.

Claire walked over to the boy and kissed him on the top of his head. "This is my son. Craig, I would like you to meet my old friend, Mr. Rigby."

Craig said, "You a real FBI agent?"

Producing his wallet, Rigby showed Craig his badge and handed him a business card.

"Do you shoot bad guys?"

"Active imagination," his mother said as a way of apology.

"Sometimes I wish I could shoot bad guys, Craig. But I'm supposed to follow the laws, too."

Claire frowned and told Craig to go wash his hands and get ready for dinner. He dutifully turned off the TV, put the remote on a coffee table, placed his hands on the chair's wheels and backed the chair up a couple of feet so he could turn it and clear the coffee table, then he rolled out of the family room.

When he was gone, Rigby turned to Claire. "What happened?"

"My fault," she said with deep sadness and followed Craig from the room.

Craig turned out to be the sparkplug of the party. While Sir Peter watched Rigby like someone protecting his wallet from a known pickpocket, and Rigby looked for chinks in Sir Peter's armor, and Claire shifted uncomfortably in her chair as if she were sitting on birdshot, Craig kept the conversation lively. Rigby learned more than he could ever possibly want to know about the St. Louis Cardinals. He learned about Craig's love for flying and how a plane flew compared to a bird. He also picked up a thing or two about pterodactyls and wondered if in his condition the boy could ever be a pilot.

The trickiest part of the evening's discussion came

when Craig decided it was time to talk about the guest and his exploits with the FBI. The boy was expecting daring-do, but considering his most recent adventure ended in failure, Rigby was not so eager to tell stories.

"I became an FBI agent to help people," he told Craig. "To make sure people get a fair shot at justice and other folks follow the law. Seeing that happen doesn't always require gunfights. Sometimes it means patience and a lot of phone calls to get information."

Craig quickly lost interest and changed the course of the conversation in a more difficult direction. "You and mommy went to college together."

"We were best friends in college," Rigby said.

Claire's butt must have found a line of that birdshot because she moved abruptly in the chair, causing the rear legs to scrape along the wooden floor. Sir Peter watched Rigby with a piece of apple pie dangling from the edge of his fork in mid-air.

"Boys and girls can't be best friends," Craig protested. "Boys can only be best friends with boys and girls with girls."

"Maybe in your school, but in college, boys and girls can be best friends."

"Is that true, mom?"

Claire nodded.

"And were you Mr. Rigby's best friend?"

He looked over at Claire and was not surprised to see her staring at him then flicking her eyes toward Sir Peter. Rigby was prepared to dissect her answer, looking for hints that the *friendship* could be renewed.

"We were good friends, Craig. But that was a long, long time ago."

He felt like the man who fell overboard and was thrown water wings instead of a life preserver. Maybe accepting the dinner invitation had not been a good idea.

"You said you had great fun at college. Was Mr. Rigby

75

part of the fun?"

Out of the mouths of babes. Rigby couldn't resist a sly smile. Sir Peter's look was more of a pout. To his pleasure, Claire smiled too, shyly, and said, "Yes, he was fun to be around. Now finish your dessert."

Craig was not through with Rigby. He wanted to know what the FBI man did after college. Rigby had exciting things to tell him because he did plenty of adventurous stuff after college, spending more than three years traveling around the world. However, he didn't want to keep the conversation on himself. He simply answered, "Had things to do. Required traveling a lot." He made it sound like a business trip.

The boy was finished now and the dinner was over. The evening had been *difficult,* to use a word the diplomats at the State Department might reserve for the situation. Coffee was served and the husband and wife Orange continued to show affection to each other with little pats and an occasional kiss.

After coffee, Craig rolled his chair back to the TV room. Sir Peter, doing a very non-royal like act, started clearing the dishes. Rigby, looking for a way to bring up the old days in a non-threatening way, asked Claire if she kept in touch with anyone from school.

"At the beginning, some. Not anymore. That part of my life is completely in the past, no connection whatsoever. That is until you showed up at my doorstep."

"More accurately, at the tomb."

"Yes, I'm sorry I left abruptly. The surprise. You…as an FBI agent. It was all too much."

Sir Peter returned for more dishes and stopped to plant a kiss on the top of his wife's head. "Still beautiful, isn't she?" he said.

"Yes, she is."

"Come, now, boys, I'm too old to have a fan club." Claire clearly enjoyed the attention.

When her husband left the room Rigby said, "Peter seems like a nice guy."

"He's a good man," she replied and he found the answer interesting because he couldn't tell what it meant. Maybe *good man* meant good provider, but there was no passion. *Good man* certainly wasn't in the same category as, 'He's wonderful!' so that meant something. Or maybe Claire simply had no interest in revealing her inner feelings to him. They weren't best friends anymore.

When Peter returned, Claire stood and took his hand. She suggested they move to the living room and talk a while, but Rigby didn't see the point. There's only so much of this lovey-dovey stuff an old boyfriend can take. He told them he enjoyed the evening and thanked them for their hospitality. He said goodbye to the boy and told Claire he'd see her at the tomb the next morning.

"It'll be all over tomorrow," she said. "The body will be there and this will be past us, thank goodness."

He said goodnight, and this time just shook Claire's hand.

Chapter 12

Rigby arrived early at the Oak Ridge Cemetery, thinking somehow the earlier he got there the sooner he'd get out of town. The cemetery officials were just unlocking the gates on Monument Ave. and a few of the construction workers were lined up to go through the gates. When the gates were opened a small caravan of pickup trucks and cars made their way to the parking lot. The workers gathered around a red pickup truck with a camper shell attached, where a bearded man in overalls and hard hat started dispensing coffee from a large pot. Rigby was offered a cup but refused and decided to walk the grounds.

He wandered to the rear of the monument where the wall had been opened for the workers to get their equipment inside. It was under this rear chamber where Lincoln's remains rested…at least until they were disturbed again today. There had been no progress in the dig since the bomb blast.

The rear of the monument stood at the crest of a small hill that sloped to a road below. A stairway led to the road. Beyond the road was a carillon, maybe twenty feet tall, standing amid trees. A small macadam path leading by the carillon started at the road, cutting through the grass in a semi-circle and leading back to the road. A concrete bench stood next to the path. Just behind the bench a dark object caught Rigby's eye.

He couldn't be sure what it was, because the bench blocked his view. Maybe some work clothes left behind or a piece of equipment covered up to protect against the elements.

He walked down the hill about halfway, stopped at a granite marker. A sign said the marker indicated the spot where a temporary burial vault had stood, holding the remains of Lincoln and his deceased sons while the great monument was being constructed. Visitors had placed many Lincoln pennies on the flat top of the granite, acknowledging their visit to the man's resting place.

Rigby didn't add a penny and didn't take one, either. He figured the caretaker counted on them for his morning coffee.

Looking back up the hill, he did not see much activity near the tomb. The workers would take their own sweet time getting started. They had a routine and nothing he could do would make them go faster.

Rigby's eyes again found the dark object right behind the concrete bench. He no longer thought it was a piece of equipment. He started to jog down the hill, instinctively looking both ways as he crossed the cemetery road, even though he knew there would be no vehicles at this time of the morning.

He pulled up as he stepped onto the grass on the other side of the road. He could see the dark object more clearly now, although it was still partially obscured by the bench. A person–or a body–in a dark Navy pea jacket and black jeans was lying on the ground.

Rigby called 'hello' hoping to wake the sleeping homeless person, but stepped lively, because the same instincts that had told him to look both ways when he crossed the road also told him he wasn't looking at a sleeping homeless person.

The blood caked near the girl's temple was partially dried. The bone in the skull had caved in somewhat, leaving a slight valley in which blood had pooled. Her eyes were open, that chilling vacant stare of death Rigby had seen too often before. He put his fingers to her neck and felt no blood pumping through the artery. She was not even twenty, he guessed. Her hair was dark and short. There were no other visible marks to her face or hands and no tears to her clothing that he could see. Despite the face twisted by the rigors of death, he decided she'd been a pretty girl in life.

Rigby sank slowly to one knee. What a terrible thing, to crush out a young life. He felt a tide of anger and sympathy engulf him. What drove people to commit such terrible acts? After all his years pursuing justice, the actual horror of crime still gripped him as if it were squeezing the breath out of him. Of course, he thought of Melanie and all he could grab onto was that at least Melanie lived.

He did not touch the body. He stood and walked around it, looking at once for both the culprit, whom he figured must be long gone, and the object used to bash in the girl's skull.

Behind the carillon were more trees and bushes and a rising hill topped with tombstones. The September foliage was still in full bloom, the leaves and shrubbery thick. To the east, a football field away, was the chain link fence marking the end of the cemetery. An arched entrance over a set of stairs allowed ingress from a street if the fence's gate was unlocked. That would have to be checked. A few steps away from where he stood looking in the same direction as the arch was what looked like an old well, topped with a concrete dome in the shape of a beehive, supported by four cement pillars. The well–if it ever was a well–was now used as a planter with flowers sprouting under the concrete beehive.

The police would have a wide search area. It was time to bring them in. Rigby ran back across the road and up the stairway until he saw some workers slowly ambling to the tomb.

"Call 9-1-1. There's been a murder."

Retreating back to the body, he saw some workers jogging down the hill. He warned them to stay away from the body and to stay on the road so they did not compromise the crime scene. Rigby's status as an FBI agent had already made the rounds after the truck blast two days earlier, so no one questioned his authority. For the most part the workers were quiet and respectful of the dead girl. One man said the girl seemed to be about his daughter's age. Another asked, "What the hell's goin' on? First the truck blows, cuttin' up the driver, now this?"

When asked if a young woman had been hanging around the tomb, the workers said no.

Rigby did another quick turn around the area. Barrel-like waste receptacles were at each entrance to the curved path running in front of the bell tower. He checked both barrels; they were empty. The time they had last been emptied would be important.

He walked back to the bench and looked around it more carefully. Nothing of interest. A few tree nuts of some kind had been cracked by squirrels, and the shells were on the path and on the grass. He saw no blood on the bench or the grass.

He thought about the explosion that decapitated the dump truck bed and wondered if the two crimes were related. Murder likes company. Crimes were usually related by blood.

Sirens echoed through the hills and dales of the cemetery. Many police in different vehicles seemed to arrive all at once. The one Rigby kept his eyes on was Detective Lisa Hunt. She was not in uniform, but dressed in a plain blue pants suit, her shield hooked to a jacket pocket.

She joined Rigby standing by the body. "You know better."

"I didn't touch anything," he said. "I found the body."

"Tell me more."

He told her what he saw and what he did, which wasn't much.

"We'll take it from here," she said.

Rigby stepped back and bowed, extending an arm

toward the body. Heaven forbid that one's jurisdiction is compromised.

The Crime Scene Unit got to work, photographing the area and the body, searching for the minutest of clues. A couple of detectives had begun a spiral search pattern, using the body as a central point.

Hunt ordered another officer to start questioning the workers. "One in three female murder victims are killed by a spouse or romantic partner. Let's see if she had a boyfriend in the crew."

Rigby decided to take a look around on his own. He walked to the bell tower, checking the ground and reading the plaques dedicating the tower and the bells to the memories of deceased relatives. Like everything else in this town, the tower had a Lincoln connection. The tablet built into the side of the tower was the stone plate upon which Lincoln's coffin had been placed in the cemetery's receiving vault.

The vault was across the roadway. He headed that way. It was not a large structure, but it had been there a long time. The historical marker accompanying it said the vault had received Lincoln's remains in 1865 and stored them until the temporary vault was built. He could see why Henry Crease kept tabulating the number of moves the body made. The vault was topped with a concrete urn, draped in concrete cloth, the words *Oak Ridge* spelled out in letters made to look like stone tree branches and surrounded by oak leaves etched in stone. The wrought iron gate allowed visitors to look inside at the four casket-sized doors to individual vaults that could hold bodies while grave plans were finished or frozen ground was dug. The sign said the vault was turned over to the state a half-century ago.

Of course, there were coins scattered on the floor. What possessed people to throw their money away at sites like this? He guessed they felt like they were playing the lottery. Spend a little and say a prayer or make a wish and if

82

the prayer or wish comes true the few cents was worth it. He wondered if any of the coins belonged to the dead woman. Obviously, her wish hadn't come true.

He left the vault behind and walked to the archway, which greeted visitors to the cemetery on the east end. At least it had been an entry once upon a time. The chain link fence separating the cemetery from the country road had a padlocked gate. The fence was placed on the outside of an old, low concrete wall, which at one time had served as the border of the cemetery. The new fence was more formidable, especially with the barbed wire running across the top.

He wondered how the dead girl had entered the cemetery. Did she scale the fence or have a key to the lock? Or did she enter from somewhere else on the grounds?

Across the road was a small dirt parking area for maybe a half-dozen cars, empty now, with a city park beyond. In the park were a stone bridge and a fountain in a little lake.

The wrought iron arch above the old entry way spelled out *Oak Ridge Cemetery* in white faded and chipped paint. Five stairs led up from the chain link fence to a flat platform of concrete under the arch, and ten stairs went down to the small asphalt path in the cemetery. Iron railings attached to concrete pillars were rusting. More nutshells were on the concrete pillars, the squirrels obviously using high places for dining tables.

He looked around and touched the handrail, noting that some of the rust and chipped black paint clung to his hand. He walked back down the stairs and followed the asphalt path that led back toward the convergence of three roads below Lincoln's tomb and the area of the old receiving vault, bell tower, and the girl's body.

The pathway ended…nowhere. It didn't go to a trail or stairway or the road. It just ended. Grass lined three sides of the path. It was from this vantage point that Rigby saw a big, black SUV hurtle around a distant corner on the cemetery road and come directly toward him at top speed. The car screeched to a halt in front of the receiving vault and three doors swung open all at once. The driver was Abby Lamont. He recognized the big boat as a Lincoln. Claire emerged from behind the front passenger door. Henry Crease, momentarily lost behind the huge car door and Claire, emerged from the rear.

Rigby closed the space between him and the new arrivals quickly before they could cross to the body.

"You don't want to go there," he said to the group, but looking at Claire.

"They said murder," Lamont said breathlessly. "Who…who…?"

"Don't know yet. A young woman about twenty."

"Oh, horrible! The poor thing," Lamont said.

"Why?" Claire hugged herself to stop shaking.

Before he could give her an answer that meant nothing, Crease said, "This dig is wrong. If I believed in such things I would say it was cursed."

"Let's not start scaring people," Rigby said.

Claire's focus was where it should be. "That poor, poor girl. This is terrible. What will happen, Zane?"

"They'll stop the dig. Whoever the girl is, we'll do the best to get her justice. That's about all we can do for her now."

"How long will they stop?" Lamont asked.

"Not my call. Detective Hunt…"

"Then I'll talk to her," Abby Lamont said. She took one step toward Hunt before Rigby grabbed her wrist and squeezed hard.

"Not now."

"Take your hands off me!" Lamont snapped. "Don't you dare–"

He squeezed her hand even harder. "A girl is dead! Respect her."

84

Claire had her hands on Rigby now, gently soothing him with one hand while peeling his fingers from Lamont's wrist with the other. He remembered Claire's soothing touch when his temper would flare so long ago. When Lamont was free of his grip, Claire led her back to the Lincoln. Crease was already in the back seat.

Rigby crossed the road and returned to the group around the body. The photographer seemed to be finished and the police were moving the body, fruitlessly searching the woman's pockets for identification. All pockets were empty except for a nearly full pack of cigarettes.

"Anything?" he asked one of the detectives.

"Nothing but a couple of cigarette butts on the ground under the body and a pack of Marlboros."

"Just bag and tag the butts, Joe," Hunt said, shooing the detective away. She sidled up to the FBI man and added, "You're tramping around too freely in an investigation area, Agent Rigby."

"Maybe I can help."

"I'm open to suggestions. If you don't think I'm qualified."

He decided whatever caused her insecurities was not his doing so he ignored her comment and told her what he saw.

"Over at the arched entry the place is scattered with nutshells the squirrels broke open. All over the pillars, the high places. Over here by the bench the nutshells are on the ground."

"So your murder suspect is a squirrel?" Her smile was poison.

"I'm saying I think these shells all around the bench were on the bench at one time. High ground for the squirrels. The victim, and probably the killer, brushed the nuts off the bench to sit down. She knew the killer. They sat and talked a while. Probably explains the cigarette butts."

"Most murder victims know their killers. A little old

fashioned, don't you think?"

Well, at least she didn't call him Pops, but he bet that's what she was thinking. He understood now. The detective wasn't brushing off his help because he was a federal officer, or even because he was a man. It was because she thought he was too old. Just like some of the brass in Washington.

Rigby looked down at the body that had now been moved from where he found her and got a glimpse of the woman's hands. A little rust and smudged black. The lady came through or over the chain link fence and went up and down the old stairway holding the rails. Her clothes seemed intact, no tears from the barbed wire. He wasn't sure Hunt would listen to anything he told her, but he suggested she look over by the old arched entrance. Then he walked away.

The coroner was on the scene and the body was placed on a stretcher. Police still searched the area and interrogated workmen. Rigby headed to his car. He wanted to look around on the other side of the chain link fence and he wasn't interested in climbing over the fence so he would drive around.

He needed to follow up on what the squirrels told him.

Chapter 13

The small dirt parking area was across the road from the chain link fence and the old arched entryway to the cemetery. The park–named Lincoln Park, naturally-sprawled away from the back road. The little parking area seemed an afterthought rather than the entrance to the park.

Rigby left his car in the road, edged up against the grass. He didn't want to scramble any tire marks or other clues that might be around. The parking area was empty, meaning the dead girl probably got a ride to the cemetery, very likely from the killer, although he couldn't rule out the possibility she had arrived on foot.

He walked around the lot, being careful to stay on the grass. Just like those little furry detectives had suggested, the clues were there, highlighted against the hard dirt.

The squirrels were not particular where they left shells. The cigarette butts on the ground near the bench indicated either the victim or the killer was not particular about where they dropped them. Rigby bet the smoker was the girl, since a pack of cigs was found on her. She had gone through a couple of smokes sitting on the bench, so it figured she smoked like a choo-choo train. If she entered the park through the gate–as her hands indicated with the smudges of rust and paint–he expected to find a cigarette butt or two on this side of the fence. Ah, there it was, in the dirt.

The butt had company, too. Next to it was a crushed Marlboro pack. Made sense; the police found a nearly full pack on the body. He couldn't prove the crushed pack and the butt belonged to the victim, but it was a solid bet.

In the dirt with the crushed pack and cigarette butt was

an empty matchbook cover. Rigby hesitated stepping onto the dirt from the grass, but he couldn't read the print on the cover. He knelt on the grass to get closer. No good, still couldn't read it. Damn, those eye exercises didn't seem to work. Okay, he had to do what he had to do. Reaching into his jacket, he pulled out a pair of reading glasses. He put them on and the letters on the matchbook cover instantly grew larger. The matchbook cover read, *The Railroad Bar.* There was an address below the name, but he'd need a magnifying glass to read that. *When did they start making the print so small on these things?*

Rigby figured he could find the place just with the name. He'd leave the evidence for Detective Hunt to retrieve. He stood, feeling only a tiny bit guilty. After all, he did offer to help and pointed her in the right direction. The detective turned him down. That's what he'd tell the Judge, if it ever came up. Who knows, maybe he was wrong about the cigarettes and matchbook.

Rigby decided his first obligation was to follow up on the truck bombing. If the Monument Bomber was working Springfield, it was a job for the FBI. He planned to be part of that investigation to catch the bastard who embarrassed him in Boston.

Rigby drove to the local FBI office, a few blocks from his hotel, past the state capitol complex. He didn't have to wait long before he was ushered into Crosby's office.

Crosby sat behind his desk. He blinked when he looked up at Rigby. Directing him to a chair, he said, "I expected a younger agent."

"Maybe the situation is more important than you thought."

Crosby was beefy and bald, somewhere in Rigby's age range. He looked like the type of guy who always had a cigar in his mouth and a pool cue in his hand and knew how to use it. He had the cockiness of the boss man about him. He'd worked his way up to a top position. Okay, he was out in the sticks, but he was still in charge.

Rigby thought about his situation. He was on a reverse escalator. Just about everyone was his boss.

"First time in Springfield?"

"First time."

"Nice town. We get to see the seamier side, of course. Nature of the business."

"Why didn't one of your guys cover the dig?"

"I'm understaffed."

"Sure, but, what's ten minutes out of someone's day to look into the coffin once it's hauled up?"

"McClavity's a hard-ass. He's the local pol. His bill. He wanted a full-time agent and I couldn't afford one on this bull..."

He caught himself and Rigby laughed. "That's what it is all right. Or was until the bombing."

"You okay? Got knocked down with the blast, I heard."

"No scratches. You let Washington know the Monument Bomber is operating here?"

"I let them know about the bomb going off near Lincoln's Tomb and Monument. The MB Task Force rep arrived this morning."

"Where is he?" Eagerness tinged Rigby's words. "I'd like to get on this right away."

Crosby leaned back in his desk chair and folded his arms across his protruding stomach. "He's gone."

"Gone? I thought he just got here."

"The report came down right about the time he arrived," Crosby said. "I called Partosian when they told me you were in the building, so he can tell you. Ah, here he is."

The office door swung open and the explosives doctor, Partosian, came in. He nodded to both men and handed a report to Crosby.

"Here's what I gave the agent from Washington. This what you want?"

"Not me," Crosby said, pointing at Rigby. "Give him

the findings."

Handing over the paper, Partosian said, "Not the real Monument Bomber. The MB uses plastic. This guy used dynamite. The MB's notes have a unique signature. No note this time. The MB hits the monuments. This guy destroyed a dump truck. Not the MB. Washington confirmed."

"But the explosion was right outside a monument," Rigby said.

Partosian took off his glasses and cleaned them with a handkerchief from his pocket as he spoke. "Coincidence. Copycat. Someone still fighting the Civil War. I don't write the script, I just read it. And the Task Force agent looked over the report and jumped back on the next plane home. He was convinced."

"Are you sure?"

Partosian stopped wiping his glasses and looked at Rigby, who realized the anxiety he felt over losing what he thought was a lead in the Monument Bomber case reflected in the tone of his voice.

"You know how this works. We do what Washington says," Partosian said in a lecturing tone. "And, frankly, I got no cause to believe any different."

"It's pretty clear this bomber isn't the MB. He doesn't have the guts for one thing. Blasting a dump truck yards away from the monument." Crosby waved a dismissive hand. "The Monument Bomber somehow got away from security and climbed into the girders in the Statue of Liberty to place his backpack of explosives. In Boston, he actually swam into Boston Harbor, in diving gear, to fix the bomb on the hull of Old Ironsides underwater. That's the way it figures anyway. That guy's got balls. This guy..." The dismissive hand followed the same flight path as before.

Rigby considered what Crosby told him. Maybe the Bomber was playing games with them; trying to throw them off the scent. He certainly played games with the FBI in Boston. Played games with him in Boston, Rigby thought with a flash of anger, remembering the homeless guy and his red windbreaker. The Bomber had some chutzpah for sure, and some skills.

Crosby said, "This is no longer FBI business. We turn everything over to Springfield PD and wash our hands of it unless they need assistance."

Rigby said, "A dead body was found at the tomb this morning. Murder."

Both Crosby and Partosian looked at him in surprise.

"I found the body. A young woman."

"Anything to do with opening the grave?" Crosby asked.

"Or the bomb?" Partosian jumped in.

"The local PD wasn't so keen on my help so I left. You have a good relationship with them?"

"Sure. Chief Braddock knows his stuff," Crosby said.

"And, Detective Hunt?"

He shrugged. "A little wet behind the ears, maybe. But she's a comer from what I hear."

Rigby said, "I'm thinking the girl's murder has something to do with the dig, given the proximity."

"But there's no proof?" Crosby inquired.

"Not yet."

"It's the locals' job to find out, not ours. They want our help and resources, course I'd be happy to assist. But until they ask..." He shook his head.

Rigby thought about the Monument Bomber lead being a dead end and then thought of the poor girl who had come to her own dead end. He thought of Detective Hunt shunning his assistance. He decided he wasn't going to wait for anyone to ask him for help.

"With the murder investigation they'll delay opening the grave. What are you gonna do with your free time?" Crosby asked.

"Get a drink," he said. "Can you direct me to the Railroad Bar?"

Chapter 14

He hefted the weapon onto his shoulder to feel the weight. Only seven kilograms, it rested easily on his shoulder. A familiar feeling, although not a recent one. He had not fired an RPG-7 in a long time, but he knew what it could do. He'd taken down Russian helicopters with this rocket grenade launcher. He had used it against a tank, and the little missile had penetrated the metal monster's skin. For his next attack, he knew it would be extremely destructive.

This time he would be on the scene when the monument exploded. This time he would be firing the explosive. No package left to be detonated later when he was safely away. He knew he would probably only have one shot. It would be devastating. His attack would be at night. The advantage would be his.

He moved the RPG-7 from his shoulder, pointing it at the floor. He needed something to conceal it, which he could carry. The RPG-7 was only 950 mm long, three feet in American measure. A large musician's case would suffice.

The risk to him was great but the reward would be greater. His previous attacks had punched holes in the monuments. They caused outrage from the American public. They caused concern about direct threats to the American homeland. Next time it would be more. So much more. He would make the shot. His brothers would be proud. They would no longer think him a coward, someone who left to escape the fighting.

He was not a coward. Had he not fought on after that

terrible attack? After Afsoon, his wife of only one month, had fallen into his arms, her life bleeding out onto his hands. He fought like a demon to kill the damned Russians. He had killed many–but not enough to make up for Afsoon. When they were gone, when they had left his country, he sought a fresh start. The Americans had been allies. America was the place for his new beginning.

Then came New York City. Ground Zero–and the Americans were no longer a friend to his people. Now they were the invaders. His brothers did not understand why he did not come running home.

They would know why it was important for him to stay in America. To destroy America from the inside with his different kind of war; his war against America's belief in itself.

He lifted the RPG-7 and loaded a grenade into the tube, lifted it to his shoulder pointed it at the apartment's inner wall. Taped to the wall were posters of many of America's monuments and historical places. A large X made by a black marker crossed out the Statue of Liberty poster. The Old Ironsides poster also carried the mark.

Peering through the weapon's sight he moved the rocket launcher from poster to poster. He paused a moment as he sighted each one then moved to the next one. Finally, he stopped moving the weapon.

Yes, that was the one. The grief would be great. The wailing like thunder and rain. The destruction would be thrilling.

Yes, that would be his next target.

Abraham Lincoln.

Chapter 15

The Railroad Bar was too far from the state capitol building to be a regular haunt for the lobbyist types, unless they felt like digging into some good eats. At least the aromas that hit Rigby when he entered the place were appealing. The bar had a feeling of a netherworld, an in-between place. Reaching toward respectability, but with the sense of *anything goes*. He reached that conclusion because the décor was nice and the bartender was partially undressed. The young woman behind the bar, in her twenties, had a pleasant face and long, blonde hair. She was rinsing out drinking glasses. Her torso was covered with a leather-laced top ending a couple of inches above the waist, exposing her silver-studded belly button and bunching up the mounds of her breasts. The pink edge of one nipple showed over the top of the leather. Without hesitation, he chose a seat at the bar.

"What up, big guy?" she said with a nod and a broad smile.

Rigby could never figure out why anyone would torture themselves with body piercing or decorate themselves with metal rings, studs or even tattoos. Especially if God had provided the beauty this young woman possessed. Then again, he remembered the scolding he received when his hair had reached down to his collar and beads were wrapped around his neck. Mild compared to what kids did to themselves today. Who ever thought anyone would think of '60s grooming styles as the good old days?

He wondered how to deal with the woman. She

reminded him of a few ladies who hung around the local bars in his PI days. The conversation here was pretty much the same, whether on a coast or in the heartland. The old PI persona would work in either place.

Rigby considered that the heartland had different mores as he asked himself how a gentleman points out a 'costume malfunction', to use the term of the day. Is the direct approach best, or should he use code words that may not be interpreted correctly? Or maybe simply write a note? He had to be careful, because the last thing he wanted was for her to call a cop.

She got down to business. "What'll you have?"

"In a helpful way, may I point out that you're exposing yourself?" Rigby flicked his eyes toward her exposed nipple.

She followed his gaze without interrupting her work and when she saw what he was indicating, she laughed. "You should see it about eleven. The whole nip gets exposed sometimes with all the rushin' round. But the nips don't hurt the tips, I always say." She winked at him. "You're a cop."

"Should've washed that off this morning."

"You can scrub-a-dub-dub, honey, but that stuff never comes off."

"I'll quit trying."

"So, you on the clock, or you want a shot? Or, you just here to see the sights?" She wriggled her shoulders and breasts while continuing to clean glasses, her smile still intact.

"Looking for a regular. Woman about twenty; short brown hair. Maybe five-foot-four. Smokes a ton."

"Half my late night clientele right there, honey."

"She might have been here last night."

"Annie-May didn't work last night. These are twelve-hour shifts I'm doin'. But only three days a week. Got a picture?"

"Afraid not."

"Gettin' forgetful in your old age?"

"I'm not old."

"Ooh…ooh," she said mockingly. "What kind a cop are you, anyway, honey? You gotta be private."

He could still play that part. No need to mention the FBI. It wouldn't do for his investigation to get back to the Bureau or to Detective Hunt. The FBI sent him to Springfield to find out about Lincoln's body. He was in the bar because of the dead girl. Maybe he was a private cop right now. Then it struck him that maybe it wasn't the girl who brought him here, but a young man and a young woman, not much older that the dead girl, who did not get justice for the crime *they* suffered so many years ago: Melanie and Zane.

He swiveled around to look at those gathering for lunch and saw a mixed clientele. Workmen in coveralls, men and women in business attire, some shoppers. Not too many young people the victim's age.

Turning back to the bartender Rigby said, "What's the night crowd like?"

"Younger bunch. Still some suits, but younger mostly, twenties; thirties crowd, different type of folks."

"Sounds like the lady I'm looking for."

"Hang. I'll keep the beers comin'."

"Appealing."

When he didn't order anything, Annie-May moved to take orders from the waitresses. He considered asking them about the young woman, but figured he wouldn't have their attention as the noonday crowd filled the tables. He would just have to come in at night.

As he rose from the stool, Annie-May came over to try to make a sale one more time. Or so he thought. She said, "You looking for this girl for business or pleasure?"

The thought that pleasure girls worked The Railroad Bar never occurred to him. The place was not low-down enough to be an obvious meat market, nor was it upscale enough to be a prime rib joint.

"You got working girls here?"

"Happens. Nothin' sanctioned by management. Most of the booty around here's free if the hook's baited right."

He nodded. "Truth is, this particular girl won't be coming in any more."

"Bummer. What happened?"

"Not good."

"They don't treat these girls right." Annie-May's words sounded angry. "The girls are just trying to survive the cruel world and it just gets crueler on 'em."

He thought the logic was right. Through the bartender's eyes he was seeing The Railroad Bar and its patrons in a new light. He also had to consider that the dead young woman may have met her end as a trick gone wrong.

"I hope she wasn't a friend," Rigby said to the bartender.

"Haven't heard no one gone missing," she said. "But, may not for a day or a week even. You been down to the Runaway."

"The what?"

"Over at the Mather Wells neighborhood. Goes by another name, a proper name. We call it the Runaway Hotel. Where some of the young runaways come here to Springfield find a place to stay. Old-time converted school. Some of the girls come in regular and a few of them will do what needs be done. You know what I'm sayin', honey?"

The school was built in 1893, the date chiseled in stone above the doorway. The building was two stories high, all red brick and big windows; the top half of the windows had to be opened with a hook on a pole. He had opened a few windows like that himself when he went to elementary school in a similar building, which was only about half as old as this one at the time. The neighborhood was east of

Eleventh Street. This part of town had seen some hard times. The residents tried to keep up a sense of community but the area didn't look or smell anything like Claire's neighborhood.

The name of the school was…well, of course, what else? That name was chiseled in stone, too, next to the front door, which stood above a long column of stairs. However, on the grass in front of the building was a new name for the place, painted rather artlessly on a board held up by three stakes: The Home of Wandering Souls.

Annie-May told him this was a charity project to keep young drifters off the streets and help turn them around. He walked up the front stairs and entered the building. A girl in her late teens, maybe early twenties sat at an old desk in the hallway, serving as some sort of monitor. She read a paperback book, her hands holding down the pages. She looked up as the door banged closed.

"Help you?"

"Maybe. I'm looking for somebody."

"Who?" One small word, but wrapped in suspicion.

"Don't have a name."

"So what else is new?"

"Maybe you can help me with the name."

"Uh-uh." She wagged her head from side to side.

He wondered why she was so mistrusting. Should he pull his badge?

"Can't help you even if I wanted to. No one has names here."

"Really? You call each other by numbers?"

"We call each other what we want to be called. Nicknames. No real names. Get away from our old selves. We can stay here and get our shit together. Figure out which road to follow."

"Looking for the Yellow Brick Road to the Emerald City?"

"Not funny. Girls come here to be protected from

98

people like you."

"And why am I so terrifying?"

"You're a father after a runaway, want to bring her back. Beat her. Abuse her."

Rigby wondered what horrible things this youngster had seen. "Sorry, Sherlock, but your deductive powers are a little off today." It was time. He reached into his inside jacket pocket and pulled out his badge.

"Oh, it's worse. You're a pig."

"Bad experience?"

She pushed back her chair and ordered him to wait. She disappeared into an office behind her.

The hall was decorated with pictures Rigby guessed were drawn by the residents. Some pictures were painted, others were drawn in pencil, and still others used crayons. No flowers or sunshine. Most were dark and sad, undoubtedly projecting the inner feelings of the artists who put up at the Runaway Hotel.

The young woman returned with an older woman in tow. The older woman had gray hair and big tortoise shell glasses, and wore a shawl. Beads were her motif. Beads at the ends of strands of hair. Beads at the edges of her shawl. Beads on her dress. The term *hippie* came to mind. He had known a few in his time.

"Those neighbors complaining again? They should practice some of that Christian charity they're so proud of preaching."

"I'm here to do justice for one of your girls. If she is one of your girls."

"Who?"

"He doesn't know," the young woman said.

"Explain yourself, officer."

"The person I'm looking for may not even live here. Tell me that and I go."

"I'm listening," the old hippie said.

"Woman about nineteen, twenty, short, dark hair, chain

smokes. And one more important thing: she didn't come home last night."

The old hippie looked at the young woman and asked, "Everyone accounted for?"

"Flute didn't get back last night."

"Wouldn't be the first time." The old hippie looked at him. "What do the police want with Flute?"

"It might not be Flute."

"And if it is? I need to know before I tell you more."

"If it is–and that's a big if–then I don't want Flute. I want her killer."

The older lady gasped. The younger one said softly, "Can't be."

"Do you have a picture of Flute around?"

The old hippie instructed her assistant to go get a picture. When the young woman ran off, the older woman asked to see Rigby's credentials. He showed her the badge.

"FBI?"

"Yes."

"I don't understand. FBI is federal."

He nodded, but kept his mouth shut. Rigby's sister once told him when their folks caught them near the broken window that if you don't say anything, you'll never be called on to repeat it. Let the lady think what she wanted to think.

The young woman returned and handed him a picture of her with her arm draped around the shoulders of another woman, both sitting on a large boulder in a park-like setting.

Rigby looked closely at the face of the second woman. The girl in the cemetery, he thought. He pulled out his reading glasses to be sure. No time for a mistake. The girl in the cemetery was Flute.

"Well?" the lady asked.

"I don't want to make a positive ID with just this photo–"

The young woman interrupted: "Flute's dead!" Tears flowed freely and she hung onto the older lady as if she were a life preserver in a troubled sea. The woman looked at him with sad eyes.

"Mind if I look around her room?" he asked, expecting to be denied. The woman just waved him on with simple directions while hugging her young friend.

Rigby went straight down the corridor, took the first left, then went through the classroom door on the right. The old school classroom had been reconfigured into three dormitory rooms all off a main entryway, which was just inside the original classroom door. Each room had a doorway covered by a curtain. Drawings of self-expression by each of the girls who lived in the rooms were pinned to the wall next to the doorway. Someplace on each paper was the girl's nickname. Next to the first curtained door was a child-like drawing of a flute. No name. Enough said.

He pulled back the curtain and walked through the doorway. The room was simple and small. Rigby's college days were well behind him but he thought this room was half the size of his college dorm room. A cardboard box of drawers served as a dresser. A folding cot was open against the wall, covered with bedding. A small half table stood against the wall alongside one chair.

A window looked out to the old schoolyard, grass poking up through cracks in the asphalt. At the edge of the school grounds was a wooden fence, broken in places. He turned from the window and banged into the chair, moving it a little. The walls of the room were decorated with a couple of posters, if you didn't count big pieces of missing chipped paint as decorations. On one wall was the skyline of New York City. The other displayed a flock of seagulls flying over a coastline. He suspected both posters spoke to the girl's urge to be free of her current circumstances.

On top of the cardboard box bureau was a flute. He wondered how good a player she might have been. He picked it up. The flute was obviously important to her. She took it along as a runaway. Maybe it calmed her down or made her think of the memories of home, the good memories. He resisted the temptation to blow on the thing and placed it back on the bureau.

Rigby did not see any notebooks, address books or diaries that could hold a clue to the girl's acquaintances and recent troubles. Placing a hand on the back of the chair, he sat on the cot. The chair rocked unevenly. On the floor, a wadded up paper that had been used to even off the legs had moved, probably when he banged into the chair.

He reached down and picked up the folded paper. It was a thick strip folded over. He opened the paper and found a receipt stub for a train ticket from Lincoln, Illinois to Springfield, Illinois. The ticket was dated in May, four months ago.

"We meet in the strangest places."

The voice startled Rigby. He jerked his head up to see Detective Lisa Hunt and a uniformed cop standing in the doorway.

"Now, I know why you were at the cemetery, but for the life of me I don't know why you should be here," Hunt said. Her tone was not friendly. "In my eyes you're just an average citizen with no right to be involved."

"I found the body. That involved me."

"Not according to the law. Keeping an eye on me?"

He heard something in her voice beyond the question. It had to do with her confidence.

"You're good," he said. "Look what you did with the matchbook cover."

"Matchbook cover?" Her eyes showed uncertainty.

"The one in the parking area across from the cemetery. It led us here."

She seemed to deflate and her eyes turned away. She was quiet a moment and when she continued her words had less bite. "The Crime Scene Unit is still working the area. We're here because the woman fit the profile for this place. You're here because of a matchbook cover."

Was he wrong or did he hear a hint of admiration in her voice? He saw an opportunity to make things better between them. "Maybe you should see this. I found it under the leg of the chair."

He handed her the train ticket receipt. She unfolded it and studied it for a moment, then said, "We don't know if it's from the woman. We don't know who she is or anything about her, even her real name."

Hunt looked at him and he wondered if she was deciding whether it would be helpful to work with him. If this case was a test for her of some sort, he was willing to help.

Ordering the police officer to look around the room, she told him she would talk to the women out front. It didn't sound like an invitation to come along, but when Rigby trailed her down the hall she didn't tell him to get lost, either.

They found the women where they had left them in the hallway. Rigby learned from Hunt's first question that the old hippie was Mrs. Rutherford.

"Same as always, Mrs. Rutherford, no real name or address for the runaway?"

"That's why they trust me, Detective," the woman answered.

"No idea if she was from Springfield or out of town?"

The younger one answered, "She's from farm country… *Was*. Was from farm country." Tears began to form in her eyes. "She wanted away from there."

"Illinois farm country?" Hunt probed.

The girl shrugged.

"Where did she go last night?"

"I don't know," the girl answered. "Flute said she had some business and went."

"Flute have a boyfriend?" Hunt pressed.

"No."

Hunt held up the unfolded train ticket stub. "Says it's

from Lincoln, Illinois to here. Flute ever talk about Lincoln?"

Negative shakes all around.

"Well, we'll get a picture and send it to the police up there," Hunt said.

"How far is it?" Rigby asked.

"Lincoln? Maybe thirty-five miles north up the interstate."

"Better to go there," he said.

"A picture will do."

"The girl may not be well known." Go the extra mile, he silently urged Hunt. Follow the lead. He wanted to root for Hunt to pass her test. He didn't want her to disappoint him, and more important, to disappoint the dead girl.

"Don't be like those cops in Maine," he blurted out.

They all looked at him strangely.

He didn't want to explain. "Never mind."

"A picture will do, Agent Rigby," she repeated with finality, establishing her position on top of the pecking order in front of the women.

"A picture–" Mrs. Rutherford began, holding up her hand to point at Rigby.

He interrupted before she could get her message out to Hunt.

"A picture just of Flute alone, that's what the detective needs." He wasn't about to give up his picture of Flute, which was safely tucked in his jacket pocket. Rigby walked toward the door before anyone could make a fuss about it.

Chapter 16

Growths of September corn four and five feet high stood against open patches of harvested areas in a checkerboard pattern stretching away from both sides of the interstate for miles. Rigby was nearing the Lincoln, Illinois exit. The drive took not much more than half an hour. He thought, again, with chagrin that Detective Hunt said it was too much of a trip.

He tried to pretend the reason he came to Lincoln was because he wanted to be more thorough than Hunt. Truthfully, he came because Hunt wanted him away from her case, because the dig would not go on until the police were satisfied they had cleared the cemetery of clues, and–perhaps most of all–he did not want to run into Claire.

Claire had made herself clear. She was happily married and she wanted the dig to end so he would go. Rigby wondered if his looks disappointed her. He pulled down the car visor and opened the mirror, careful to dart his eyes at the road as he drove. Hoping to see the face of a college boy staring back at him, instead the face carried lines marking the passage of years, topped with hair more gray than black. He snapped the mirror cover closed and flipped up the visor.

He exited the highway. To the right, by a railroad track, was a state park with glorious trees breaking up the flat landscape. He crossed a bridge over what a sign said was Salt Creek and into Lincoln on Route 66.

"I get my kicks on Route 66," Rigby said aloud and thought of the old TV show with Tod and Buz crisscrossing the country in their snappy Corvette convertible. They were the envy of every boy in his school. Now here he was on the famous road in a plain vanilla rental car with no sidekick or hope for adventure. Guess you can't be Tod and Buz forever. Hell, Tod and Buz weren't Tod and Buz forever. They were cancelled after three or four years.

Lincoln was a lively little town built around a big, old courthouse plopped in the middle of the town square, with neighboring buildings and storefronts of distinct late nineteenth and early twentieth century architecture. Asking at his hotel, Rigby was told Lincoln was the spiritual and governmental center of Logan County, so naturally it was also the population center with probably no more than 15,000 residents.

He drove by the train station and decided that would be a good place to start his investigation to find the identity of the dead young woman. It was the train ticket stub that brought him here.

The station was made up in part of derailed cars that had been attached or placed next to the depot. He assumed the cars were used for restaurants and waiting rooms. There were some cabooses and dining cars. Lincoln was like many Midwestern towns that came to life when railroads ran through them. This little addition to the depot served as some kind of homage to the town's existence.

He parked the car, walked around to a red brick sidewalk entryway and passed under the *Lincoln Depot* sign. Three people stood in line at the ticket window. Pulling his badge, Rigby interrupted the transaction going on between a white-haired clerk and a young woman and her five-year-old child.

"Sorry, folks, got some police business."

Showing the photograph of the dead woman and her friend, he slid the photo to the clerk, who wore a nametag that read *Eddie*.

"Eddie, ever see this woman?" He pointed to Flute.

Eddie took the photograph and studied it closely, as if

he were looking for Waldo hidden in a sea of beachgoers, then pronounced firmly, "I don't know."

"You don't know if you ever saw her?"

"Maybe I have. I see lots of people."

"She might have bought a ticket to Springfield in May."

"Mister, that was months ago."

"Possibly shuttles back and forth if she's got folks here."

"Then she'd be a regular and I'd recognize a regular like Miss Sue and little Helen here."

"Is that me, mommy?" the little girl asked upon hearing her name. Sue shushed her.

"I guess she wasn't a regular, then," Rigby said. "And you don't remember her?"

Again Eddie stared at the picture, looking for hidden meaning.

"Can we move this along?" the man behind Sue asked.

Rigby took the photo back from Eddie, walked it over to the man and asked if he recognized the girl. When he shook his head Rigby asked Sue the same question and got the same result.

He thought the next best place to stop was the police station, although he didn't know what reaction he would get there if Lisa Hunt had sent the picture of Flute along as she promised to–probably with a warning to be wary of a snooping FBI man.

He considered another avenue to pursue. In his PI days, when he didn't have the luxury of police authority to back up his play, Rigby would try to find the local know-it-all, the town gossip, to get information. Most towns had at least one. It was worth a try without having to involve the police right away, and he figured Eddie might know who that person was.

"Tell me, Eddie, who might know the comings and goings around here, official and unofficial, if you know what I mean?"

Eddie knew what he meant. But it put him right back with the local authorities.

"You want to see Deputy Gable. He's over the old courthouse. Usually works security at the entrance."

Rigby headed back to his car and realized he could easily walk to the courthouse square, so he headed up Pulaski Street. A historical marker affixed to the side of a building caught his eye, and he quickly scanned the words. It noted this was the site of the Rustic Inn, in which a counterfeiting gang met to hatch a plot to steal Lincoln's corpse. Rigby laughed and wondered if the Judge had superpowers willing him to walk this way to see the marker so he'd keep his mind on the reason he was in Illinois. Well, today his mission was to find out about the murdered woman and that's what he intended to do.

Rigby reached the town square and the impressive courthouse. A whole city block, three stories high, it was made of large stone blocks and smaller stone bricks, topped in the center of the building by a large dome. Clock faces were on each side of the dome, facing the four directions of the compass. The building had the look of early twentieth century architecture.

Rigby went up the steps and into the building. A metal detector stood inside the door. Any public building, even this far from the power centers of the country, felt concerns over possible terror attacks. He wondered if a place like this would be a target for the Monument Bomber.

He flashed his badge at the young sheriff's deputy on the other side of the detector and walked through to the beeping sounds of the device that had detected his gun.

"Deputy Gable?"

"No, sir, he's on break. You can find him upstairs. Sometimes he stretches out on a bench in one of those old courtrooms."

Rigby looked up the staircase and then at the dome. It

was even more impressive from the inside. The inner dome was made of stained glass and was smaller and separate from the outer dome. Climbing the stairs, he came upon some murals. A sign said each wall represented the county seat in what became Logan County with the town's name and date inscribed on the mural. One wall had the open spaces of Elk Hill in 1819; then Postville in 1839 with its two-story courthouse. Mt. Pulaski took over the county seat in 1848 earning its own mural, and finally Lincoln in 1857. Naturally, portraits and statues of Abraham Lincoln could be found in the courthouse, along with some other Illinois dignitaries.

Rigby found the courtrooms and poked his head inside the first one, noticing its early twentieth century charm. He moved on to the second courtroom just as the door opened and a big man in a sheriff's uniform exited.

"Deputy Gable?"

"That's right," the man responded with a wide grin. "Deputy Clark Gable. Guess who I'm named after? My mother had a thing for him." At just under six feet and just over 250 pounds, with no mustache and long, graying hair the deputy looked nothing like his namesake.

"My name's Zane Rigby, FBI." Rigby showed Gable his credentials. "Mind if we talk a moment."

"Don't mind at all. Step into my office," he said, pulling open the door to the courtroom.

They entered the empty courtroom and sat down in the last row of benches.

"This here's a famous courthouse. Built in 1905. On the National Register of Historic Places. The dome's a beaut!"

"I am impressed," Rigby said cordially.

"This town's the only one named for Mr. Lincoln before he became president," Clark Gable said. It sounded like he gave this spiel often to visitors. "He christened the town by spilling watermelon juice on the ground."

"Really." Did Rigby sound bored? He hoped so. Rigby

should have expected this. You look for the town gossip you have to expect a chatterer.

"He rode the circuit here. When he was in the state legislature he helped get the bill passed that created the county so they named the town after him."

Rigby wanted to say, *Frankly, my dear, I don't give a damn*. He did say, "I'm trying to identify a murdered woman."

"That so? Got some national security issue here in Lincoln?"

"I'm looking for a connection to this woman." He pulled the picture from his pocket and pointed at Flute. "She may or may not be from around here. But I understand you keep a good tab on the comings and goings in Lincoln."

"Just doing my job," Deputy Gable said. He studied the picture. Finally he said, "Could be."

"Could be what?"

"Could…be," he repeated as if stalling for time so he could study the picture longer. "Could be that girl."

Rigby waited for a further explanation, and finally it came.

"A few months back I came out on my lunch break. Brown bagged it that day and went outside to sit on a bench. A young woman was there on the bench and she was eyeing my sandwich. I figured she was hungry, so I shared my sandwich with her. Turkey on wheat with a nickel-sized splash of mayo, always bring the same thing. She chomped it down like a wolf. Said she spent her last dollar on a train ticket to Springfield."

"Did she mention her name? Where she came from?"

"No name. Said her folks farmed near Clinton. That's east down the state road."

"And that was a few months ago?"

"Yeah. The springtime, I think. I talk to lots of folks, but this one I shared my sandwich with. That's why I remember. Pretty thing. She was interested in my name, too.

Most folks are." He laughed. "But I remember her saying she watched all the old movie channels on satellite to escape... Clark Gable, all the old stars. I thought it sad. Didn't like the farm living much. She part of a terrorist plot?"

"A victim of terror," Rigby said.

"Too bad." Suddenly, he snapped his fingers. "I remember now, remember something else she said. Said her folks flew the biggest Stars and Stripes in the county, down by Clinton way."

Illinois Highway 10 brought Rigby back to the wide-open spaces of the great prairie. There was cornfield upon cornfield. The farmers were kind enough to place signs by the roadside identifying the types of corn, the different hybrids. He didn't recognize any of the names. The extent of his knowledge about different kinds of corn was that there is yellow corn and white corn and some of it you can pop. That was about it.

The open spaces were broken up by an occasional farmhouse, some probably built in the 1880s, others more modern. Trees and grain silos dotted the countryside along with a handful of telephone cell towers. Flat, endless roads marked by numbers instead of names crossed the flat, endless road on which he traveled. Rigby felt like a sailor on a ship at sea far from land.

Finally, he arrived in Clinton, and wondered if all the towns on this road were named for presidents, although he knew this town was around before the president of the same name. When Rigby saw a farmer by the side of the road he pulled over and asked about the big American flag. The farmer had no trouble identifying the Blair Farm and offered directions.

It was off in the country, down more flat, endless roads with plenty of corn and cows, and the occasional slow tractors hogging the road. The drive took longer than he would have liked. Finally, Rigby came to a white, two-story farmhouse and red barn, a silo nearby. Red, white, and blue bunting adorned the porch. A sturdy flagpole stood in front of the porch with an enormous American flag hanging limp in the breezeless afternoon.

Rigby pulled the car off on a gravel drive to an area where other cars were parked in front of the barn. Greeting him as he exited the car were three dogs, each a mixed breed, with tails wagging and noses twitching as they closed in for a good sniff. After a day of hustling around from murder site to a bar, the Runaway Hotel, and the town of Lincoln he figured he had a lot to offer them. Rigby patted each dog in turn, then led the parade to the house, climbed the front stairs to the porch and, being an equal opportunity patter, rubbed the tiger cat sitting on top of the rail at the head of the stairs.

The front door was open behind a screen door, and he could see inside the house to a front parlor of comfortable and well-used furniture and walls decorated with family pictures. However, the screen made it difficult to identify anyone in the pictures. He could smell the aroma of cooked food drifting down a hallway from the kitchen, certain that he got the whiff of a fresh baked apple pie. Rigby knocked on the wood frame of the screen door.

It took a second knock before he got a response from the back. A female voice called out, "Coming. Got to undo my apron."

Soon a middle-aged woman approached the screen door. She wore a plain print dress and her hair was pulled up in a bun. A smile on her face faded as she neared the door. Rigby sensed she was afraid of him for some reason and he spoke up to reassure her.

"Good afternoon, Ma'am, name's Rigby."

"One moment, please," she said and then in a louder voice called out, "Artie. Come down here."

Rigby wondered if she was pretending to call for a man

so that he would not think she was alone. She stayed a few feet back from the screen door. The dogs were gathered around his feet, wagging their tails and waiting for the opportunity for the door to open so that they could bolt inside the house.

The call to Artie was not phony. A sound of clumping boots descending the stairs announced the man's arrival. Soon a man wearing blue coveralls with the button on the left shoulder unattached, as if he were in the process of changing, joined the woman. The woman pointed at Rigby and started to knead one hand with the other.

"Help you?" Artie asked in a not unfriendly way.

"My name's Zane Rigby."

The woman cut him off and spoke up now that her husband was standing by her side. "Are you with the Army?"

Strange question, Rigby thought. "No."

A wave of relief washed over her and the smile returned to her face. "I didn't know. I didn't know how they did these things. Our boy's in the service. I thought you might be bearing bad news. How silly of me."

She put her arm around her husband and squeezed.

Rigby felt he had been hit in the stomach by Muhammad Ali. She was so relieved that he wasn't bearing bad news about her son, but if Flute were her daughter Rigby was still the dark angel she feared. Her relief would be momentary and the shock would be great. He prayed that the dead girl was not her daughter.

"So you sellin' somethin'?" Artie asked.

"Mr. and Mrs. Blair, I work with the police. I wondered if you can identify the young woman in this photo?"

He had the picture out of his pocket and held it up on his side of the screen. The Blairs approached and Artie pushed open the screen door. All three dogs and the cat scampered into the house.

Holding open the screen, Artie took the photo and shared it with his wife. "Yeah, the one on the left is Mary, our daughter. What's up?"

Somberly, Rigby said, "Then I'm afraid I do come with bad news."

He gave them all the time that they needed. Nearly half an hour went by and the outright bawling of both parents had subsided to sniffles, occasional outbursts of more tears, and constant hugging. The Blairs were seated on the sofa in the living room. Rigby sat in the rocking chair and did his best to hold the chair still, not wanting to rock the thing because the motion seemed somehow casual and disrespectful.

Finally, conversation began in fits and starts. When they requested information, he told them what he knew, which wasn't much. They were looking for a motive for this terrible act and he couldn't supply one and neither could they.

"I...we...we didn't know she was in Springfield," Mrs. Blair said.

"You didn't notice the postmarks on the letters?"

"No letters," Artie Blair said. "E-mails." He shrugged. "Didn't know where they came from. She must've borrowed a computer or used one in the library or somethin'. We didn't want her to go, mind you. She sort of ran away. Sort of. There was lots of yellin' and stuff, but when she walked out we didn't block the door. We just asked her to stay in touch 'cause we'd worry."

This brought more tears from Mrs. Blair and a break in the conversation.

Artie Blair said, "She never liked the isolation of this place. She needed more people. We knew we couldn't keep her here forever, so we didn't stand in the door when she packed up. The day she turned eighteen she up and left."

Only eighteen, Rigby thought and he felt his shoulders slump.

114

"We thought she was in Chicago," Mrs. Blair said. "That's where runaways go, don't they? The big city. She mentioned Chicago in her e-mails a couple of times."

"Did you save any of her e-mails?"

"I think the last one's still on the machine," Artie said. He hugged his wife again, stood up from the couch and motioned to Rigby to follow him as Mrs. Blair buried her face in a handkerchief, sobbing silently.

The computer was on a desk off an alcove in the kitchen. Blair fired it up and connected to his e-mail file. The note from Mary Blair–Flute–was short and five days old. It read: *Doing okay. Have a chance to make good money soon. Have friends. Having fun with Chicago. Love, me.*

"Any idea what the money project was?" he asked. Blair didn't know.

"Did Flute, I mean Mary, keep in touch with anyone else? Did she e-mail her brother in the service? How about friends from here?"

"If she did, we don't know," her father said. "She was rebellious. You know how kids get. Especially one that's going to leave home. We don't even know how she got to the train station."

Rigby's drive back toward Lincoln was a good twenty miles above the speed limit. He wanted to get his information on Flute to Detective Hunt. He promised himself he wouldn't gloat.

He heard the familiar ring of his cell phone. He pulled it from the vest pocket.

"Yeah?"

"Zane?"

Claire. He could recognize her voice on one word, its sound permanently imprinted in his memory. There was a tremor in her voice.

"What's the matter, Claire?"

"Someone tried to run me off the road!"

"Are you all right?" Now there was panic in his voice.

"I'm scared."

"Where are you?"

"At home with Craig."

"I'm near the town of Lincoln. I'm coming. Call the police."

"I'll wait for you. We're okay here. But I'm scared."

"I'm coming."

He clicked off the phone and wondered why Claire had called him and not her husband. Rigby jammed on the accelerator and the speedometer climbed to ninety-five.

Chapter 17

It was not cool enough to wear regular gloves so he wore the see-through kind, the one the food processors use at fast food restaurants. These, too, looked suspicious and out of place, but he was carrying the letter that would go to the FBI. He'd had these gloves on ever since composing the letter, to protect against leaving any telltale signs. He pulled his hands into the sleeves of his lightweight jacket as far as possible; only the tips of his fingers could be seen by passers-by. He had pulled the gloves tight so the material clung to his fingers. They would be difficult to spot unless someone stared at the envelope in his hand. No one would have a reason to do that, he thought. Still, he watched the eyes of the people walking down the street and frequently looked over his shoulder to see if anyone following him was fixated on the letter he held.

He enjoyed this cat-and-mouse game with the FBI. He thought himself very good at it. He had tricked them so well in Boston. It had cost him only $200 and some secondhand clothes he picked up in various thrift shops to send the decoy into the FBI trap.

When he sent his first letter, warning of his New York attack, he doubted they believed him. He had set up a diversion there as well, but it was not needed.

Now they would believe him. That is why he could laugh about this new letter. He walked more than one step ahead of the FBI. That was the American expression, wasn't it–one step ahead.

From his humble beginnings no one could ever imagine he would turn out as he had. A man like that movie character–James Bond. That is how he saw himself in this duel he had created against the evil Americans. But then, no one could see the wars that ravaged his country. Who would have dreamed he would leave his country of birth to settle in the United States, only to then see his new country attack his old one?

While the war carried on in Afghanistan, he would open a new front at home. Not by killing people–although many Americans deserved to die–but by killing their beliefs. Turning them to see what the rest of the world thought of them. This was a war they did not expect.

Feeling the envelope in his fingertips, he knew he would fool the FBI again and this time with the help of his rocket launcher he would destroy Abraham Lincoln. Destroy! Yes, this will give him great pleasure. Whatever news he made with his earlier actions would pale by his next attack. This would tear at the heart of the Americans. He liked that very much.

He had passed a number of mailboxes along the route he had taken that afternoon. Now he felt he had come far enough. He approached the mailbox at the next corner, dropped his letter in, and walked another two blocks before removing his gloves and disposing of them in a city trash receptacle.

Chapter 18

"A big, black pickup truck with tinted windows," Claire said. She held Rigby's hand in both of hers. It felt good. They were in the living room of her house. Craig sat in his wheelchair looking out a window into the backyard. He was quiet and restrained, much different than the gregarious kid Rigby met on his first visit. The boy, too, was scared.

"I left work early...Craig has a doctor's appointment. I was on my way home when suddenly this...this big pickup was on me. Someone in a hurry, I thought. I slowed so he'd pass. I was on a two-lane road. Straight...flat. Nothing was coming the other way. But he didn't go around. He slowed, too. Then he came right up on my rear bumper."

"He? Did you see the driver?"

"No. Not really. I saw a baseball cap low over a face. Maybe a she, doubt it... But whoever, the driver seemed large...it was a big vehicle and the driver wasn't dwarfed by it. You know how small women in big vehicles look lost? Not this time."

"What was on the cap?"

"It was a Cardinals' cap. Red with the intertwined S, T, and L for St. Louis."

"None of the Cardinals would do that to you, Mom," Craig spoke up, defending his heroes.

"Someone was wearing a Cardinals cap, Craig. I didn't say it was a player." She lowered her voice to a whisper. "I'm worried I scared him. When I got home I was a bundle of nerves."

"He'll be okay." Rigby reached out with his free hand

to give a reassuring squeeze on Claire's upper arm. He did not want to pull his other hand away from her grip. "Maybe it was an obnoxious teenager–"

"Being dangerous! He bumped my car twice. *Twice*. There's a dent in the bumper. The second bump he accelerated, pushing my car to the edge of the road. My tires skidded on the gravel. I was afraid I'd fly off the road."

"What happened?"

"Once the cars separated…when I skidded…he pulled around and sped away."

"Did you get the license? Anything distinctive about the car?"

"I closed my eyes, Zane."

She said this with a sense of terror and exhaustion. He pulled his hand free of hers and enveloped her in a hug. He buried his face in her hair and smelled the wonderful, familiar scent of Claire. Still the fragrance of lilacs about her. She sobbed into his shoulder and then whispered in a low voice her son would not hear, "Does this have to do with the terrible things going on at the cemetery?"

How to answer? He did not understand how all the pieces fit: the exploded dump truck, the dead girl, Claire's moment of terror. They all had some relation to Lincoln's Tomb, but there could be other explanations for each incident.

He wanted to tell Claire everything would be all right. That the person who pushed her off the road was a crummy driver, not a killer, but he had no way of knowing that. He felt guilty. Claire feared the worst, and in fearing the worst she had called him. She held him close. He did not want her to let go. He took the coward's way out and did not respond to her question. He justified his non-response by telling himself he really didn't know the truth. He just squeezed her tighter.

When Rigby sensed she was ready to break free, he let go and said, "You have to talk to the police."

"I suppose I should, but I have to take Craig to Dr. Rittinghouse. We have the last appointment of the day and I can still get us there. But I'm afraid. I know it's asking a lot, but will you come, please?"

He wondered where Sir Peter was but didn't ask. "My pleasure."

Rigby followed Claire's directions until they reached a warehouse district, where she instructed him to park in front of an old brick building. A motorcycle repair shop stood next door. A mechanic worked on a large chopper in front of the garage revved the engine, setting off a loud *vroom*. The guy smiled with satisfaction over a job well done.

Rigby looked at Claire. "A doctor's office?"

"He's a genius," Claire said, getting out of the car to retrieve Craig's wheelchair from the trunk.

Self-described *geniuses* often work or live in places like this. Rigby decided that's why they thought of themselves as geniuses. The warehouse was a fairly clean structure, as warehouses go, and the artificial plants by the front door were as green as could be, but the place was still a warehouse. They moved down a corridor of corrugated sheet metal walls past a large, open storage area and arrived at another walled off section in the rear. Claire opened an unmarked door and Craig wheeled inside; Rigby and Claire followed.

No flasks and bubbling potions. No work areas stocked with chemicals. The office-laboratory was spacious, filled with computers and odd-looking machines. A grouping of chairs and a couch by the door served as a waiting area. A woman at a desk was closing down her computer for the night.

"Dr. Orange, we didn't think you were coming."

"Is it too late?"

"I'm sure he'll see you."

The doctor was working on a computer at a desk against the back wall. He seemed lost in concentration. The woman walked to the back of the large room and whispered something to him. He stood and approached them.

Tall and lean in a white medical coat over an open shirt collar, the man had classic features, tight skin over pronounced cheekbones, a narrow nose and flowing black hair he wore down to his collar. Stripped to his waist and mounted bareback on a pony, he would easily pass for an Indian warrior of old.

"Who have we here?" The doctor walked straight toward Rigby and looked down on him from his superior height.

"Friend of the family." Rigby extended his hand. "Zane Rigby."

"Bernard Rittinghouse," he said, taking Rigby's hand briefly, and then turning an inquiring eye on Claire.

"Zane helped me with a problem I was having today."

"Ah, another specialist. That makes two of us. Are you good at your specialty, Mr. Rigby?"

"Depends who you ask."

"I'm asking you," he said.

Rigby wondered if this was some sort of dog-pissing contest marking territory. Okay, he could keep up.

"I can do the job and I can handle the instruments." *Bang-bang.*

Turning to Claire, the doctor said, "It takes a bit more than that to be a specialist." His gaze stayed on Claire a bit longer before he faced Craig. "And how's my patient?"

"Okay, Doc. But no tingly feeling yet."

"I see. All right, we should take a look." To Rigby he said, "Do you mind?"

Claire said, "I'll stay with Zane. Let me know if you need me."

Rittinghouse nodded and led Craig back to his computer. Rigby watched as the doctor hooked Craig up to some wires and then concentrated on the computer again.

Rigby and Claire sat down on the couch. He put a

122

reassuring hand on her shoulder and left it there. Claire sighed deeply. She did not acknowledge his hand nor try to remove it. She stared at the floor, seeing something inside her that he was not privy to.

To break the silence he said, "Strange bedside manner your doc has."

"He's a genius, really. That's why I take Craig to see him. He's the only one that can help."

"Do what?"

"Make Craig walk again."

Rigby removed his hand from Claire's shoulder and put it on her chin, turning her face in his direction. God, she was beautiful, but her features were so sad.

"Aren't you hoping for a miracle? That's even out of a genius' league."

"Oh, no, Zane. He's made great progress. Rejuvenation of the spinal cord nerves is his life's work. He's a brilliant man. He studies stem cells, DNA–knows it all. I know he'll make Craig walk again. Why should I think anything different?"

She was right. Cling to the impossible if that's what keeps you going.

"You see," she started softly, then looked at the floor again, "it's all my fault. Craig's condition, I mean. I yelled at him. This was two years ago. A silly argument like mothers and sons have all over the world throughout history. He ran into the backyard and climbed into his tree house. He was angry, still screaming…and what do I do? Like an idiot, I go outside and yell back; no, I won't take his guff, not this day…" Tears glistened in her eyes. "No, I'll stand up to his carrying on. So I yell back and he gets more angry and steps out on the tree limb to scream at me and…and falls to the ground…cracking…his spine."

Claire cried. Rigby draped an arm around her and told her she didn't mean to hurt the boy, but he could feel that he was holding pure guilt. They sat in silence for a while until they heard Craig's chatty voice. He pushed himself toward them, followed by Rittinghouse.

The doctor said he could talk to Claire now and she said that it was all right to speak in front of Rigby. From his look, the doctor did not want to, or at least didn't think that was the professional thing to do, but he sat down in a chair opposite them.

"Craig's doing fine. I'd say he's almost ready."

"For what?" Rigby asked.

The doctor shot him a look. He took the question as one of impertinence and Rigby guessed he agreed, but didn't care. He was worried about Claire. Worried about the kid, too. With all the guilt that overwhelmed Claire, he felt she was susceptible to quackery.

Claire said, "Dr. Rittinghouse has been working on a special method to restore nerves; allow disabled people to walk. He thinks Craig's an excellent candidate."

Rittinghouse leaned back in his chair, sticking his long legs out in front of him, and said, "I smell a non-believer."

Rigby had seen a few cut-rate charlatans and scam artists in his PI days. The ones he encountered since joining the FBI were usually more sophisticated. He couldn't tell about this guy. He considered dropping the fact that he was a cop, but he didn't want to put Rittinghouse on guard. Maybe he'd tip his game by just talking. Rigby said, "Natural to be skeptical."

"Three things hold back scientific progress." Rittinghouse held up three fingers. "One, aversion of those in power to take risks. Two, negativity. A belief that progress can't be achieved so what you're seeing is smoke and mirrors, forgery and fakes. And, three is money."

"No fair," Rigby said, "that last is a universal ingredient named by all who fail."

Rittinghouse eyed Rigby for a time before responding. When he spoke, his words came rapid-fire with an air of superiority. "In South Korea, doctors at Chosun University

Joel Fox

and Seoul National University transplanted stem cells isolated from umbilical cord blood into a patient who could not stand for nineteen years, and she's now walking. In Portugal, stem cells removed from within a one-inch section of a person's upper nasal cavity are implanted in the injured area after scar tissue is removed. These stem cells produce new nerves and promote healing. Olfactory cells regenerate. That's why your sense of smell comes back after you've had a cold. My strategy to have the disabled walk again is even more dramatic, more certain."

"And that is?"

"Still a trade secret, but it's coming along fine. This will be a world-renowned breakthrough of great complexity. But in the simplest terms, I fix what's broken. Isn't that your specialty, too?"

Rigby had his doubts about all of this, but understood that when it came to biology, the frog he dissected in high school had a higher IQ than him. He'd ask Smitty to check this guy out. Still, even if all he said were true his method was experimental, and Craig should not be a guinea pig.

To Claire, Rigby said, "You ought to get a second opinion."

"She can do what she wants," Rittinghouse said. "But few will understand. My method will work. I talk it over constantly with my brothers and sisters. I come from a family of doctors and am descended from doctors." He pointed to a picture on the wall of eight people of varying ages, all wearing doctors' smocks.

"Dr. Frankenstein in the family?"

Rittinghouse didn't see the humor. Rigby looked at Claire and her son, and thought again about Sir Peter. He should be part of the decision-making process for his son. Rigby had to ask: "Where's your husband?"

"With a client, I suppose. I couldn't raise him on his cell."

Rittinghouse stood. To Craig he said, "Not too long

125

now. Keep taking those pills so you'll be ready when the time comes."

Craig said he would. Claire thanked the doctor. Rigby didn't say a word.

Chapter 19

Rigby dropped Claire and Craig off at their home. Claire invited him to come inside.

"Are you still upset?"

"Much better, thanks to you. And, Peter should be home soon."

He didn't see the point of hanging around if Sir Peter was on his way. "If you need me you have my cell number on the business card I gave Craig."

"How do you think I called you when I was run off the road," she reminded him with that wonderful, warm Claire smile.

He smiled back, squeezed her arm and walked to his car.

Rigby drove back to town to find Lisa Hunt. He needed to let her know he'd identified the dead girl and talked to her parents. He also weighed what he should tell her about Claire's escape from the crazed pickup driver. All this he wanted to say to Hunt's face. When he was told on the phone that she was at police headquarters, but could not be disturbed, he changed course. He headed to the Runaway Hotel.

Lights were on throughout the old school as Rigby pulled up in front. He was playing a hunch, but it seemed reasonable. If it paid off, he expected to gather a whole crop of new information about Flute, nee Mary Blair.

Inside the building a different girl sat at the monitor's desk. She was short and dark and played a hand-held video game. Rigby asked to see Mrs. Rutherford.

"Okay," the girl said without asking who he was. "She

went to the cafeteria. Wait here."

The girl left her post, and once again Rigby scanned the pictures drawn by residents and posted on the wall. This time he looked with a purpose for the author's signature, hoping to find something that Flute had drawn. He found it above the fire alarm box. The small, flat drawing of a flute, similar to the one he'd seen earlier in the day next to Flute's dorm room door, was in the corner of a picture of a city skyline. The drawing appeared sketchy and child-like. The city skyline was bleak and dark, all blacks and grays. However, in the corner she'd drawn a baby carriage, and inside the carriage was a crude drawing of a baby, pink and flesh tones, standing out against the ominous background. Was the baby Flute finding her way in the big city?

"It's you, is it?" Mrs. Rutherford strode up the hallway.

"I wonder if I can have this picture of Flute's." Rigby pointed at the artwork.

"What for?"

"To send to her parents."

Mrs. Rutherford looked surprised.

"Yes, I found them. They live about fifty miles from here. Flute's real name was Mary Blair."

"Mary," the young girl said with a sense of wonder, as if discovering someone's real name was unlocking a treasure chest.

"Yes. Send it to them. And let them know I did my best by her," Mrs. Rutherford said.

"I'm sure you did." He unpinned the drawing from the wall.

"Anything else?" Mrs. Rutherford raised an eyebrow in inquiry.

"Yes. I'd like to talk to Chicago."

For the second time within a minute he surprised the woman. S*tunned* would be more appropriate. She looked at him a long time, as if he were a wizard.

"Did you tell Detective Hunt about Flute's best friend?"

Mrs. Rutherford shook her head slowly. "She didn't ask and Chicago doesn't live here anymore. How did you know?"

"References to Chicago in Flute's e-mails back home. Her parents thought she meant the city. Given your set-up I figured it was a nickname. Where's Chicago now?"

"Gone. Ran off and married last week. She probably doesn't know about Flute."

"No forwarding address?"

"We don't keep those kind of things," Mrs. Rutherford said. "We're a home while they're here."

"But I know," the young girl said. "She told me where her man lived."

The address was an apartment in downtown Springfield, above stores. *Address* was too strong a description for what the girl gave him. More or less directions from cross streets to where he could find the staircase leading up to the apartments above the storefronts. She did not know which apartment belonged to Chicago.

By the time he arrived at Capitol Ave. between 5th and 6th the city was shutting down for the night. All the commercial places were closed except for the occasional restaurant. No problem in finding a parking spot. He moved along the storefronts on the north side of the street looking for the narrow stairway he was told would be there. Above the stores were large windows, a few lights on. Rigby wondered if he was in the right place. The large windows could have been apartments, but they appeared to be offices.

Near the end of the block, set back in a dark alcove, was a door. There were four thin mailboxes in the wall next to the door with the letters A to D marking each box, no names. He turned the handle and the door opened. Behind the door was a set of stairs that would make an aerobics instructor weary. He took the stairs two at a time until halfway up, and then switched to one step at a time. When he reached the top he was puffing. What happened to the guy who used to run cross-country in college? He'd gained thirty pounds over the years, but Rigby chose to believe that was nature's fault. If age is going to be a bummer when it comes to eyesight, hearing, and all sorts of things, at least it can be an excuse for a few extra pounds.

The hallway at the top of the stairs was wide, reflecting the design of a grandiose building from the early years of the twentieth century. All the doors were on his right-hand side toward the street. As he walked the corridor, the floor creaked beneath his feet.

The first door, with a big wooden A in the center, had a sign identifying it as an insurance agent's office. Office B was an accountant's office; Office C belonged to a lawyer. Certainly, these were not apartments and Rigby wondered if he got the directions wrong or if the young woman was told where Chicago's husband worked rather than where he lived.

Office D had no identification and light was escaping from under the door. After climbing all those stairs he decided he was entitled to find out if this was the right place. He knocked.

From inside a female voice said, "Forget the key again, stupid?"

The door opened. A young woman of eighteen or nineteen stood there wearing only a black thong and a tight T-shirt, her nipples protruding in the appropriate places. A tattoo of Asian letters ran from her hip down the front of her left leg to the top of her knee. She had raven black hair with facial features that probably went all the way back to Caesar.

With no embarrassment she stood at the door staring at him as if he were the oddball in this situation and said, "You're not Don."

"But, I'll bet you're Chicago."

"You win the bet. You a friend of Don's?"

130

He felt uncomfortable carrying on the conversation dressed the way she was–or rather undressed the way she was–but she didn't seem to mind.

"I don't know Don, but I know Flute."

A smile covered her face like morning sunshine. "I should've told her what Don and me was cookin', but he made me swear. I was gonna call. Honest. How's she?"

The open room was partially an office with a desk and worktable by the windows. Apparently, Don conducted some sort of business from the place, but it was also living quarters for the newlyweds with an opened sleeper sofa, small dining table, sink and pint-sized refrigerator in view from the open doorway. Rigby wanted to ask her if he could come inside, but given her state of undress he didn't want her to take his approach the wrong way.

He hung his head and waited for a moment. She sensed something was wrong and her smile faded to sunset.

"I'm afraid I have bad news." He paused. He wanted Chicago to steel herself, but the pause was as much for him delivering the bad news as for her receiving it. "Flute was murdered."

"No!" the woman wrapped her arms around her torso and shuddered. "No, it can't be!"

"Maybe you should sit down," he said.

She shook her head. He didn't know whether she was responding negatively to his suggestion or if she were trying to reject the idea that her friend was dead.

He gave her some time before saying, "I have to talk to you about Flute."

"Not here." Without closing the door she went over to a box that apparently served as a clothes bureau, pulled out a pair of jeans and a sweater and put them on. She slipped into a pair of sandals, picked up a key from the dining table, and came out to the hallway, closing and locking the door behind her. "This way," she said, leading him back down the hallway toward the stairway to the street.

131

They settled into a corner booth of a restaurant, about a block away, that had seen its best days when Eisenhower was president, and ordered coffee. Her first words since they left her room told Rigby why she wanted to get away. "Don'll be home soon. And, he don't know all about me. He don't know I lived in the Runaway and it's best to keep it that way. Are you working the case?"

Rigby guessed he was in his own way. "Yes."

"Poor Flute. She had so much to live for."

"Good things were happening to her?"

"Duh! She was pregnant."

Rigby considered this for a moment. "Who was the father?"

Chicago sipped from her coffee cup and said nothing.

Rigby's patience was running thin. "Look there's a killer out there. He killed Flute, someone close to you. He may have tried to kill someone dear to me. He may be reckless enough to kill indiscriminately with bombs. I need your help to find him."

"I don't know. Honest. She told me she's going to have a baby. I was so happy for her."

"You were her best friend?"

"Guess."

"And she didn't tell you who the father was?"

"No."

"I don't believe you."

She stared hard at Rigby. "Just like my old man."

"Don't hold out on me," he said.

"Why the hell should I?"

"This is for Flute," he reminded her.

She remained silent.

"Was she dating anyone?"

"No one special, if that's what you mean." She drank more coffee then said, "You think her lover boy killed her?"

He ignored her question. "What did you two do together?"

"Hung. Bar hopped."

"Did you work?"

"When we could. Flute ran errands for some lawyer in town, you know, delivering letters and packages. He let her use a bicycle."

"Do you think the lawyer could be the baby's father?"

"Naw. She called him a fruit. He wouldn't be interested."

"You wouldn't happen to know his name? Or the names of any of the guys she went out with?"

"We didn't go in for names and I never met the guy," Chicago said, and drank more coffee. Rigby realized he hadn't touched his.

"Do you know the name Mary Blair?"

Chicago shook her head.

"Tell me about Don."

Chicago stiffened and sat up straight. "He's not in this. He's a good man and he rescued me. That's enough. Leave him alone."

Remembering what the bartender at The Railroad Bar told him about the pleasure women, he said to Chicago, "I'm looking into a murder here. I have to ask some tough questions, but I need truthful answers."

"I want Flute's killer fried. Ask me."

"Is it possible Flute didn't know who the father was?"

"Huh?"

"Did Flute turn tricks to survive?"

Chicago said no, then took a long drink from her cup, emptying it. Rigby pushed his untouched cup over to her.

"I know what you're thinking. You think me and Flute both screwed to survive. It was tempting at times, I admit that. But it ain't so. We got by. We worked when we could. Had some savings. My brother sent me money. And in the hotel we got fed couple'a times a day. Just ain't so, and don't go round telling stories. What would Don think of me?"

He wondered what Don thought of her and considered

133

asking him. "Thanks for your help. Let me suggest that you fill Don in on your past. It's best he hears it from you."

"You gonna tell him?" Her voice trembled with fear.

"Not me. The police."

"The police," Chicago said as if she suddenly understood the meaning of a modern art painting. "Then who the hell are you?"

"The guy who bought you a cup of coffee," he said, throwing a couple of bills on the table.

Chapter 20

Arriving at Municipal Center East on Monroe Street, home of the Springfield Police Department, after seven p.m., Rigby told the officer behind the glass window that Detective Hunt wanted to see him. The officer called Hunt, had a brief conversation with her, then dutifully reported that Rigby must be mistaken, Detective Hunt did not want to see him.

"Call her back and tell her she does want to see me. Tell her I know the who and I'm working on the why." He was surprised to be talking like the Judge.

The officer sighed, realizing she was being dragged into something she wanted no part of, and made the call. Soon he was directed to an interrogation room, bare except for an institutional table and chairs and a two-way mirror on one wall.

Hunt showed up carrying a soft drink can. She offered him nothing. She looked at Rigby with tired, dull eyes, the skin around them puffy. It had been a long day for Rigby, too, since he'd found Flute's body, but he thought he had held up okay. He made sure to sit up straight and show some energy for Hunt.

"I don't have the time," she said, sitting opposite him.

"Just the facts, Ma'am."

"So tell me."

He started by telling her he found out the name of the dead girl.

"Who told you?"

"Clark Gable."

"What's the girl's name, Vivian Leigh?" She didn't

smile.

Rigby laughed. What else could he do? "Give me a minute to explain. I took a drive to Lincoln."

When he finished she said, "Why didn't you get me this info sooner?"

Rigby took a deep breath and told her about Claire Orange being run off the road.

The detective bristled, her shoulders narrowing to her neck like a volcanic eruption about to spew forth and cover him with invective. When she spoke, however, it was just the hiss before the eruption. "Trying to solve the case all by yourself?"

There was that confidence thing again with Hunt. She didn't think he trusted her. He hoped to correct her impression. "I tried calling you earlier, but they wouldn't put me through. You can check with the desk."

That seemed to settle her a bit.

Rigby said, "I have more for you."

"You've been a busy boy. Do tell."

He told her about Chicago. How he latched onto her, the woman's friendship with Flute, Flute's job with the gay lawyer. Topping his narrative with the big piece of information he believed would lead them to her killer, he said, "Flute was pregnant."

Rigby leaned back in his chair, intertwined his fingers together to create a headrest as he put his hands around the back of his head. He had a 'look at me' smirk on his face and was proud of it, expecting his revelations and how he came by them would leave Hunt gasping for air trying to keep up.

She took a sip from her can and said, "Well, I see you still got some fuel in the tank. Not bad for an old-timer."

Is that supposed to be a compliment?

"Too bad it's mostly wrong."

A smile now broke on her face, bright and cheerful and disgusting. Her confidence had returned.

"You saying the victim wasn't Mary Blair?"

"Yes, Mary Blair. The Clinton police called a little while ago, so I knew the victim's name. They called at the request of Mary's parents. Her parents called the police because of your visit so I'll give you that one. But, I also got the autopsy report and Mary Blair was not pregnant. Maybe she was screwing her boss, the lawyer, and figured telling him she *was* pregnant could get her money, but he panics and kills her. We found a rolled-up wad of bills hidden in her things at the Runaway. We'll find out...already got the guy here. Denied everything, of course."

It was Rigby's turn to show respect. He nodded at Hunt. "But not all is packaged neatly. Chicago said the lawyer was gay. She called him a fruit. Why would he be screwing Mary?"

"She called him a fruit because his name's like a fruit. It's Orange. The lawyer's name is Peter Orange."

Any cockiness he possessed when he entered the police station flowed out of him like sands in an hourglass. He thought of Claire being run off the road and wondered if it had been Sir Peter at the wheel of the black pickup truck. Claire could not find him anywhere. Was he right there with her, refusing to answer her call? Poor Claire. How would she take the news? Her experiences this day had already left her shaken. How could she not be devastated to learn her husband was being questioned under suspicion of murder for killing his young mistress? He was worried about her. God forgive him, he couldn't squelch the thought that raced through his mind: Claire might be *available*.

Rigby shook his head forcefully, trying to dispel the thought. How could he even think that?

"How did you learn about Peter Orange?"

"What's the matter, Special Agent Rigby, don't you think I can investigate a crime?"

"I think you did a great job," he said humbly.

Hunt stopped the soda can an inch from her lips and lowered it, staring at him all the while. She must have decided his comment was sincere because she said, "Thank you."

He nodded. "You say Orange denied everything. Are there cracks in his story?"

"We know Flute worked for him from time to time. We know he gave her gifts. We found the guy's business card inside the rubber band holding the cash in her room. The rest is speculation. He's not under arrest yet, just here for questioning."

"Have they determined the time of the murder?"

"Midnight. Little after."

"Then I guess I can't be Peter Orange's alibi."

It was Hunt's turn to be surprised. She placed the can gently on the table and said, "What did you say?"

"Does Orange's wife know about this?"

She shook her head.

"I had dinner with Mr. and Mrs. Orange last night. Left before nine. "

"I was about to send someone to talk to her," Hunt said. "Maybe I'll do it myself."

"Mind if I go along?"

"I think that'd be really interesting."

Claire was surprised to see Detective Hunt and Rigby standing under the porch light when she opened the door. She looked anxious, which didn't surprise him considering the day she had been through. That was only the beginning, dear, he thought.

"Zane," she said, but did not take her eyes off Lisa Hunt. "And...Detective Hunt...together."

Hunt offered her hand and asked if they could come in.

"What's wrong? It's Peter, isn't it? There's something wrong with Peter?"

"Why do you think that?" Hunt asked.

"You're the police. I can't get a hold of him. He's been hurt."

"No, he's okay," Hunt said. "May we come in?"

They followed Claire into the living room and took seats.

"What brings you here?" Claire demanded to know.

Rigby looked at Hunt. This was a local matter, as she was so quick to point out, so he would let her handle this tough part. He would be there to comfort Claire.

"Mrs. Orange, we're conducting a murder investigation," Hunt began. "The woman near Lincoln's Tomb."

"Yes, of course. The tomb." A small smile captured Claire's lips and perhaps relief crawled over her body, maybe giving her a chill, for there was a quick shiver, as if a burden had been thrown off her. "You need some history? The killing has something to do with the excavation."

Detective Hunt shook her head. "No, I don't think so. Mrs. Orange…"

Hunt paused for a moment. Rigby fixed his stare on Claire. Here it comes.

"There's a connection between the murdered girl and your husband."

"Connection? What do you mean *connection*?"

"She did things for him."

"You mean…sex?" Claire was afire with barely controlled rage. Rigby wondered if Sir Peter had wandered before, and the sneaky thought that no respectable man should have scampered across his brain again: *Claire might be available*! Stop it! He yelled at himself inside his head. Claire needed his help, needed him to be strong for her. Focus on the questions and answers.

"I don't know," the cop said. "What I do know is she ran errands for him. You don't know this girl, Mary Blair? She also went by the name Flute?"

Claire said, "I don't know those names."

Hunt produced a picture, a better copy than he had of the girl.

Claire shook her head and chewed on her bottom lip.

"This young woman, Mary, told her friends she was pregnant. She had a roll of money stuffed away in a drawer with your husband's business card. She wasn't pregnant, but maybe she was blackmailing him."

"Then they did have sex?"

"I don't know that. I'm creating a what-if scenario. I'm asking you if your husband has been acting strange lately. Any signs that may indicate he was cheating on you? Too many late nights? Phone calls made or taken behind closed doors? You know what I mean."

Claire shook her head slowly. She balled up a fist and ground it into the palm of her other hand like a pestle in a mortar. The possibility that she was the victim of a philandering husband hurt her.

"I can't say, really," Claire said with a sob. "He was hard working. He's always been that since we were married. He works late and takes business calls away from the family. I don't know." She paused for a moment and made her voice stronger when she added, "I know this: my husband would not kill."

"Have there been...?" Rigby stopped asking the question. How far could he venture into Claire's private life? How far would she let him?

Hunt noticed his incomplete query and said, "Have there been what?"

He thought Hunt should be asking the personal questions. Well, somebody had to ask, and he started it.

"Problems," he said. "In the marriage?"

Claire glared at him for a long time before she answered, "Are you suggesting Peter is guilty because you want him to be guilty? Because you want him out of the way?"

No, that's not what he was suggesting. Or was it? Was a subconscious hope surfacing in his question? He looked at Detective Hunt, who eyed him oddly. What was she thinking about Claire's accusation?

Softly he said, "This is a murder investigation, Claire. My questions are not personal. I'm trying to get at the truth. The truth will likely clear Peter, but we have to know." He reached out to lay a comforting hand on her shoulder, but she turned away.

Hunt picked up the questioning, since he'd done such a marvelous job securing helpful answers. "You didn't know your husband had a young woman working for him, running errands?"

"Why should I? He doesn't tell me about the janitor or the mail boy, either. Why are you trying to implicate Peter?"

"Was Mr. Orange home last night?"

"Yes."

"All night?"

"Yes."

"What time did you go to sleep?" Hunt asked.

"Eleven."

"And your husband went to bed with you?"

"No, he was reading in the office he keeps here."

"What time did he come to bed?"

"I...I guess I don't know. I was sleeping."

Rigby asked, "You didn't get up at all during the night? Go to the bathroom?" He did that more often since he'd hit fifty, and Claire was his age.

"Yes. Once."

"When was that?" Hunt picked up the questioning again.

"About one."

"You're sure?"

"Yes. I saw the digital alarm clock."

"And your husband was sleeping beside you when you awoke."

"He was...well. No, no he wasn't."

Hunt looked at Rigby and Claire reacted to the look

with an anxious yelp. "So what? He always stays up late when he's working. Going to bed at two a.m. is not unusual for Peter."

Hunt pressed: "But you never heard him throughout the night. You don't know if he was in or out of the house. Either way because you heard nothing?"

She did not respond verbally, but her silence was enough for Detective Hunt. Claire seemed to shrink a bit into the sofa. She appeared vulnerable and weak. Tears were building up behind her eyes. She showed concern for her husband. He suspected she was also afraid for herself. Afraid Sir Peter might be guilty and that guilt would reflect poorly on her; what the neighbors and her co-workers would whisper about her; how her lifestyle would change without her husband's income. It was a natural reaction. Rigby wanted to wrap her in a bear hug, but he knew that was not appropriate for all kinds of reasons.

"Does Peter have a lawyer with him?" Claire asked Hunt.

"He's been advised of his rights. He was willing to answer questions without a lawyer, but has since asked for his attorney. We're waiting for him to arrive. That gave me the opportunity to see you."

"Can I see Peter?"

"Soon."

"Then until I see him, I don't think I should talk to you without a lawyer present. A wife can't be made to testify against her husband." The tears did not come.

"All right then." Hunt rose from the chair. "If you think of anything that will help us, no matter which way it goes, I hope you'll be in touch."

"You expect me to turn against my husband?"

"Yes…if it means justice for that poor woman."

Hunt turned to go. Rigby tried to make eye contact with Claire, but she was looking at the floor. As he followed Hunt he could hear Claire rise behind him; her footsteps followed them to the front door.

The detective was already on the porch when Rigby stopped just outside the door. He turned and said, "I'm sorry Claire. I'm going to do everything I can to help."

"I wonder if that's true," she said angrily and slammed the door shut.

He turned and saw Hunt, her head cocked to the side, which made her body somehow look like a question mark.

"We were a couple in college," he said. He put his head down and headed for the car.

Chapter 21

Congressman John McClavity and Abigail Lamont were waiting outside police headquarters when Detective Hunt and Rigby returned. It was no coincidence they were there. They had been looking for Hunt and said the officer at the front desk had told them that if they waited around long enough, she would return. When Rigby started to leave, McClavity ordered him to stay.

"You're here to see the exhumation is carried out properly, Agent Rigby, and that's what we're here to talk about." Turning to Hunt and pointing the pinky finger of his right hand at her, McClavity said in a demanding voice, "We must continue the work in the tomb. You must clear the dig."

"I'm paying for the construction crew to sit around and do nothing," Lamont added. "It's an expense that hurts, because I have less to donate to the museum and other causes in this town. The world will be better when we discover the truth about Mr. Lincoln."

The world wasn't going to change one speck whether Mr. Lincoln was in his grave or not, Rigby thought. On the other hand, the local economy was in for a downfall once the truth was out, because Abby Lamont wouldn't be throwing her money around on contractors and security guards.

Hunt said, "I understand your impatience, Congressman McClavity, and I understand about the cost, Mrs. Lamont. I want to make sure that we've turned over every stone–and there are a lot of stones out there. You understand this is a murder investigation and I'm in charge."

"Perhaps not for much longer." McClavity's tone bore a touch of menace. "I've been in contact with the mayor and the chief."

Hunt was surprised at McClavity's revelation. Rigby wasn't. He had seen the congressman's intimidation before and was just as disgusted that he was trying it on Hunt, like he'd done with the young librarian. Rigby suspected Hunt hadn't played the political game in her job. Big shots, or those who felt they should be treated like big shots, routinely went over the heads of field operatives to get their way. Hunt shot Rigby a look, figuring Rigby was probably the only ally she had in the little circle, but the truth was he didn't have a dog in this fight.

"That's not kosher," she finally said, trying to good-naturedly deal with the threat.

Abby Lamont spoke up more soothingly than her companion. "Mr. Lincoln is special, don't you see? Everyone cares. Everyone wants to know the truth. Everyone who is part of the Honor Guard, like you, should care."

Hunt's gaze drifted from the circle. She was weighing what everyone who wants to do their jobs and deal with outside political pressure had to put up with. Rigby could almost read her mind: *Doing it my way–the right way as I see it–will get the job done. On the other hand, doing it my way could get me fired before I got to the end, then the job doesn't get done.*

Finally, the detective looked at the congressman and said, "You can dig tomorrow afternoon."

"I'll hold you to that," McClavity said, pointing an index finger at the cop this time.

"Thank you," Lamont said. "I know what you're doing is important, but what we're doing is important, too. Very, very important. If extra, you know, *resources* helps move the investigation along, you can come to me."

Some outsider listening to the conversation could

almost take that last statement as a bribe, but Lamont probably didn't mean it that way. Rich people always talk like that. They call it *doing business*.

When McClavity and Lamont retreated, Rigby offered to accompany Hunt inside. He knew she was going to question Peter Orange again, with his lawyer present this time, and he wanted to sit in. She told him he was not part of the investigation and to go home. From her tone, he thought she meant Washington, D.C., not the hotel.

He wanted to go home, too, and he meant Washington. Since it was late, he had to settle for the hotel. He slept fitfully and awoke tired. The previous day had been a long one and he could feel it in his bones.

He lingered over a late breakfast and killed more time back in the room reading the newspaper. Hunt wanted him nowhere near the murder investigation. Claire wanted him nowhere near her. As best as he could tell, the Judge wanted him nowhere near Washington, D.C.

He noticed a short paragraph in a list of brief news items on an inside page of the paper's front section. Domestic terrorist experts told the Associated Press the Monument Bomber was expected to strike again soon. The FBI had no comment on the speculation.

Rigby cursed himself for being fooled by the Bomber in Boston. He wanted to be part of the investigation, to bring the guy to justice. Instead, he was far away from the center of action. He cursed again and mumbled a little wish that this guy wouldn't trick the Bureau again.

He decided the best thing for him to do was forget all about the Monument Bomber by following up on some things bothering him right here in Springfield. He would start in the city library. It had been gnawing at him that McClavity had been so eager to open Lincoln's grave. He understood Abigail Lamont's desire to get on with the job; she was paying for it and running up big bills. McClavity's impatience puzzled him. He thought he should try to get a look at that folder McClavity stored in the Sangamon Valley Collections room.

He walked to the library, dodging businesspeople and tourists. A group of Japanese tourists walked slowly in front of him, staying close to their tour guide, who was offering a history lesson. At least, he guessed she offered a history lesson. His Japanese learning stopped after he mastered the word *hai*, meaning *yes*. He figured if he ever got to a Geisha house, that would be the only word he would need.

The same young woman who manned the Sangamon Valley Collections desk a couple of days earlier sat there as he ambled in just before noon.

"Hi, Miss, remember me?"

"You're…the man with Congressman McClavity a couple of days ago," she said, her tone indicating uncertainty.

"That's right. I'd like to look at the file the congressman and I were looking at that day."

The woman frowned. "I don't think I can do that, sir. It's the congressman's file."

"But I was with him looking at it. You know that. He wants me to see what's in it." The devil clearly had taken over his conscience.

"Well, sir, if I only had a note or something."

"Should I write you one?"

"From the congressman, I mean," she said.

"What's this? What's this?" A female voice fired off a couple of verbal rounds from the doorway.

Rigby turned to see Mildred Huffington, the receptionist for Claire and Crease. She approached the desk. "Hello, Nancy, how's your mother?"

"Hi, Mrs. Huffington," the woman behind the desk responded. "She's doing really well. The pills are working."

"That's great. I'll get over to see her soon. Just made a peach cobbler that will have her smacking her lips." Reaching a hand toward him, she asked, "Is Special Agent

Rigby spooning with you?"

Nancy blushed, but looked at him with different eyes. "I didn't know you were FBI."

Huffington said, "Nancy's a fine guide if you're a stranger in Springfield."

The woman was trying to fix him up. He appreciated the thought and Nancy was probably thirty, so she fit right in the middle of his scale of the desirable age range, twenty-nine to thirty-one. Okay, maybe the range is more liberal than that. It had to be or he might as well become a monk.

Nancy said, "He wanted to look at Congressman McClavity's special file."

"Special file?" Mrs. Huffington said.

"I was looking at it with him a couple of days ago. I need to do some more research."

"Really." Mildred rubbed her hands together. "Shall we see what's in it?"

Nancy hesitated. "I don't know."

"Come, Nancy. If it were that secret he wouldn't leave it here at the library, would he? Besides, we're all working on the same thing: history, young lady. Unlocking history."

Mildred Huffington was firm in her position and reminded Rigby of his second grade teacher. You didn't say no to Mrs. Carrington unless you wanted to stay after school. He felt sorry for Nancy. With McClavity, Huffington, and himself, he'd never seen a librarian bullied so much since Harold Hill tormented Marian in *The Music Man*.

Nancy opened a drawer and pulled out the requested folder. Mildred took the folder and directed him to a study table.

"This should prove interesting," Mildred whispered as she took a chair.

Rigby sat across from the president of the local chapter of Busybodies Anonymous. She opened the folder and started leafing through the pages. From upside down and across the table most of the pages looked like photocopies of old newspaper articles. He saw the copy of the newspaper photograph in which he had identified McClavity's grandfather, Samuel.

"Why would he want to dredge all this stuff up? Fire devastating city blocks. Awful thing." Mildred seemed to be speaking to herself. She did not share any of the news from the articles she read. When she started muttering again, Rigby spoke up.

"Tell me."

"All these stories about this fire. The local papers at the time covered it for days and it appears the congressman collected every article."

He reached across the table and pulled one of the photocopies toward him. Turning it so he could read the page, he learned more about what set off Mildred's mutterings.

A fire had roared through blocks of Springfield's commercial real estate in 1922. The fire started in a warehouse late at night. The reporter rather prosaically described how the fire lit up the night sky as if noon had burst out at midnight. Containment of the fire took some time and before it was put down, four city blocks were ashes. Most of the buildings lost were warehouses and business establishments, although two homes went up at the edge of the fire. No lives were reported lost, but fire officials were still going through the charred building remains as the story was written.

"Aha!" Mildred declared. "This never found its way into a McClavity campaign brochure." She flipped a second page over to Rigby. The newspaper was dated four days after the one he was reading. The paper reported on a suspect who might have set the fire. It was not a hobo trying to keep warm, as first conjectured in the days following the fire. The police arrested a well-known citizen by the name of Samuel McClavity.

Tittering from Mildred brought the prospect of more gossipy news. When he finally caught up with her after reading the pile of old newspaper stories, he learned that Samuel McClavity was found guilty of setting the Springfield fire, which destroyed four city blocks, the bones of one person were found in the ashes. No one was ever reported missing so the victim was never identified, and Samuel was institutionalized for his manic action, having been ruled insane. He gave no defense for the reason he set the fire.

When Rigby finished reading the last account he glanced up at Mildred, who looked like the snake that swallowed the rabbit, all content and puffy with excitement. She had a lot of information to send through the telephone trees of Springfield if she chose.

The congressman obviously didn't think his grandfather was a reliable source. Rigby tried to make a connection between what he just learned and the Lincoln dig McClavity so adamantly supported. All those other people who'd identified Lincoln. Twenty-three of them. They all didn't lie. Rigby tried to figure what this all meant to McClavity and why he needed to know if Lincoln's body was in the grave. Maybe he should just ask him.

Huffington stood and asked Rigby to put the file back together and return it. She said goodbye to Nancy.

"Don't you want to look at your research?" Nancy asked.

"Can't now, dear. Took up too much time with this. My lunch hour is over and I've got to get back to work."

Huffington left. Rigby assembled the clippings and returned them to the folder, but not before he took a photocopy of the article detailing Samuel McClavity's involvement in the fire.

As he returned the file to Nancy he asked her, "What's Mrs. Huffington's research about?"

Nancy gave him that uncertain look again and he

repeated the words Huffington used to secure the McClavity file. "We're unlocking history, dear."

She smiled and said Mrs. Huffington was doing research for Dr. Crease on the Lincoln Guard of Honor.

He thanked her and started to go. Nancy asked, "Do you need a guide to see Springfield, Agent Rigby?"

He looked at her smiling face full of anticipation and said, "I've seen too much of Springfield already."

He walked out of the room thinking it was time to put the screws to a congressman. That ought to tick off the Judge.

Chapter 22

Rigby called McClavity's office from his hotel room. The call was passed on to his young assistant, Lenny Poler, who said his boss was out for the morning, circulating around the district and taking care of constituent problems. Poler told him the congressman would be back for the opening of the grave.

"So you think the body will be there?"

"I don't know any more than you," Rigby said. "Probably less, since you're with the congressman all the time."

"Oh, no, he doesn't talk about that."

"Why not? He's extremely interested in it."

"Who isn't? Those of us who know about it, I mean." He said this in a self-important way, putting himself into the elite group of those who knew the secret about opening Lincoln's grave.

"Those grave robbers over one hundred years ago were on to something," Poler continued. "They expected to make money with the body when they returned it. You could make a lot today by just showing it off."

"I'm sure the congressman isn't interested in making money off of Mr. Lincoln's remains."

"You misunderstand, Agent Rigby. I was just saying how interesting this would be to people everywhere."

Rigby told Poler he'd see his boss later and hung up.

He wondered what Detective Hunt had learned from Peter Orange, and again thought of Claire. From the heights of her trust, calling him when she had been run off the road, to her angry response last night, he had fallen a long way.

He wanted to go to her, but thought better of it. She needed time to consider what was happening in her topsy-turvy life.

Still, he wasn't interested in hanging around the hotel room until it was time to go to the cemetery. He pulled on his sports coat and opened the door.

Claire was on the other side–walking away.

When she heard the door open she stopped and turned. He was surprised and confused. She gave him a faint smile.

"You caught me," she said. "I guess I changed my mind."

"Don't," he replied. "Come in?"

"Well, I…since I'm in the neighborhood."

He stepped aside and she walked in. He closed the door. Claire walked to the window and took in the panoramic view of Springfield offered by his room near the top of the hotel tower. He waited for her to speak. Clearly, she had something on her mind. He removed his jacket, tossed it on the bed and sat down.

Finally, Claire said, "I want to apologize for last night. The way I received you and Detective Hunt."

"No need. Understandable under the circumstances."

Claire turned from the window. Her look had changed. Fear lived in her eyes. "What do the police think?"

She referred to Sir Peter. Not knowing what they thought, he shook his head.

"I was upset at the news last night, as you can imagine. But Peter came home and he's explained everything. The girl just worked for him, that's all. It was nothing. That's what the police concluded, right?"

"The police don't confide in me."

"Well, they'll reach that conclusion. Have to. Peter did nothing wrong."

Her loyalty was touching and, for all he knew, well deserved. "Where's Peter?"

"Took Craig out. Man to man sort of thing. Craig knew Peter and I were very upset. Peter needed to explain some things to him."

She took a step toward Rigby, reached out and touched his knee. "Thank you for staying my friend."

He used every muscle in his body to hold himself rigid, not stand up to kiss her on the lips. Beautiful Claire. She begged to be kissed whether she knew it or not.

He started massaging his knee. She pulled her hand away.

"Does your knee hurt?"

"I think it's going to rain," he said.

"That happens to you, too?" She laughed. "I never believed that kind of stuff when I was younger, but now–oh boy."

She sighed and looked at him with those big, brown doe eyes, then shook her head slowly. "Sometimes, I just don't know how to cope. What happened to Craig…the threat to me…now Peter. I don't know how to come out from under."

"You're doing fine. You're a strong woman."

"Once upon a time. When we parted after college…I was strong then. You were itching to see the world…"

"I wanted you to come." He reached out and touched her hand.

"I know. But I wanted something for me…to be a professional, to be an academic. I couldn't wait to get my doctorate. You, Zane, you were the wild one. Wild by my standards, anyway. That's probably what attracted me at first, you being so different." She paused. Reflected. "FBI. Somehow that fits. Adventurous, but a bit on the conservative side."

"I do have to wear suits and ties," he said.

She smiled.

"I wished you had come with me," he said softly, still remembering his feelings after all these years. "I waited for weeks hoping the phone would ring before I left the country. No cell phones then. Once I was gone that was it."

"I wanted a settled life, Zane. You knew that. No travel. I did enough of that as an Army brat. I was strong when you left...real strong, keeping to my plan. I let you go." She paused, looked away.

"I guess I let you go, too." He didn't try to hide the regret of that decision, so long ago, not to try everything he could to convince Claire to travel with him. Yet, he could never see himself waiting around an apartment or taking an odd job while she studied for her advanced degree.

She looked at him for a long time, smiled gently. Just as quickly the smile was gone.

He stood up next to her, close enough to smell the captivating scent of Claire. He felt himself getting warm in his neck and face. Claire had the look of innocence, but she was a witch who could boil his blood with a touch. He turned away from her. Trying to escape his thoughts, he said, "Will you be at the tomb when they resume digging?"

"When it *ends,* you mean. Finally. I feel so responsible for bringing this on. I'll feel even guiltier if that dig has anything to do with the girl's death and my husband ensnared in a trap. You won't let anything bad happen to Peter, will you Zane? Promise?"

He could promise nothing but he would promise Claire anything. "Of course not. He'll be fine."

"I wish I could be sure. The police let him go, but said they'd want him for more questioning. You'd tell me if they suspect anything about Peter? You wouldn't keep a secret?"

He told her what she wanted to hear.

"I wish I could know everything will be all right. That we'll be protected." The nervousness was back. The uncertainty. She looked past him at the digital clock on the nightstand. "We'll have to get to the cemetery soon." She looked up into his eyes. "Cemeteries are not always cruel places. Remember?"

He knew instantly to what she referred, and would never forget. Their eyes locked. Through the shadowy sparkle in her eyes he could see back through time to a young couple holding hands, kicking through freshly fallen autumn leaves. The trail led into an old cemetery called Rolling Hill, set on the side of the hill during colonial times. The forest had nearly reclaimed the old place, but gravestones still stood, many inscriptions on the stones illegible, scrubbed obscure by the elements and time, other stones dirty or moss covered. The young couple rested against a great oak tree and amid the memorials to the dead, they experienced life. Gentle kisses, light touching, exploring hands. She encouraged him by unfastening the top button on her blouse, as if showing him how it was done. He was a fast learner.

Claire looked away from him, lost in her own thoughts, her own memories. When she spoke there was a catch in her voice. "I haven't forgotten."

Putting a finger to Claire's chin, he gently guided her face back toward his. He could feel the years fall away. He was certain that in the mirror of her eyes he could see brown hair instead of gray, a thin face no longer jowly.

She reached up slowly with trembling hands and undid the top button on her blouse, just as she had done all those years ago. As he had done all those years ago, he reached toward the next button, took it in his fingers–and then stopped.

What the hell was he doing? He took a deep breath and stepped back. She was offering herself to him. She was insecure and needy, and he had started to take advantage. He should slap himself upside the head. He looked at Claire again, seeing her through different eyes. The smoke of passion cleared. Claire was frightened. The life she knew was threatened because the man she loved was in danger. She would do anything to protect him. She would even seek help from an old lover whom she thought could provide that protection.

He pulled his hands away and took a couple of steps

back. She looked at him with uncertainty.

"I think I hear the sounds of drilling," he said.

Claire played her part, turned to the window. "No, it can't be. We're too far away for that."

"But they'll be drilling by now. We should go to the monument."

"Yes," she said softly, "I suppose we should."

He took his jacket off the bed and slipped it on while Claire took the time to brush her hair with her fingers and button her blouse. He escorted her to the door.

Exiting the room, she looked back at him and said, "Thank you, Zane."

Chapter 23

Claire accepted Rigby's offer to drive her to Oak Ridge Cemetery. The drive was made in silence. No discussion of what did, or did not happen in the hotel room. No more questions about Peter Orange and his standing with the police. Rigby didn't know if Peter was guilty or not, but he was determined to remain a strong arm to hold onto for Claire no matter how it went down. She could have his arm and his faith and he'd leave it at that.

Of course, he realized that when the coffin was opened and Mr. Lincoln's remains were where they were supposed to be, he would be ordered back to Washington, and Claire would not even have him as support.

Rigby glanced at her sitting in the passenger seat and wondered what she was thinking. She looked straight ahead, her expression sad. Even as the historian of the Lincoln Presidential Library and Museum, he doubted she had Mr. Lincoln on her mind right now.

Echoing from the inner burial chamber, the sound of drilling through concrete reverberated across the open grass field in front of Lincoln's Tomb. Rigby parked on Monument Ave. because he was told the parking lot was occupied by big trucks and equipment used to break up ten feet of hundred-year-old concrete.

Walking to the ornate tomb, they passed a phalanx of security people and police. Each time they passed another checkpoint Rigby had to produce his FBI identification and Claire her library ID. He started to think there was a 747 parked nearby.

158

The crowd gathered for this momentous event was smaller than he had anticipated. Besides security and workmen, it seemed only a few officials had shown up. Whoever was in charge of confidentiality on this project ought to be drafted by some of the misfits in Washington who couldn't keep a secret to save someone's life, the usual price paid for their failure.

Claire and Rigby made their way to the tomb. As they reached the tomb, the drilling stopped. Rigby saw workmen filing out of the rear chamber, some plopping on the grass, taking a break. He decided to use the opportunity to see what progress had been made.

Instead of entering the tomb from the open rear chamber where the work was being done, Rigby proceeded through the door to the hall where he'd seen Claire for the first time. Claire followed him inside, still not saying a word.

After he'd flashed his ID to yet another police officer, he wandered into the hallway leading to the rear of the tomb, Claire in tow. Smaller statues of Lincoln, perhaps two or three feet high, stood on pedestals at the first turn in the hall. One bronze was of Lincoln as a young soldier, at attention, his left hand on the hilt of a sword held at his side. The other was Lincoln on horseback, holding a rifle.

They walked the length of the hall to the next turn. This elbow in the hallway was more cluttered than the first. Objects from the burial chamber had been moved along the hallway to make room for the diggers. Two statues on pedestals held their places here, too. One was Lincoln riding the circuit as a lawyer, a tall man in a tall hat on horseback, the other a standing President Lincoln, a man of large feet and powerful hands, one hand grasping his jacket lapel, striking a pose in front of the presidential chair, a seat of power.

Scattered in front of the statues were a number of flags on poles. Besides the American flag and the presidential flag there were seven flags from different states. The Illinois flag was obvious, but Rigby was less sure why the Kentucky and Massachusetts flags and others were present. He wondered if they rotated the state flags on a regular basis.

Past a metal gate was the burial chamber. The area was covered with dust and debris. A huge hole had been dug through the floor. Jackhammers sat on top of piles of concrete rubble. Other mounds of concrete were visible outside, through the opening that had been cut into the back of the tomb wall to bring in heavy equipment.

Rigby nodded to a dust-covered worker holding a pick and sitting on a chunk of concrete and asked if he could look down the hole.

"Unless you're afraid of ghosts."

Some ghosts, he was. Ghosts from his past like Melanie and like Claire and those bastards in Maine who…. *Focus.* The U.S. government had spared little expense in sending him on this important mission and he had a job to do. That job was to see if Abraham Lincoln was in his grave. He stepped forward and looked into the hole.

The workers had reached the metal bars securing the concrete around the coffin and were cutting them away.

"Not long now?" he said to the worker.

"A bitch," the worker replied. "They locked him up but good. Coffin's inside metal bars…concrete poured right through the bars. Broke a couple of bits…the damn engine drinking gallons of oil so it won't blow. The final chipping we're doin' by hand."

Rigby actually meant his comment to be taken as a question, hoping the worker would confirm that this crazy project was almost over. He looked at Claire.

She was concentrating on the dust-covered coffin deep in the hole. Her academic side must've taken possession of her. He thought he'd ask her some questions about the tomb and bore the worker so much that he'd stop paying attention

160

to them.

"That inscription over there on the wall, 'Now He Belongs to the Ages,' what's that?"

Before Claire could answer the worker said, "That's what Stanton said, the Secretary of War, when Lincoln kicked."

Okay, maybe he wasn't going to bore the guy. He turned away from the worker and saw inscriptions to Mary Todd Lincoln and her sons on the wall behind them. "The family?"

Claire started to say something, but again the worker replied, "The wife and three of the boys. The oldest and only one to become a man, Robert, he's buried in Arlington. They used to be right there where you're standing but in 1930 they added this inside corridor so they had to move the crypts to where you see 'em now."

Even the workers around here are historians. Claire smiled at Rigby, sensing his frustration. He had to get her away from the dust-covered professor here. "Come, I want to ask you about those flags, odd assortment."

They walked to the corner as Claire explained the flags represented states in which Lincoln and his ancestors had lived. The worker called out that he would soon resume the banging and for their ears' sake they should vamoose.

They vamoosed to the terrace level at the front of the obelisk, by the bronze Lincoln statue. Rigby decided to find out what Claire was thinking. He wanted to know how she was feeling about all that had transpired between them in the last hour. Before he could speak, she pointed to an old stone plastered into the obelisk and asked if he knew what it was.

"Yes, it's an ancient stone with magical powers put in place to change the subject at hand."

The stone's powers must also make people deaf because Claire went on as if she didn't hear a word he'd said. "It's called the Roman Stone. The words are Latin.

Before 1930 you could actually walk to the top of the obelisk, but this stone was used to close the entrance. It honors an ancient Roman ruler who freed the serfs and offered them citizenship. It was a gift from the people of Rome to Abraham Lincoln while he was president. You know what happened to the Roman leader? He was assassinated."

Footsteps ascending the stairs to the terrace signaled they would not be alone much longer.

A security guard appeared, accompanying Bernard Rittinghouse. The doctor carried a black bag like the doctors of Rigby's youth, when house visits were still in order and gas was twenty cents a gallon. Yes, the *good old days* people talk about.

The security man said, "Dr. Orange. Your guest is here. Don't want folks wandering so I brought him to you."

Claire thanked the guard, who saluted and left.

Pointing to the bag, Rigby said to Rittinghouse, "Coming to see one of your patients in the cemetery?"

"You never know when a doctor is needed," he said stiffly.

Claire was about to step between them to cut off any bickering when another voice called out. "There you are," Detective Hunt said, reaching the terrace. "Ready for the big event? A beautiful day. Hardly a cloud in the sky."

"It's going to rain," Claire said. "Zane's knee hurts."

Hunt gave a look of bewilderment, Claire smiled and Rigby made a face at her.

"Can I talk to you a moment, Agent Rigby?" Hunt asked.

Claire pulled Rittinghouse by his jacket sleeve and they wandered off as the banging from inside the tomb grew louder.

Hunt moved closer to Rigby and said, "I see you and Dr. Orange are getting along fine again."

"It's hard to be mad at me for long."

"I doubt that. So, you and Mrs. Orange doing okay?"

"You already asked that." He waved to new arrivals on the terrace, Henry Crease and Abby Lamont.

The two approached as if they were wearing the masks of comedy and drama. Lamont was all smiles and a gelatin of excitement, quivering all over. Crease frowned sourly.

"What a glorious day," Lamont said. She wore some fashion designer's best, a pants-suit of orange and blue leather studded with precious stones, topped by her Abe Lincoln leather jacket. Every society queen should have one. "Mr. Lincoln's truth will save the world and we're all here at the beginning."

"The beginning of what?" Rigby asked. "I thought this was the end."

"Well, maybe...the, ah, end of the beginning," she said. "There'll be a revival of Lincoln, I think."

"Just because Mr. Lincoln did a bang-up job as president in his time doesn't mean he'd do as well in our time," Rigby said.

"You're wrong, Agent Rigby. He's a man for all times. We sure could use his leadership today."

FBI agents are not supposed to get into political debates while on the job and he supposed it wasn't wise to joust with a *benefactor,* so he didn't press the issue.

In the uncomfortable silence that followed he tried to change the subject and asked Crease how his paper on the Lincoln Honor Guard was coming.

"Paper?"

"The one Mildred Huffington is helping you research."

He was surprised. "You know about that? Well, who has the time to start that?"

Some yelling came from the burial chamber, but no one could hear what was being said. Claire appeared from the back of the terrace and shouted, "They've called for the crane."

As a group they descended the stairs and walked

around the back of the tomb to the opening in the rear wall of the burial chamber. A small crane on tank-like treads, operated remotely, had been maneuvered through the break in the wall and hovered over the hole in the chamber. Workers were lowering cables into the hole, where Rigby assumed other workers were carefully attaching the cables to a device placed around the coffin.

He looked around at the small contingent outside the tomb and saw some familiar faces. Congressman McClavity was there along with his assistant, Lenny Poler. The younger man saluted Mildred Huffington with a raised fist and she responded in kind.

McClavity sidled up to Rigby and whispered, "The moment of truth."

When the moment elongated to a few minutes, Rigby filled the silence by whispering back at him, "I read about old Sam and the fire."

McClavity looked at Rigby with shock, his secret somehow revealed. He asked anxiously, "Do-do you think he did it?"

"They found him guilty and institutionalized him, didn't they?"

He was quiet for a moment. "Yes, yes they did." He turned his attention to the whirring of the crane's motor.

As the crane began slowly pulling the coffin to daylight for the first time in over one hundred years, all the chattering stopped. An eerie but respectful silence enveloped the place. People strained to be the first to get a glimpse of the coffin.

Suddenly, there it was. The faded red cedar outer coffin, covered in a fine layer of dust, was wrapped in net-like webbing coming together in a metal ring attached to the crane's hook.

The crane rolled back through the wall and then gently lowered the coffin onto a small platform constructed for the occasion. Without a word workmen freed the ring from the hook and neatly dropped the webbing onto the platform, leaving it in place for the task of returning the coffin to the grave. The workers stepped back, and one by one removed their hard hats.

Abigail Lamont and McClavity stepped forward. When they reached the coffin, Lamont reached out and placed her hand lovingly on the box. After a moment she looked around and said, "Reverend?"

Rigby had not noticed the minister before, but now the man stepped up, holding a bible and dressed as if he were prepared to lead Sunday morning services. He asked all to bow their heads before proceeding to deliver prayers over Mr. Lincoln's remains. When the minister was finished the congressman made some comments about the momentous occasion and then he called a worker forward to open the outer box. With hammers and crowbars the lid and side of the cedar box were removed.

Inside the outer box was a black coffin with metal studs, its inner lead lining exposed. A workman lit an acetylene torch to cut open the lead around shoulder height. Claire leaned toward Rigby and whispered, "They used plumbers to open the casket in 1887 and 1901. They had to do the same thing."

He nodded. The task was done with only the sound of the torch. No one spoke. After the workman finished and backed away from the coffin, no one moved. A bird's chirp carried through the hushed crowd. The congressman finally motioned for a worker to lift the cut piece of metal.

The guy Rigby had chatted with in the burial chamber approached with a small crowbar. He slipped it under the lid and pushed down, breaking the seal on the coffin. A hiss of air escaped. Gasps rose from the crowd. Silence descended again. The workman put down his crowbar and, joined by a colleague, grasped the metal square. With effort they lifted the piece off the coffin.

Chapter 24

Abraham Lincoln.

The Judge bent over the table and took a closer look. The letter seemed authentic. Her experts would confirm that shortly. All signs pointed to the Monument Bomber, warning he would soon strike again. Once again, in a letter to the FBI, he had named a target, but the letter was vague.

Abraham Lincoln would be his target. Which Lincoln? The Bomber did not mention a specific monument to Lincoln, of the many that existed around the country. He wrote simply that Abraham Lincoln would be his target because Lincoln was the man Americans put above all others. America's *special prophet*, he called Lincoln.

The Judge stood straight and moved away from her aides standing around the desk. The bomber had promised something spectacular this time. What did that mean? Was he again creating a smokescreen to lead the Bureau in a false direction?

The Judge rubbed the pressure building between her eyes. She had to catch this bastard. Already there was talk she was not up to the job as Director of the FBI. She had been on the job such a short time. Failing to bring to justice such a high-profile terrorist could undermine her position. She would not let that happen.

If only Rigby had nailed the bastard in Boston. He had let her down. Everything indicated he was the man for the job, but he had been hoodwinked and that cost the Bureau. It had cost her. Now she would have to be personally involved in bringing this investigation to a sound conclusion.

At least Rigby's incompetence would not interfere any longer. He was off on his wild goose chase looking after Mr. Lincoln's bones.

Suddenly, she whirled and looked back at the Monument Bomber's letter sitting on the desk.

Lincoln!

Chapter 25

Abigail Lamont eagerly leaned over the coffin, then let out a ghastly scream. She swooned and collapsed, her head hitting the side of the coffin as she fell to the ground. Rigby was pushed forward by the crush of people all eager for a look.

The coffin was empty.

McClavity covered his face with both hands to block out some unseen horror, ignoring the fallen Lamont at his feet. Claire, standing next to Rigby, screamed as if she had just witnessed a man murdered in cold blood. Henry Crease stood in disbelief. Mrs. Huffington, at the edge of the crowd, sobbed uncontrollably, and was comforted by Lenny Poler. Dr. Rittinghouse stood quietly by a tree, twisting the handle of his black bag in both hands. Detective Hunt looked around the crowd as if the body-napping suspect was in the group. The workman who had been so informative in the burial chamber kicked the ground in disgust.

Rigby moved over to Mrs. Lamont, who was receiving assistance from the minister. Lincoln's relative had a bruise on her cheek that would darken quickly. She coughed as she came out of her faint.

When the din reached a crescendo, McClavity demanded quiet. Silence was not easily achieved, but finally it came. The congressman said, "We will discover the truth. There's an FBI agent here who will find the whereabouts of Mr. Lincoln's body. Please don't tell anyone what you saw. Don't talk to the press."

As if that admonition would work. It was like telling people to rush off to the nearest reporter. Of course, the reporters would be told of Rigby's involvement. Now, he was expected to be the hero. All they wanted him to do was win the game by kicking a field goal with one second left from his own one yard line. Impossible.

As if leaving a funeral, members of the crowd solemnly walked away. Rigby put an arm around Claire and asked her if she were all right.

"This was not supposed to be," she said through tears.

He tried to cheer her by saying, "You were the one who discovered the hand. You were the one who put the world onto this historic truth."

His words did nothing to calm her. She repeated, "This was not supposed to be," and she cried.

Rigby escorted Claire away from the scene. Maybe she could give him more insight into the grave-robbing attempt and the subsequent openings of the coffin. He would also consult with Smitty, though he really saw no clear path to discovering the missing body. Whoever wrote the note was long dead and had left no clues. Why the body-napper made no contact after the original note was a puzzle. Had he somehow lost the body? Had he been afraid he would end up in jail? Was he killed in an accident?

Rigby decided to involve Claire in his thinking and try to get her to believe they could right this wrong, even though he didn't believe it himself. "We have to discover who wrote the ransom note."

Claire responded by crying harder. He squeezed her shoulders.

"Zane Rigby."

Rigby turned to see Detective Hunt wading through the workmen toward him. "Agent Rigby, I need to talk to you."

Now she needs to talk to him. This high-profile case was under his jurisdiction and she wanted a piece of it. He could say no and teach her a lesson.

"I'm escorting Claire out of here," he said to Hunt, "I'll catch up to you."

She frowned, but stopped her pursuit.

Rigby hailed Henry Crease. Claire had come to the cemetery with him, but he needed to report the astounding development of the empty coffin to the Judge. He needed Crease to drive Claire away from the cemetery.

After getting her to Crease's car Rigby reassured her that everything would be all right. She just shook her head. He told her he would have to call on her later to go over details about the Lincoln grave-robbing attempt and the 1901 reburial.

After Crease and Claire drove away, he decided not to go back to the tomb and look for Hunt. The call to the Judge was more pressing. He headed for his car and the local FBI office.

Rigby was sitting with Crosby in his office, facing the speakerphone when the Judge came on the line.

"You got thirty seconds," the Judge said.

"Lincoln's coffin was empty," Rigby reported.

"Astonishing." He could hear the surprise in her voice. She paused. "McClavity must be in a twist."

"He says the FBI will find the body."

"I don't have time for this." She made no effort to hide her impatience.

"You've got to be ready," Rigby said. "It will come back to you. This is front page."

"The Monument Bomber's front page, too, and he's back."

Rigby looked at Crosby, who shrugged, indicating he didn't know anything about that. Rigby leaned forward in his chair. "He wrote again?"

"Yes. We're on it," she said dismissively. "I sent you to Illinois to find Mr. Lincoln's body, Agent Rigby. Do your job and find the body. Or show them you're trying at least. Mr. Crosby will give what assistance he can, but keep it limited. This is a waste of time. Right now I've got more important things to worry about. Report to the Associate Deputy Director."

She paused. Rigby thought for a moment she had hung up. Then she said, "Anything odd going on by you?"

"Just the usual," Rigby said. "Abraham Lincoln's body is missing from its grave."

"I mean besides what you just told me," she said in an irritated voice.

Crosby said, "A truck was bombed outside the Lincoln Monument. A woman was murdered, body left near the monument."

"Hmm." Another pause. "Okay, Mr. Crosby, I may be back to you. Agent Rigby, look for the body."

There was no goodbye.

Crosby reached across the desk and punched off the speakerphone.

Rigby said, "What do you think she meant, that she would get back to you?"

He shrugged. "She's the Director and I'm in charge here."

"Ever talk to her before?"

"Conference call, not one-on-one."

"I think it has to do with the Monument Bomber maybe being here."

"Not that again." Crosby laughed. He stood up and walked to a cabinet, from which he took a bottle of water. He waved one in Rigby's direction. Rigby turned it down with a shake of his head.

"She's obviously thinking of the bomber," Rigby said. "When she hears about the strange goings-on around the tomb she says she might get back to you. What I'm hearing is there's a connection between the incidents at the tomb and the bomber."

"You're trying to build a roadster with just a steering wheel and a tire. There're not enough parts. Forget it."

"Are *you* going to forget it?"

"The bomber's not in Springfield," Crosby said.

"Then you'll have time to help me find Lincoln."

Crosby laughed. "Nice try. That's your headache."

"The director told you to assist."

"Indeed. And you know what I'm going to do for you? I'm going to let you use the telephone. Can I show you one in a private office?"

Rigby smiled at the SAC and took him up on it.

In the private office, he dialed Smitty at the Smithsonian. He trusted he'd get straight info from her. He wasn't so sure what he'd get from the characters he was dealing with here.

She was glad to hear from Rigby and asked if there was any news from the Lincoln Tomb. He told her the news and told her to keep it to herself.

"Just ask and I'll be on the first plane out there."

"I know you would, kid, but I need your help there."

"You call me kid one more time and you'll be talking to air."

"The quicker you get me some information I need, the quicker I solve my problem and can get back there to show you the town."

"A date?" He could hear the excitement in her voice.

Rigby didn't think that's what he should call it. "Tell you what, I'll take you to the Lincoln Memorial."

"Done," Smitty said, not catching the sarcasm in his voice. "What you need?"

"What we talked about. The Lincoln Guard of Honor and the grave robbers."

"I have some stuff, not much. The guys who attempted to rob the grave, Mullins and Hughes, they got a year in jail and then disappeared from the world. At least, disappeared from a researcher who only had a few hours to follow their trail. Same with Swegles, the guy who was with them but snitched to the Secret Service. Got a great description of what went on in a book written by John Carroll Power.

Fascinating stuff."

"Yeah, I'll bet."

"Power was custodian of the monument for twenty years and was with the Secret Service the night of the grave robbing. Do you want to know about that night?"

"They didn't open the coffin, right?"

"Opened the marble sarcophagus and pulled the coffin out a bit, no more."

"Then skip it. The coffin went back into the sarcophagus."

"No it didn't."

"It didn't?"

"Well, I guess it did."

"It did or it didn't, Smitty?"

"Wrong, Z. It did *and* it didn't. Not *or*."

What frustrated Rigby was that he knew Smitty was smarter than him, so he figured he'd missed something.

"Tell me."

"The coffin went back into the sarcophagus for only six days."

"And..." He said impatiently when she paused.

"The people in charge of the monument didn't want another attempt on the body. So they took the coffin out of the sarcophagus and moved it to the side of the catacomb out of view until they could put together a team of loyal supporters who moved the coffin in the dead of night."

His interest was actually piqued. "Where did they move it?"

"They lifted it up and took it outside around the monument and entered Memorial Hall on the other end of the monument. Then they went to the labyrinth of corridors–I take it mostly dirt pathways–under the terrace at the foundation of the obelisk. Power wrote that the terrace leaked and there was no ventilation, making the place smell rancid."

"Who would've thought," he mused. "So that's where it

was buried."

"They meant to bury it."

"Please, Smitty."

"Come on, Z, would I make this stuff up? It's too bizarre even for your favorite researcher with outlandish fantasies that sometimes include you."

He ignored her and said, "You mean they didn't bury the coffin?"

"Not for two years."

"Guess they just forgot," he said sarcastically.

"No. The digging and burying was hard work for the old guys. Get this: Lincoln's coffin was above ground covered up with wood planks sitting under the terrace in the foundation while visitors were paying respects to the empty sarcophagus in the catacomb. What finally prompted them to bury the coffin was another grave robbing."

"Another attempt at Lincoln?"

"No, some extremely wealthy New York merchant, Alexander Stewart. Ever hear of him?"

"No."

"Neither did I, but I looked him up, which is the difference between us, besides the obvious," she said. "Stewart started the first department store in America."

"Tell me about the Lincoln Guard of Honor."

"I am telling you. This group that buried the body again was the forerunner. They were younger men than those who ran the Lincoln National Monument Association. They had to recruit the younger men to move the 500-pound coffin."

"You're saying the older guys couldn't handle it?" he said, perhaps a bit too defensively.

Smitty continued: "When Stewart's body was kidnapped and a ransom was paid to get it back, Lincoln's friends realized the president's body was not out of danger so they went and moved it to another part of the underground labyrinth and buried it at that time. Then a

174

group of loyalists formed the Lincoln Guard of Honor as a legal organization, outwardly to honor his memory with ceremonies each year. But in reality it was a secret society dedicated to protecting the remains. When Mrs. Lincoln died a couple of years later, she only remained in her crypt two days, then the secret society boys came by one night and buried her next to the president under the obelisk's foundation."

"These guys assumed a lot. Did you check them out?"

"Come on, Z, I only got two hands. All were upstanding members of the community as far as I can tell. And, Robert Lincoln, the son, he knew what was going on. He approved. In 1887, they finally moved the Lincolns back to where they were supposed to be...kind of. They buried them below the floor under the sarcophagus instead of in it. Took the time to look at the president's remains to verify he was in the coffin and put him and the Mrs. six feet under. But due to structural flaws in the monument, the bodies had to be moved again for a tomb reconstruction in 1901. When the president's body was returned to the sarcophagus after reconstruction, Robert wasn't satisfied the body was safe so they dug deeper, ten feet, and buried the coffin in a steel cage under concrete and got rid of the sarcophagus. They opened the coffin one last time to identify the body."

"Did you check out the people who looked at the body in 1901?"

"Every one I could. The youngest, Fleetwood Lindley, was fourteen. He's buried in Oak Ridge too, died in '63. There was one oddball in the group though. His name was Samuel McClavity. Institutionalized for setting a fire in 1922."

Which reminded him to drop by the congressman's office when he had a chance.

"I've got to go, Smitty. Keep at it."

"Now wait a minute, Z. I'm not your slave. Don't you have a whole FBI that can do this stuff for you?"

175

"I can't get fast enough help through the bureaucracy. The Judge doesn't consider me priority. You'll help me, won't you...Veronica?"

"No fair," Smitty said as he clicked off the phone.

A knock on the door was followed by Crosby's assistant sticking her head in the office to tell him that he had a call on line three. Interesting, since nobody in the outside world knew he was here except the Judge.

Rigby picked up the phone, "Yes, Director."

"I'm not a director, I'm not even a chief, I'm a lowly detective."

Lisa Hunt.

"You were supposed to come see me, not run off to the FBI office."

"Given what we didn't find in the coffin, I thought I better do the job I was assigned to do."

"Admirable," she said, "but I still have to talk to you."

"What about?"

"Let's leave that for when we get together."

"All right," he said cautiously, "my place or yours?"

"I don't think either will do. Ask someone there to direct you to the Dirksen statue. See you there in fifteen minutes."

Hunt clicked off her phone before he could respond. *Why the mystery?* He had the sense Hunt played by the book. Whatever she was cooking up had him curious.

The Illinois state capitol building on Second Street looked like many a state capitol building Rigby had seen: a large center dome, expansive wings, stone columns, the building made of what appeared to be limestone block construction. The wide lawn in front of the building was dotted with statues. There was one of Lincoln, of course, closer to the street. Back by the capitol door stood a Stephen Douglas statue. The coal miners' lobby must be strong in the state because he saw a statue for miners.

The statue Rigby was looking for was to the left of the main entrance of the building near the street. Senator Everett McKinley Dirksen. Rigby remembered him from when he was a boy. You often heard him quoted even today, when some commentator was talking about unimaginable government budgets. "A billion here, a billion there, and pretty soon you're talking about real money," the old senator once said. Or something like that. Not enough of that money got down to the working stiffs like Rigby.

He had to laugh at the statue. It was unique. The replica of Dirksen, standing in an oratory pose, was not the only figure standing on the large block base. At his ankles facing him on one side was an elephant and on the other side was a donkey. They were animated creatures, the donkey wearing a hat and jacket, the elephant holding an oil can. What all this meant he had no idea, unless Dirksen had the ability to bring together warring political sides. But an oil can? He remembered Dirksen had a distinctive, raspy voice. Maybe he needed the voice well oiled to operate.

"Remarkable man," Lisa Hunt said, walking up behind him.

"Remarkable statue," he responded. "This your usual meeting place?"

"It will serve."

"Secrets? You have an interest in finding the missing president? I remember when Crease introduced us, he said you belonged to the modern version of the Lincoln Guard of Honor."

"Right now I'm interested in a more recent body."

"Flute?"

She nodded.

"I don't know anything more than I've already told you so I'm afraid I can't help."

Hunt glanced at the statue before allowing her gaze to fall back on him. "I asked you to meet me here because I want to talk to you unofficially. Trying to clear something up."

"About what?" A strange feeling came over him. The detective wasn't meeting him here to gather information, but to hear his side of the story. "You suspect me of something?"

"Let's not get ahead of ourselves," she said. "I just want to talk to you. Giving you some professional courtesy."

"What about?"

"You and Claire Orange."

Hunt's statement was like a tranquilizer dart. It nearly paralyzed him. In a softer voice, he said, "What?"

"Last night at Dr. Orange's house she nearly accused you of wanting her husband out of the way."

Yes, she had, he thought. That line jolted him.

"Dr. Orange was distraught with the news about her husband."

"Then how do you explain her coming off the elevator with you in your hotel this morning?"

"Are you spying on me?" Rigby said indignantly. He wondered if this young police detective had him followed and he was burning. He also realized how suspicious his relationship with Claire must look to Hunt.

"The police station is around the corner from the hotel. You were seen with Dr. Orange."

He calmed himself before speaking and tried to keep a steady voice: "Remember I told you someone had run Claire off the road."

"I remember."

"She's upset. You would be, too. Being run off the road…her son's in a wheelchair and some weird doctor has her believing the boy can walk again but there's no progress, then her husband is questioned about a murder. Claire's world was crumbling and I was an old friend who had been close with her before."

Hunt looked doubtful.

He tried another tack. "You saw me with Claire. We

were old friends. So you're thinking maybe I want to eliminate her husband by setting him up–"

"I didn't say that."

"But, you're thinking it. Trying it out for size. That's why we're here. Look, if I wanted to eliminate Peter Orange as a rival for Claire and you think I'm willing to kill to do it, then why not just kill Peter?"

She was slow to answer, but when she did, she talked more about her confidence problem than about him. "Maybe because you don't think I can solve a complex case."

"That's not what I mean and you know it."

Hunt said, "So you're saying you were just comforting your friend and had no designs on her."

"An old friend in need. Remember, Claire called on me when someone tried to run her off the road because she trusted me."

"She didn't call her husband?"

"She did, but she couldn't find him." This was not the time, and Rigby wasn't in the best situation to raise any suspicions about Peter Orange being the driver of the pickup truck. "She trusted me. She even asked me to stick with her when she took her boy to see Dr. Rittinghouse."

"Rittinghouse." Hunt repeated the name as if testing a swallow of wine inside her mouth. "I know that name. Rittinghouse. Kicked out of med school. Bit of a tabloid scandal."

"He make off with the dean's wife?"

"Nothing like that. Scientific scandal. He was a cutting edge researcher. Pushed the envelope on cloning. Made the trustees of the SIU Med School uncomfortable. They kicked him off the faculty. He's still practicing medicine?"

"In a warehouse. Still doing cutting edge stuff, apparently," Rigby said. "He's trying to get Claire's son to walk again."

"Which brings us back to Dr. Orange," she said.

"You can connect me to Claire, but there's nothing to

connect me to Flute."

"You found the body. You were there first. Maybe you knew where to look. Where were you when Flute was killed?"

"In my hotel room. Asleep and alone."

"Not very original."

"Do I need a lawyer?" Rigby demanded, trying to force an end to the questioning, which seemed to be going out of control.

"You remain a person of interest," she said, "so I'd say you need some good luck."

Chapter 26

The one thing Rigby had to do was the last thing he wanted to do. He should be trying to solve Flute's murder…clear his name. He should be searching for Lincoln's missing body, as futile as that seemed. However, he had to see Claire first. He couldn't let her discover Hunt's suspicion about them from someone else.

Rigby went to the Presidential Library and Museum and walked up to Mildred Huffington's desk. Her drooping eyes and deep frown reflected sadness inside. Seeing Rigby and knowing they shared the truth about what was discovered at Oak Ridge brought new tears to her eyes. He asked to see Claire. Mildred sent him back without even calling her on the phone.

Claire sat behind her desk doing nothing, her empty stare fixed on Rigby as he entered the office. It was the same empty stare he got from the statue depicted in the Lincoln Memorial poster on the wall.

"What an awful day," she began. He realized that for the second time he was the bearer of bad tidings.

"I just came from talking to Detective Hunt," Rigby said.

Now she looked at him eagerly. "About Peter?"

He shook his head slowly and said, "About…us."

Claire sensed something ill. She sagged back in her seat as if prepared to take a blow. He hoped she could withstand the one he was about to deliver. He closed the door.

"Hunt is suspicious about you and me. About what you said last night…that I wanted Peter out of the way."

"But–" He cut her off by holding up his hand.

"And one more thing. We were seen together coming from my hotel."

"From your room?"

"From the room, from the elevator…I don't know for sure."

"What does she think? What did she say?" Claire wrung her hands together. "Is she going to spread gossip? What of my family?"

"Easy, Claire. Hunt was testing out a wacky theory because of what she heard you say. I think I persuaded her she's on the wrong track."

Rigby wasn't sure he moved Hunt at all, but he wanted Claire to lighten up.

She became more agitated. "Her theory is that you trapped Peter so you could have me. You're in danger now. So what are you going to do? Find a replacement suspect? Sacrifice Peter to save yourself?"

"That's what you think of me?" Rigby snapped. Had she forgotten so quickly that she had come on to him in the hotel room? This wasn't the Claire he remembered. She would not be so accusatory. Not of him. "Don't be foolish. It's all a misunderstanding. It'll pass. And, I don't *sacrifice* people. I'm going to find the real killer, whoever it is."

Rigby let that last thought linger a moment because he certainly hadn't eliminated Peter Orange as a possibility. "I want justice for Flute. Not just to protect myself. Not to ruin your marriage. Getting justice for people like her is why I joined the FBI in the first place."

Claire's eyes still sparked with anger toward him, anger that was building. He paused a moment then lowered his voice. "Do you know why I'm not married?"

She didn't answer, but he could see was curious.

"I was almost married…once. Melanie Sussex, an English girl. I met her on my world travels. A sweet lady. Besides you, the only woman I ever loved. We were in our early thirties and after spending ten months in England and getting her to say yes to marriage, I took her home to meet the folks. We were going to spend three months at the family home in Massachusetts, travel a bit. Then go back to England. I was prepared to live there with Melanie.

"A month into our stay we set out for a week-long camping and hiking trip to the far reaches of Maine. You know how I like to hike."

Claire didn't respond, watched him closely. He could see her anger was still there, but her eyes had clouded.

"Late one night Melanie and I were sitting at our campfire when three hunters happened upon us. They were…very drunk."

He stopped, pushing down the anger and pity welling up in his throat like bile. He needed to fight off the old demons, tell the story straight for Claire's sake.

Once he felt he had a grip he resumed. "They were very drunk. Hunting season was over so these guys were lawbreakers. They didn't care. This was the weekend they could get away so they came to hunt no matter what the law said. I bet they were all upstanding members of their community. Probably a hardware store owner or a school vice principal. But this night they'd drunk themselves into monsters. They were out night hunting, they said. *Night hunting!* That's how drunk they were. They complained they couldn't find any prey–until they found Melanie and me…"

The tall man with the two-inch scar under his left eye had done most of the talking since the three men had come out of the woods, drawn to the campfire.

"It's dangerous to be carrying those weapons around at night," Zane said.

"But we need these guns, friend. How else we gonna bag a moose?"

"Two moose," said the stocky man wearing a bright orange hunter's hat with earflaps down over his ears,

although the night was warm.

"No, no, two meese. Two mooses is meese," said the third man with a three-day growth of beard and a blue bandanna wrapped around his neck western style.

The three men guffawed.

Scar moved to his left over near the fire. Zane decided sitting on the ground was not a wise thing. He stood up and helped Melanie to her feet.

"My, isn't she a pretty thing," Scar said.

"Wonder what she looks like under that sweater," Blue Bandanna said.

"Enough," Zane snapped. "Get out of here."

"Yeah, come on, sweet thing," Orange Hat said. "Let's see your breasts."

"Both of 'em. Two breastses," Blue Bandanna said. He was the only one that laughed.

Zane curled his hands into fists. He regretted not taking a gun along on the hike. He knew Melanie would object. Looking down at the campfire, he wondered if the log sticking out of it would be too hot to hold. Before he could react the butt of a shotgun caught him on the back of the head and sent him spinning to the ground. The stocky man with the orange hat threw force behind his blow.

"Stop!" Melanie called out in her crisp English accent. "Leave him be. I'll do as you ask. You look and then you go."

Zane protested, but Melanie ignored him. She pulled her sweater over her head and began working the buttons on her blouse. She had trouble weaving one button through a hole and in frustration tore at her blouse, ripping it open as the last two buttons popped off and flew into the fire. Melanie gave each of the 'night hunters' an ugly look and then reached behind her back, unclipped her bra and slipped it off her shoulders, dropping it to the ground.

"Yahoo!" Blue Bandanna hollered while his companions ogled the topless woman.

"Don't stop there, darlin'," Scar said.

Zane tried to jump to his feet, but Orange Hat clubbed him again, this time using the metal barrel of the shotgun. He collapsed to the ground, dirt flying in his mouth and eyes. He spat out the dirt and rose slowly to his hands and knees, using his shirtsleeve to rub the dirt from his eyes. When he pulled the sleeve away from his face he saw Blue Bandanna had removed his shoes and was dropping his pants.

Claire gasped, feeling the terror poor Melanie must have felt. Rigby continued.

Melanie had unbuttoned her jeans to comply with Scar's demand, but now she froze watching Blue Bandanna. He didn't stop with his pants. His tugged his jockey shorts to his stocking feet and stepped out of them, exposing himself and his desire.

Blue Bandanna advanced on Melanie. Zane screamed, "No!" and jumped to his feet only to be batted back to the ground by Orange Hat, who clubbed him repeatedly with his rifle. Blood oozed from a slash on his scalp.

Melanie started to run, using the campfire as a barrier between her and Blue Bandanna. But she had forgotten about Scar. He came up behind her and wrapped his arms around her, pulling her off her feet.

Melanie and Scar fell to the ground, Scar under her, holding her in a bear hug. Blue Bandanna grabbed the cuffs of her pant legs and pulled the jeans from her body. While Scar kept her pinned, Blue Bandanna made short work of her panties.

"Stop! Please, stop!" Melanie cried as Blue Bandanna dropped to his knees and pulled her legs apart.

Orange Hat shoved his shotgun into Zane's neck and cocked the weapon.

Zane tried to turn away, but the horror of the scene

held him. Scar on the ground, his arms wrapped around Melanie, and Blue Bandanna mounted on her, grinding away. Melanie struggled but couldn't do much.

When Blue Bandanna finished, he rolled off of her and traded places with Scar. The fight was gone from Melanie as Scar took her. She lay there, not moving, her left cheek resting on the ground, her eyes staring across the campground at Zane. He had not moved, the shotgun still pressed against his neck.

"Yeah, man, go!" Orange Hat cheered as he watched the action. The campfire painted an eerie shadow of the woman and her attackers on the surface of the white tent at the edge of the camp.

When Scar was done he ambled over with a grin on his face, took the shotgun from Orange Hat and told him, "Get your piece."

Orange Hat wasted no time obliging. Melanie did not resist. She continued to stare at Zane. He could see the fear, the rage, and the shame in her eyes.

When Orange Hat backed away from Melanie he howled like a wolf. Soon his companions joined him, the trio acting like animals, but these were the worst kind—mad human animals. Zane closed his eyes.

The night hunters dressed and disappeared into the woods.

Zane staggered to his feet and crossed the campground to Melanie. He reached out to embrace her but she pulled away. She huddled in a ball, her legs pulled up to her chest, her arms wrapped around her knees. And she wailed.

The numbness that had enveloped her began wearing off. She looked at Zane now with fury.

He had not protected her!

Rigby paused, took a big gulp of air. His cheeks were wet. Still...after all this time, the tears came so readily. He let them sit on his cheeks, unashamed.

"We reported the crime to the Maine state troopers. I felt that if the rapists were brought to justice, the wound in our relationship would heal. The Maine cops figured the guys were long gone and that they were not from around there. Probably from New York, maybe Canada. The cops made an attempt to do some tracking but gave up quickly.

"Melanie became distant. She decided it was somehow my fault, suggesting the camping trip to that lonely spot, and then not being able to stop the monsters. I wanted us to see a counselor. I knew a counselor would tell her I wasn't at fault. But she didn't want that. She decided a week later all she wanted to do was go home. Back to England...alone."

Rigby pulled a handkerchief from his pocket and dabbed at the tears. He realized he had finished the story staring at the wall.

"I didn't give up. I went back to Maine to prod the cops. I did some investigating myself. I still felt if the bad guys were captured Melanie would come back to me, but nothing happened. I only ran into dead ends. It was over those cold months that I determined to find justice for people like Melanie and me. Because of Melanie's encouragement I had decided to give up my career as a private investigator and already had been accepted to law school. I'd use the law degree as an avenue to get into the FBI. I rushed through law school in two years. I applied for the Bureau and got in before I was too old.

"Over the course of the next couple of years I tried contacting Melanie. My letters were not returned, my phone calls not accepted. I won't be able to fix my relationship with her, and I won't be able to change what happened in the Maine woods, but some small piece of me will heal if I get justice for this dead girl."

Rigby finally shifted his gaze to Claire, who sobbed. He did not try to comfort her. He left.

Chapter 27

He didn't get far.

Detective Hunt, Henry Crease, and a uniformed police officer stood at Mildred Huffington's desk. As Rigby approached he heard Crease say, "That just can't be."

Hunt was the first to notice Rigby. She ignored Crease and said, "I see you and Dr. Orange are together again."

"What is that supposed to mean?" Rigby snapped. He wasn't going to allow Hunt to spread her gossip and innuendo in front of Claire's co-workers.

"Never mind," she said. "I'm not here to see you. I'm here to see Dr. Orange."

With that, Hunt motioned the officer to follow her. They marched toward Claire's office. Crease followed, as did Mildred, who said as she passed Rigby, "Claire's in trouble."

That turned him right around to join the parade.

Claire was wiping the tears from her eyes when Hunt led everybody through her door. "What is it?" she asked as she jumped to her feet. "Peter?"

"No. It's you. We just confirmed some new information."

Glancing at Rigby Hunt added, "Looks like I was wrong about you." Turning back to Claire she said forcefully, "Dr. Orange, you'll have to come with me."

"What for?"

"I have some questions for you about the murder of Mary Blair."

Claire stared at Rigby with terror in her eyes. She shifted her gaze to the detective. "This is wrong. You're making a terrible mistake. I didn't do anything!"

"We'll talk about it at headquarters," Hunt replied.

Crease snapped, "Preposterous! Dr. Orange wouldn't hurt a fly. Where's your proof?"

"This isn't a courtroom and you all aren't the jury. Gomez." Hunt gestured to the cop, who put a hand on Claire's arm.

"You're making a terrible mistake," Claire repeated. She was terrified. Once again she looked to Rigby with pleading eyes.

He spoke in an even tone meant not to rattle Hunt: "Arresting the wrong person is messy. I've been there. Best to be sure."

"This is not an arrest and I suggest everyone here stay clear of police business."

"You can't haul her out of here without a reason," Crease said.

Hunt thought for a moment and finally said, "I have reasons. Dr. Orange was out the night of the murder. She told Agent Rigby and me she was in bed, but her husband told us she went out to get some of her son's medicine she'd accidentally left in her office. Security tapes and records show she never entered this building that night. She also fabricated one other little item. She said she never knew Mary Blair. The night of Mary's murder, Dr. Orange picked Mary Blair up at the Runaway Hotel."

A spasm shook Claire's body. Despite Gomez's restraining hand on her arm she fell back into her chair. Everyone looked at her, stunned by what they had heard.

Something inside of Rigby would never believe Claire Spencer Orange could commit murder. He knew this woman to the core…or thought he did. Hadn't he just recently told himself this was not the Claire he remembered?

"You told me you didn't go out that night," Rigby said to her.

She shook her head. "I know. I'm...I'm sorry."

Mildred quickly chimed in: "Don't talk without a lawyer present."

"I have to," Claire said. "I have to tell everyone here I didn't do it."

"Whatever you say can be used against you," Hunt warned. She ordered Gomez to read Claire her Miranda rights, which he did.

"I thought she wasn't under arrest," Mildred protested.

"She's not. But if she wants to talk to you then I'm protecting myself and this case."

Claire looked around and said, "Doesn't anyone believe me?"

Again there was silence and Rigby could see Claire weakening.

Rigby told Hunt, "This is hard for any of us to believe." He hoped Hunt would defend her position and reveal a little of what she knew.

Hunt hesitated, obviously conflicted about presenting her case to a group of Claire's friends and co-workers. However, he suspected she also wanted to show she wasn't capriciously damaging the reputation of a well-known member of the community.

"Dr. Orange was in her husband's office the day of the murder. According to people we talked to at the law office, she seemed upset when her husband came back after a long lunch with this young woman, Mary Blair. Dr. Orange didn't know Mary worked at the office and asked around, discovering the girl did deliveries and had been on the payroll for a few months. Dr. Orange talked to the young woman and discovered she had a good opportunity to make a lot of money. The meeting was that night. When she learned Mary had no transportation other than the bus system, she offered to drive Mary to her meeting at about 10 p.m. A secretary in the office heard this arrangement being made, and told me about it; Peter Orange apparently had not been aware of it. When it came time to leave the house and take Mary to where she had to go, Dr. Orange made up a story to tell her husband."

Claire cried, "Yes it's *true*, but not the conclusion. I didn't kill her." She stopped, gathered herself before going on. "I was upset about my husband and Mary. I-I wanted to know if there was more to it than a friendly lunch. I didn't want to go through what my mother went through with my father. She was so unhappy. I thought..." A long pause, as if Claire was reviewing her thoughts before speaking. "...if I offered Mary a ride to her business opportunity, I could talk to her and learn the truth. If there was anything between her and my husband."

"Where did you take Flute that night?" Rigby asked.

"To the Railroad Bar. She had me drop her off outside. She was going to meet her contact at the bar."

"Did she tell you about the opportunity? Who she was going to meet, and why? That's pretty late for a business meeting."

"She didn't want to talk about it. She said it was a strange meeting time and place, but the opportunity was something different so it didn't put her off. Her business wasn't why I offered her the ride anyway, so I didn't ask again."

"What did she tell you about your husband?"

Claire hesitated then said, "That he was a nice man. Generous. Offering tips how to get ahead in the world and occasionally buying her lunches so she would eat well once in a while."

A tear collected in the corner of Claire's eye. She was probably thinking she had doubted a good man, and if all this stuff was true Rigby had to admit Peter Orange had some positive points.

"Why didn't you speak about this after the woman was murdered?" Hunt asked.

"I was scared. I didn't know what anyone would think

about what I'd done, especially Peter."

Hunt said, "Okay, I've gone way beyond the lines. Let's go. More questions at headquarters."

Claire went along with Hunt and Gomez. For a long time after she was gone the panicked look in her eyes remained with Rigby.

Chapter 28

He pulled his taxicab into the small parking area next to the Lincoln Memorial. It was early morning, the first hints of dawn creeping in from the east, a brisk breeze caused him to zip his jacket closed. He made his way along Lincoln Memorial Circle watching the trees to his right, looking at the walkways and pathways leading away from the Memorial, trying to discern the best escape route.

It would be darker when he came with his RPG-7. Off to his right stood a grove of trees, which shielded the Korean War Memorial. Ahead of him, past the steps leading up to the Lincoln Memorial on his left and the Reflecting Pool on his right, were more trees and a pathway to the Vietnam War Memorial.

These Americans were always fighting wars then setting up memorials to them. Too soon they forget the death and destruction they brought to other places in the world. They were doing it again in his home country and in other places. He wondered where these bloodthirsty savages would build monuments to the new wars.

If he were still teaching these Americans lessons when new monuments were built to America's current wars, he would make certain those monuments became targets, too.

Reaching the bottom of the steps up to the Memorial, he turned his back on it and looked to the left and then the right. Not only were the trees closer to his left–north–but beyond the Vietnam Memorial and the edge of the park area he knew was Constitution Ave., and across the street the National Academy of Sciences and the Federal Reserve Building. This is where the city with all its streets and alleys and office buildings began. To the south were Independence Ave. and more of the park and the Tidal Basin and the Franklin D. Roosevelt Memorial. He had considered the Roosevelt Memorial as a target, but the one he stood before was better known here in America and around the world. Perhaps next time.

The north would offer more protection; more ways to flee from pursuing agents of the American state. He would plan his escape to the north. He would have more than one vehicle waiting for him. Perhaps as many as three vehicles, all taxicabs. He would be able to get to one of them before any American agent could find him. His taxicab would be one vehicle, and he would borrow others from his colleagues. A taxi driving around Washington at midnight was not so strange. That would help him escape.

He slowly turned toward the Lincoln Memorial. Like a Greek Temple it was. Sitting atop a rise with dozens of steps to reach it. From his position he could see through the majestic columns, holding up the monument's roof, to the large seated figure inside. Yes, even he was impressed at this mythmaking, at the Americans' penchant for doing everything big. He'd heard an American expression once and wondered if it applied here: *The bigger they are, the harder they fall*. He would see to it that America's ego fell hard.

Open for business, he thought of the memorial. Open and ready for a missile to crash into the statue unmolested. He would have no trouble at this distance hitting his mark; he had done it many times before.

He turned and walked away from the monument down steps to the Reflecting Pool. Looking back to gauge the distance to the monument, he thought the statue was still well in the range of the RPG-7. From here, he could drop the weapon into the water of the Reflecting Pool and dash straight for the trees and Constitution Ave. beyond.

He scanned the monument area looking for uniformed

officers. If this were any other country but the United States he would expect to see soldiers holding machine guns at a monument such as this. All he could see were one Park Ranger and two police officers talking at the bottom of the stairs, each sipping from a cup of coffee, none paying attention to their surroundings.

Perhaps one of the few tourists standing on the steps of the memorial or in the circular drive–and he only counted four of those in this early morning–was an undercover official. It would not matter. He would consider all people at the memorial as enemies the night he conducted his mission, and he would be ready for them.

He brought up both arms and stretched them toward the sky. Once he held them in that position for a count of three, he moved them out to his side and again counted to himself for three seconds. Finally he moved them forward, holding his arms rigid, sighting the statue down the length of his arm. Someone would think he was stretching his muscles, not lining up a shot he was certain he could make, a shot that would be heard back in Kabul.

This time he held his arms in a rigid position for a ten count. When he was certain he would be comfortable with this distance, he dropped his hands and headed north toward Constitution Ave. He decided he would have to make this trip many times to work out various escape routes.

Chapter 29

Rigby wanted to go to the police station with Claire to give her support, but Hunt would have none of it. She ordered him to stay away, far away, from Claire and from her.

Hunt's interest first centered on Peter Orange; then him; now Claire. At this rate she was bound to collar the right person by naming everyone in town.

Once in his car, Rigby took the road to Chicago. The woman, not the city. He needed Chicago to tell him the truth this time. The hot tip that Flute worked for a gay lawyer showed Chicago either liked to play with words, didn't understand what Flute meant when she said she worked for a 'fruit' or was an outright liar. Since her information that Flute was pregnant proved false, he was betting on the latter.

A light rain started to fall, proving his sore knee right again. He wished he had such intuitive powers to help with the detective work.

Chicago was in her apartment alone, this time fully dressed. She was not happy to see Rigby. "You're trouble," she said when she pulled open the door.

"Especially when I'm lied to." He walked into her apartment without being asked. He decided to be no nonsense with Chicago this time. He would let the PI in him take over. "You didn't tell me the truth."

"Did so," she said.

He decided to fight her lies with a few guesses stated as truth, a subtler form of lying. Perhaps not in keeping with the Cowboy Code he liked to follow, but this wasn't a

Saturday matinee.

"You and Flute offered the locals treats with a trick."

"Lie!" Her face turned red. He saw her eyes cut to the open door to make sure no one was standing there. She walked over and closed it.

"I've been talking to people at The Railroad Bar."

"They'd say anything for an Abe."

Abe? Oh, him again, a five spot. "You and Flute turned tricks. Amateur night. But there was a need for money. Maybe your husband knows about it."

"Bastard!" The epithet fired from Chicago's mouth was followed by something else from her mouth. She spat at his feet.

Rigby raised his voice: "The bastard's the one who killed Flute. Don't you get it? I'm going to find out who it was. You said she was pregnant. You lied."

Chicago's expression changed. Her hard appearance softened and she looked at him with curious eyes. "Flute said she was going to have a baby."

"She was blackmailing whoever she was screwing."

"No, she talked about a baby. She had no reason to lie to me about that if it wasn't so. We went window shopping for baby clothes. She even drew up a picture with a baby in it."

He remembered the drawing he took off the wall at the Runaway Hotel. Flute had put a pink baby against a depressing black and gray landscape. He hadn't sent the drawing to her folks yet.

"I saw the drawing," Rigby said.

"When Flute showed me the picture she said the baby was going to free her from the Runaway, and she pulled out a roll of bills. The last time I saw her, right before Don and I ran off to get married, she said she had a date with the father soon. She was going to get even more dough. Maybe that's the night she got killed."

Flute was given a lot of money, more than for turning a

trick, but probably appropriate if she was blackmailing some married guy who thought she was pregnant. Peter Orange still remained on his list.

Rigby asked Chicago, "When Flute said she was working, you decided the guy was gay?"

She seemed puzzled by the question. "Why not? She called him a fruit."

"And Flute didn't have a steady customer?"

She hesitated.

"Your best friend's dead. Murdered. God damn it!"

Chicago hung her head. "Okay. Okay," she said slowly, trying to convince herself of something. She blew out a breath before she went on, still looking at the floor. "She did it for money once. *Once!* Hated it. Unclean. *Yucky*, she said. Flute had religion and what she'd done played on her mind."

He considered what Chicago was telling him and although he did not trust the woman, he tried to figure out if there was another way to look at the facts. Flute said she was going to have a baby but she was not pregnant. She had her best friend convinced she really *was* going to have a baby. Her drawing showed the baby as the only bright point in her dark world. Maybe it was a false pregnancy reading from a store-bought kit. What was that roll of money all about? Plus, Chicago said Flute was going to get more money when she planned to meet the father, probably the night she was killed, but she gave up doing tricks. He wasn't sure he believed that. The facts all added up to one thing in his mind: *blackmail*.

Suddenly, another possibility hit him.

Chapter 30

The Railroad Bar was rocking. A DJ ran music past the sound barrier and Rigby wondered how much his ears would hurt if he had the 100 percent hearing of his youth.

Annie-May, the blonde bartender, stood behind the bar wearing a purple T-shirt with a low plunging neckline that must be very good for tips. She was talking to a young man, about her age, in a suit and tie, sitting at the bar. Rigby recognized the guy: Congressman McClavity's assistant, Lenny Poler.

Pushing through the young crowd, each person holding a drink in one hand, he reached the bar. Poler was earnestly trying to convince Annie-May of something as he held both her hands in his.

Even over the music Rigby picked up the conversation, maybe because the song being played was by The Doors–his generation–so it didn't sound like noise.

"Come on, babe, I work for a congressman. I can get us in. A congressman can open any door."

"That's so sweet of you, honey, but Annie-May works that night and can't skip out and lose the job."

"You don't believe me, do you?" Poler said.

Rigby took the stool next to Poler. Annie-May pulled her hands away and turned to him with her flashbulb smile. "How can I help you, honey?"

Poler looked over at his competition. Rigby spotted instant recognition in his eyes. "Agent Rigby," Poler said, thrusting out his hand, "Lenny Poler with Congressman McClavity."

Poler must've seen him as a stamp of validity in his

quest for Annie-May's hand, or whatever other parts he was after, for he turned to her and said, "Special Agent Rigby of the FBI will tell you I work for the congressman."

"I remember you." Annie-May laughed, to Poler's surprise. "You were in a couple of days ago. Special Agent, huh? I thought you were just a private dick, but you're a really big dick, huh?"

Somehow her bright smile and playfulness made the provocative come off as endearing. "One of the biggest," he said.

"So what's it this time, business or pleasure?"

"A beer would taste good. Anything dark from the tap."

Annie-May went off to get his beer. He turned to Poler. "How's the boss?"

"All shook up, as Elvis would say. The thing at the tomb sent him off to the bottle. In fact, that's the reason I'm here. He's over in a corner booth and I'm here to drive him home."

"Why do you suppose he's affected like that?"

"You seen the office. The place is a goddamn shrine to Lincoln."

"You don't approve?"

"I think it's a bit…over the top, to be kind." Poler took a drink from the tall glass in front of him. "I'm going to check in with the boss. Want to say hello?"

Rigby nodded and told Annie-May he'd be back as she placed the beer on the bar. He left it there to hold his place. Following Poler across the dance floor, Rigby wove between dancers. He had trouble slipping through the narrow channels.

Congressman McClavity had a corner booth all to himself. Someone observing him might think he was listening intently to the music, but Rigby got the feeling he was staring off into a world he visited alone. The glass in front of him was half full with what looked like scotch and stood alongside a backup glass of the same liquid filled to the brim.

Poler tapped on the table to get his boss's attention and said, "You got company."

McClavity did not seem happy to see Rigby. He did not invite the agent to join him for a drink, instead saying, "It's been a bad, bad day."

On that they could agree. McClavity turned away, as if ending the conversation before it began would send Rigby off. Not likely. McClavity might be upset about Lincoln's missing body, but Rigby's primary concern wasn't Lincoln anymore. He wanted to find Flute's killer. He felt personally invested in the crime, with police suspicion on him, and now Claire sitting under a hot lamp. The last time he had been personally invested in Mr. Lincoln was when he got his birthday off from school.

Poler stood by the table. Rigby remembered what the guy had said to Annie-May. He'd told her he could take her someplace special because a congressman can open any door.

Rigby said to McClavity, "Who has the key to the padlock on the chain link fence for Oak Ridge Cemetery's gate facing Lincoln Park?"

McClavity showed surprise, not expecting such a question. "I don't really know. The cemetery management, I suppose."

"Could you get it?"

"By simply asking?"

"Yes. As a congressman."

"Why would I?"

"I'm exploring possibilities."

"I don't care for the implication, sir," McClavity snapped. "You're supposed to find Mr. Lincoln's body. I can assure you the body is not in this bar."

He didn't want to talk about Flute's murder. Maybe if Rigby kept him talking, that subject would return. "You want to talk about Mr. Lincoln? Fine, let's do that. But maybe you should ask Mr. Poler to leave."

"Lenny can be of valuable assistance, remembering points from our conversation, tracking down something we might need."

"Good. Then let's start our conversation about that person in the picture you showed me at the library and maybe Lenny can do some tracking for us."

McClavity drained the scotch from his half-filled glass and placed it at the edge of the table. "Lenny, would you please get me a refill."

Poler was surprised by his turn in fortune, but he obeyed, probably anxious to get back to wooing Annie-May. Once he disappeared through the forest of dancers Rigby said to McClavity, "Let's discuss what your grandfather told you about the day Lincoln's coffin was opened."

McClavity hesitated, said, "Um," and fell silent.

Rigby came to his rescue. "My guess is Samuel McClavity never told you anything about that day. Or if he did, you discounted it because he was in an institution for the criminally insane. That's what they used to call it then, right?"

McClavity took a sip from his backup glass and placed the glass slowly and gently on the table.

"The truth is, Agent Rigby, I never met my grandfather. Not once. My parents wouldn't let me see him because he was in the institution. He died when I was thirteen. I never talked to him once."

"Do you know why he started the fire?"

McClavity didn't answer promptly and Rigby added, "You must have read the court record."

"For insurance, I suppose. He owned one of the buildings that went up."

McClavity acted uneasy and Rigby suspected it was difficult for an upstanding member of the community–a congressman no less–to discuss a wayward relative. His old PI instinct had a hunch it was more than that. There was something to do with his push for the McClavity bill and the desire to see if Lincoln was buried where he was supposed to be.

"You expected Lincoln wasn't in the coffin. You feared it."

"Why would I?" he demanded.

"You had to satisfy your suspicions about your grandfather. I imagine the conversation around the dining room table didn't paint him in a complimentary light. You probably wondered if this man, Samuel McClavity, who could set a fire that destroyed all those buildings, could also steal Lincoln's body after the viewing was over."

"There's no indication of that," McClavity said. He took a deeper drink this time.

Rigby said, "According to the newspaper accounts of the fire, somebody died."

"That's right. They said a hobo, a drifter. Broke into a warehouse to spend the night out of the cold."

"Maybe. But no one was reported missing. Yet, they found bones. A body had been burned up. Was that your grandfather's warehouse where the bones were found?"

Sweat beaded along McClavity's hairline. The movement of his hands, thumbs rubbing frantically against index fingers, the lower lip rolled under the row of top teeth told Rigby all he had to know about McClavity's blood pressure.

"I suppose those bones aren't around for DNA testing," the FBI agent said and watched McClavity actually start to shake.

There was no way to prove or disprove this theory. It must be torture on McClavity thinking what his kin might have done to his hero. Rigby guessed the congressman only wanted to know the truth if it vindicated Samuel. He would prefer that the 1922 fire burned up the body of a live person rather than a dead one.

Poler returned with another glass of scotch. Rigby realized that, in McClavity's condition, questioning wasn't going to get him anywhere. He stood up. Let him sweat a while. He wondered whether he would tell Crosby about his assessment of Samuel McClavity. He didn't want to start a rumor that probably could never be substantiated.

Rigby returned to his beer at the bar, the glass dripped with condensation from the heat of the room. He picked up the glass, but instead of drinking he put it against his forehead, the cooling moisture relieving some of the heat.

"What ya doin'?" Annie-May asked.

"Trying to discover the secret of life."

"That's easy. It's money. So you got no worries." Annie-May turned off her bright smile, put her elbows on the bar and leaned forward. "You know, I saw a picture of that murdered girl. That's the one you came askin' around for the first time?"

"Mary Blair. Flute, they called her," he said.

"Yeah. Flute. I remember. Too bad. You was right. Once I saw the picture. She did come here on occasion."

"Where did you see her picture?"

"A lady cop brought it by."

He was pleased that Hunt had been working the case hard.

"What did you tell the lady cop?"

"Just that I recognized the face. Didn't know the name. But I told her about you." This came with a smile from her and a frown from him.

"What did you tell her about me?"

"That you were around askin' questions. She described you pretty good. I knew who she was talkin' 'bout right away."

"The part about being real handsome is a dead giveaway."

Dumb, yes, but it got him that isn't-he-cute-as-apuppy-dog smile. The problem was, there was nothing to smile about. Snooping around would not endear him to Hunt after she'd demanded he stay far away from the investigation, and it may just fuel her suspicion about him.

"Did you tell her I first showed up days ago?"

"She asked when you first came in, but I couldn't remember exactly. She seemed more interested that you were here than me recognizing that girl, Flute. Once I mentioned you, she talked about nothing else. She took notes."

He laid a fifty on the bar. "Keep the change."

"You have a more persuasive style than your young friend who works for that congressman," she said.

"I'm buying some information."

"Maybe you didn't pay enough," she said.

"What's the going price?"

"Supply and demand. I supply the right answer, I demand the price."

Like he said, endearing somehow.

Rigby said, "You told me certain things are sometimes for sale in this place."

"This here's a free trade zone," she responded with caution.

He tried to put her at ease. "Not official. Want to know if anyone was shopping for a young woman to play a surrogate mother."

Sure it was a long shot, but it allowed the pieces of the puzzle to come together. The money. The baby. Flute not being pregnant, at least not yet.

Annie-May leaned closer. He wondered if it was because she wanted to be heard over the music, or so that others would not hear her. "That's a strange one. Strange enough that it would stand out." She paused and looked at the fifty on the bar. "Yeah, I remember."

"Did Flute get the job?"

"She talked about surrogate moms and all. Didn't say

she was doin' it. Just brought up the conversation."

"Who was selling?"

"Can't say."

"Can't say or I didn't pay enough?"

"Can't. Don't know. Flute brought up the subject and we all joined in. Guys and gals. Some of the guys said I should do it."

"Why? 'Cause you want a baby?"

"Come on, Mr. Special Agent. These were guys. They said a baby would love my big boobs. You ask me, the only babies were those guys who was talkin'. It was just bar talk is all. Wasn't tied to anyone special. Not Flute. Not anyone buyin' or sellin'. Just talkin'."

But Flute brought it up, he thought. He guessed she was thinking about it. Deciding.

"Not much to go on," he said.

"Fifty dollars worth," Annie-May responded.

Chapter 31

Rapping on Rigby's hotel door stirred him from sleep. He turned over and looked at the digital clock: nearly seven-thirty in the morning. He'd slept much later than usual. He had many dreams, none of them good. They all seemed like wisps of smoke now. He threw back the blankets, found the hotel robe and tossed it on as he shuffled to the door.

Crosby stood on the other side of the door.

"Getting your beauty rest, Rigby? Let me tell you, it's working." He snorted and walked past Rigby into the room without being asked. Rigby closed the door.

"What brings you here so early?"

Crosby rubbed his partially bald head. "McClavity."

"On our butt to find Lincoln," Rigby muttered.

"On *his* butt. Dead."

"No! I saw him last night." Not a very professional comment, he thought, but that's what came tumbling out of his mouth.

"I know."

"Of course, you know. That's why you're here."

"That's why I'm here," Crosby repeated and sat down in the chair at the desk.

"How'd he die?"

"That's the million dollar question, I'd say. He was found lying at the bottom of the main stairway in the Old State Capitol. Neck broken. Did he fall down the stairs? Or was he pushed? That's what we need to learn. Couple of my agents already talked to his aide. He told us McClavity was in the dumps last night, drinking at The Railroad Bar. He said you came into the bar and talked to McClavity for a while and when you left, McClavity was even more in the dumps. What'd you talk about?"

"Abraham Lincoln," Rigby said without hesitation.

"Well, that makes sense." Crosby put his hand to his chin and struck a thoughtful pose. "Poler said his boss insisted he needed to be closer to Lincoln and he made Poler drive him over to the capitol before going home."

"Poler just left him there?"

"He said the boss insisted. And McClavity has an apartment in the city not too far away. Poler wasn't concerned."

"Did he tell you McClavity was drunk?"

Crosby nodded. "Although Poler's spin on his boss's condition was a bit more diplomatic. McClavity arrived just as the night man was leaving. According to the guy, McClavity talked his way inside with some sort of persuasive argument, he being a powerful congressman and all."

"I know how he does it…did it," Rigby said, correcting himself with due respect for the deceased. "He tells them he controls some of their salary with federal funds. Didn't the night man hear him fall?"

Crosby shook his head. "He thought McClavity had left. He didn't see him anywhere when he locked up. The guy who opens up in the a.m. found McClavity at the bottom of the stairs a little before six. He called the cops and the cops called us."

A murdered congressman was the responsibility of the FBI. The question remained, was this congressman murdered? When Crosby said he was headed for the Old State Capitol, Rigby told him to wait in the lobby while he dressed.

The Old State Capitol building was preserved in a square in the center of town just a block from the hotel. The Greek revival building was made of large stones with four stone pillars at the entrance that Samson would have enjoyed pushing down. A red-colored dome sat like a hat atop a pillared tower centered on the top of the structure. Rigby walked up the steps with Crosby and turned back for a view across the lawn to the storefronts and buildings beyond. He saw the Lincoln-Herndon law offices across the mall, the legend painted in thick black letters between the first and second floors of the wood-framed brick building.

He turned and followed Crosby into the building.

A wide staircase in front of them led up to the second floor. McClavity's body lay twisted and broken at the bottom of the stairs. Rigby looked up at the platform above the stairs, which provided a landing for two more sets of stairways that continued up to the second floor, one to the right and one to the left.

Detective Lisa Hunt approached from somewhere. "Too early in the morning for this sort of thing," she said.

"Then I guess there's never a right time."

"Any verdict from the doc?" Crosby asked.

"Confirmed the broken neck from the fall. He's bruised and cut. Hit a lot of stairs on the way down. Doc will take a closer look but no other readily visible signs of trauma. No knife wounds. Bullet wounds. Nothing."

Rigby could see the bruises on McClavity's face where he'd struck the stairs and floor in his fall. He had blood caked on a gash on his forehead and a split lip.

"Until we know for certain there was no foul play we'll take our appropriate jurisdiction," Crosby told Hunt matter-of-factly. "Working in cooperation with your good offices," he added.

Rigby waited for Hunt to express indignation that Crosby didn't think her capable, but all she said was, "Those are the rules and I play by them."

"Where do you suppose McClavity hid out when the night man thought he was gone?" Rigby asked.

Crosby shrugged. "This place is a museum now. Lots

of nooks and crannies. If McClavity felt he had to be close to Lincoln, this was as good a place as any. Why do you think he wanted to be so close?"

Crosby and Hunt stared at Rigby. He had a good idea but he wasn't ready to share it. He said, "I'd like to look around, see the nooks and crannies."

"Be my guest," Crosby said stiffly, understanding Rigby had ignored his question. "I can even supply you with a guide. One of the docents has already checked in for work this morning."

Rigby was taken to a side room and introduced to a lady who would look comfortable under whale oil lamps. She wore a long period dress sweeping the floor behind her and a cap over white hair. They were kept in the side room until the congressman's body was removed and then told they could walk the corridors as long as they gave a wide berth to the investigators and, of course, touched nothing.

The lady expressed her regrets at the accident that took McClavity's life. Nonetheless, she soon fell into her rote explanation of the old building and the things that went on there. She was good, reciting events and dates and telling stories of personalities and politics. The star of nearly all her stories was none other than you-know-who. She said this was the place where he gave the 'House Divided' speech. Rigby made a mental note to look that up and see what it was.

They climbed the stairs and peeked into the small Supreme Court chambers where Lincoln tried many cases, the Senate chambers and Representatives Hall, where a stovepipe hat on a desk and a shawl on the chair behind the desk indicated where Lincoln once sat. The docent told Rigby that over 75,000 people viewed Lincoln's open casket in this hall over a two-day period in May of 1865, before it was taken to the Oak Ridge Cemetery. There were enough witnesses to believe Lincoln was where he was supposed to be at that time, he thought.

The docent showed him the governor's reception area and informed him Lincoln spent most of his time running for president in this room, greeting visitors, well wishers, and office seekers. So many people had come to Springfield to see him that his home and law office proved too small to handle the crowds. She stopped a moment and studied the room.

"That's funny," she said, "the rail is leaning in the corner."

He looked at the long split rail that had probably been part of a prairie fence at one time. "Looks out of place in this room."

"Not at all. The split rail was one of the greatest marketing tools in American political history."

"How's that?"

"Mr. Lincoln was known as the rail splitter. Someone carrying a split rail identified himself as a Lincoln supporter. Even better, since this was mostly an agrarian nation in 1860 most people looking out over the horizon probably saw split rail fences and thought of Lincoln."

Fine, but Rigby preferred campaign buttons; easier on the shoulder.

"The rail is usually against the wall over there, not leaned into the corner of the room."

She removed the velvet rope used to keep spectators out of the room and started to walk inside when he put a restraining hand on her shoulder.

"What are you doing?"

"I'm going to put the rail back in its place. The old wood-burning stove blocks the view in the corner."

"Leave it be," he said. "Anything out of place has to be looked at by the investigating team."

"Oh," she said. She stepped back into the hallway and replaced the velvet rope.

McClavity could have fallen asleep in this room and moved the rail to be more comfortable. The night man had gone when McClavity awoke, and his mix of booze and sleep and the dark interior of the building could have led to his tragic fall.

Or somebody could have clubbed him with that rail.

Rigby thanked the docent for serving as guide and made sure she got to her car before returning to the main floor lobby. Detective Hunt had gone but Crosby was waiting for him.

"So what do you think?" Crosby asked. "Accident? Murder?"

"How about suicide?"

That brought him up short. "Never crossed my mind. No reason to. And, that's not the typical method, jumping from the second floor, usually not fatal. What do you know?"

Rigby considered whether his tough attitude with McClavity the night before at the Railroad Bar might have pushed him in that direction.

Crosby grew impatient with Rigby's silence. "You sure you told me everything you and the congressman talked about last night?"

"I may have solved the mystery of Lincoln's missing bones."

"You what?" Crosby's voice echoed through the old building, turning the heads of a couple of cops.

Rigby took Crosby's arm and led him to the rear of the stairway away from curious ears.

"From McClavity himself, I learned his grandfather was at the opening of Lincoln's coffin in 1901." Rigby went on to explain his suspicions that Samuel McClavity somehow stole the president's body and burned it up in the warehouse fire twenty years later. He told Crosby McClavity feared it to be the truth, even though there was no way to prove it. He concluded: "Maybe when he saw the bones were missing he decided to jump."

Crosby looked at him, dumbfounded.

Rigby filled the silence. "If he did jump from the second floor he must have hit the stairs and bounced down to the lobby, causing those cuts and bruises."

Crosby was still trying to get his arms around the idea that Lincoln's remains were destroyed in a fire. "But there's no proof…"

"None. Just the suspicion built by McClavity's fear. Certainly not enough to tell the Judge the search is over. But the odds aren't bad that this is what happened."

"Unbelievable," Crosby muttered.

"Before we shut the door on this, let's have the medical team check McClavity for splinters."

Crosby shifted gears and his expression said so. He was no longer thinking about the possible suicide. Rigby had his attention. Rigby told him about the split rail in the governor's reception room and the docent's surprise that it had been moved.

Rigby concluded, "Anyway, we'll confirm it with the investigation. I'll talk to the docs."

Crosby cleared his throat and stepped away from the stairs. "We are not investigating."

"Don't let Hunt pull that local jurisdiction crap. She knows a congressman's death comes under the FBI."

"And the FBI is investigating," he said. "I guess I should have been more precise. When I said 'We are not investigating,' I should have said *you* are not investigating."

"Why not? I know more about McClavity and what made him tick than anyone on your staff."

"Maybe so, but I have orders directly from the Judge. She just called when you were on tour with the docent. You're going back to Washington."

"Washington? No. Not with what happened to McClavity," Rigby said. He didn't add that he had to remain in Springfield to assist Claire by finding Flute's killer.

"Sorry. I'm just the messenger boy here."

"Why's she got it in for me?"

"When she called me about McClavity I told her you were here with me. She said McClavity was my concern, not yours. The Bureau heard from the Springfield police, Rigby, about you spending time on the girl's murder. She said the murdered girl was not your concern. The Judge said you showed bad judgment again and had to be recalled."

"Because I was helping the cops?" Rigby held his arms out, palms up in a manner expressing his skepticism. "Come on, Crosby. I'm smelling a rat. That wouldn't be you, would it?"

Crosby issued a part snort, part laugh and placed a hand heavily on Rigby's shoulder.

Rigby tensed, uncertain what would come next. He stared hard into Crosby's eyes. He wanted the truth and he wanted Crosby to know it. Crosby did not blink.

"That's what she said. Send you home cause you're messin' where your not supposed to be messin'." He hesitated only a brief moment, then went on: "But she said something else, too. The Bomber made a new threat, like she'd told us in my office. What she didn't say was the target is Lincoln."

"Lincoln? Here?"

Crosby shook his head. "Don't know. Just Lincoln. The letter wasn't specific. Could be Lincoln Memorial, Mount Rushmore, any dozens of sites honoring Lincoln around the country–"

"And here," Rigby said. "In Springfield. And that's why she doesn't want me here."

Rigby could feel the blood rise in his temples. The Judge did not want him to have a second chance. All those years of good service to the Bureau and to the country, and one miss and he's blackballed for life. He'd have it out with the Judge when he got back to Washington, but he would delay his return trip to help Claire and even take a shot at stopping the Lincoln attack in Springfield. That's where it had to be, he decided; that's why the Judge wanted him

214

away for here.

"Do you remember what was in the Bomber's letter?"

Crosby studied Rigby for a moment. Then he shrugged and pulled a Blackberry from his pocket, tapped on a couple of keys and turned the screen toward Rigby, who took the device from Crosby and read:

Abraham Lincoln is America's special prophet. He is not a great prophet. He is America's prophet. For that he will not withstand the shooting star which will appear on a moonless night.

Rigby looked up from the screen. "That's it?"

Crosby nodded.

"That says nothing. There are so many monuments and statues to Lincoln. I even saw a statue in Hawaii of a young Lincoln wielding an axe. They're everywhere. Is the Judge going to wrap them all up?"

"The Judge doesn't think he's going to hit Lincoln. She thinks he's doing a head fake. Like Boston, when he told us he was after Bunker Hill and he hit the ship in the harbor. The Judge thinks all this Lincoln stuff isn't real. He's after something else."

"But just in case it is real, she wants me away from here."

"Don't look at it that way," Crosby said.

"How much time before I ship out?"

"To do what?"

"To fix something here."

"Nothing you can do about it."

"I've got to help a friend in trouble."

"Come on, Rigby. Guys like you and me are close to the end. Don't risk it all. Go back and take your lumps." Crosby paused, than added firmly, "The Judge said she wants you on the next plane to Washington and she ordered me to see that my people put you on it."

Chapter 32

Rigby arrived at Reagan National Airport at five o'clock in the afternoon. He grabbed a taxi and headed straight to FBI headquarters not knowing whether the Judge was in her office or not.

She was there.

She refused to see him.

The Judge's perky assistant informed him she was engrossed in the problem of the Monument Bomber and now she also had to deal with the death of Congressman McClavity. The Judge was not currently concerned with the whereabouts of Mr. Lincoln's bones. The assistant screwed up her face and said she was relieved the hand in the jar had been shipped to the lab in Quantico, that she didn't have to look at that scary old thing anymore. When she finished talking about the hand she handed Rigby an envelope.

"The Director said I should give this to you when you arrived," the assistant said.

The Judge had been expecting him and she had an answer for his anger. He opened the envelope and withdrew the folded paper inside. Opening it, he read his new assignment. He would be involved in background checks on minor political appointees. That was the kind of duty reserved for rookie agents or those in the doghouse. Message received loud and clear.

Rigby's mind and energy still churned on the events in Springfield. Flute's murder; Claire's troubles; Lincoln's empty coffin; now McClavity's death. On top of all that, the Monument Bomber had reappeared—and his target was Abraham Lincoln. Maybe something to do with Lincoln and

Springfield, but Rigby was in D.C., expected to talk to some college professor about her former student who had been appointed to the Federal Elections Commission or whatever.

He wasn't going to do it. No, he was going to make himself useful and help deal with important things like the bomber and Lincoln. He felt his anger rising like mercury heated in a tube. Put a cap on it, he thought. He looked at the young woman before him and without a nod or wave turned on his heel and exited her office.

In the hallway, he leaned against a wall. He thought about what the Judge's assistant said. Lincoln's hand had been recently shipped to the lab. He recalled a document in the thin file the Judge gave him when she first assigned him to the case in Springfield. The hand had been verified as real by the FBI Lab–a perfect DNA match. The DNA from a fragment of bone sent from Springfield matched Lincoln's DNA from skull pieces saved at the time of the assassination and stored at the National Museum of Health and Medicine, located on the grounds of the Walter Reed Army Medical Center in Washington. The report verifying the match said the hand itself was due to arrive in a couple of days. Then the hand ended up as some kind of weird trophy on the Judge's desktop.

Rigby wondered why the hand had been sent to Washington in the first place. The test had been completed on the bone fragment. The hand belonged in Springfield for reburial. Maybe the person sending it for testing was unaware the sample was sent ahead of time. He needed to see that report again, but he didn't have it with him. However, he knew how he could see a copy quickly. He walked back into the Judge's office.

The Judge's assistant was surprised to see him return. He smiled at her and turned on the charm.

"I wondered if you could show me the original file that was copied for me before I went to Springfield."

She looked at him skeptically. "Wasn't that a new

217

assignment from the Director in the envelope?"

Of course she knew it was, but he was ready with an answer. "Yes. But I need to write a report on my activities in Springfield and I left so quickly that I forgot my copy there. I need to see some items in the file to complete my report."

The assistant's dubious look didn't leave her eyes.

"I'm not going to take it away," he assured her. "Just want to peek at it right here for a minute."

The assistant relented. She walked to stacked boxes labeled IN and OUT and dug to the bottom of the OUT box; obviously behind on her filing, Rigby thought, which was probably a good thing for him. She came up with the correct file and motioned him to a small round table with one chair in the corner of the reception area. He thanked her, sat down and opened the file.

He shuffled through the pages and quickly found what he wanted. Henry Crease had sent the hand to Washington. Rigby guessed Crease probably didn't think it was real and didn't mind sending it across country.

Crease wouldn't have sent the hand if he knew the bone chip revealed it truly belonged to Lincoln. He would have waited for the test results from the bone chip, if he had known about it.

Rigby turned over the next page of the report and looked for the spot where the name of the sender was supplied: Dr. Claire Orange. He thought of poor Claire. Her misery–and his–had started with the hand.

Claire was the authority sending the bone chip, but a medical man, one who made sure the procedure had been carried out properly, had handled it. Dr. Bernard Rittinghouse.

There was something about Rittinghouse that set Rigby to itching. He guessed it made sense that Claire would rely on him. Claire found the hand. She knew Rittinghouse because of her son. She called him a wizard in many scientific disciplines, including DNA. Still, Rittinghouse set off that itching even a thousand miles away.

Rigby thanked the assistant, told her he could write his report now, and returned the file. He left the Judge's office.

If the Judge wouldn't talk to him, Rigby hoped someone in the Bureau would. He knew where to start. On the phone in Crosby's office when he reported Lincoln's coffin was empty, the Judge told him not to bother her with Lincoln any longer but to report to Associate Deputy Director Paul Duncan.

Okay, Mr. Duncan, you're on. Rigby didn't know much about the guy. He had been in West Coast field offices his entire career until the Judge brought him to Washington. Rigby didn't know the connection between Duncan and the Judge, but counted on the fact that Duncan must be loyal to her, so he would tread carefully in talking about her.

Duncan agreed to see Rigby when he showed up unexpectedly. He was ushered into the office.

Duncan, a tall man, looked younger than Rigby expected. Part of the Judge's new regime that she would mold in her own image. He shook Rigby's hand and directed him to a sofa in the corner of his office. Duncan sat across from him in a rocking chair.

Rigby said, "The Director told me to report to you on the Lincoln situation."

"There is no Lincoln situation anymore for you," Duncan replied. "There's probably no Lincoln situation for anyone. Mr. Lincoln's missing bones are low priority for the Bureau right now. And, since the Director recalled you, that ends your involvement."

Loyal to the Judge, just as he expected, but loyal to the point of shutting out all other theories? He would probe.

"I was in Springfield long enough to see some strange things going on. There was a murder in Lincoln's cemetery. And now the bomber is threatening Lincoln. There could be a connection. Springfield could be the target."

"How did you know that the bomber was targeting Lincoln?" Duncan gave Rigby an icy stare, and he realized he had exposed Crosby to the wrath of Washington.

"Something I learned when I got back here," Rigby said, hoping to keep the brass away from Crosby.

Duncan accepted Rigby's explanation. "Could be one of many targets when it comes to President Lincoln. But the real target is somewhere else. We're sure he is trying to throw us off the scent like he did with you up in Boston."

The way in which he said it made Rigby understand the Judge had passed down her disrespect of him to her subordinate. Rigby wasn't interested in getting into personality battles. He charged ahead with his theories. "Look, Mr. Duncan, there are threads that have to be followed. The way Lincoln's hand was handled–"

"President Lincoln is no longer your concern." Duncan's voice was sharp, uncompromising.

"Lincoln is a concern for all of us. And not just the missing bones. I think Lincoln is the real target–"

"Enough." Duncan stood and indicated with an upward sweep of his hand that Rigby should do the same.

Rigby not only left Duncan's office, he exited the building.

Outside, Rigby called Wendell Muboto at the FBI Lab. They had worked well together on a kidnapping case a few years back. He asked Wendell to take a quick look at the records on the DNA sample of the hand. He wanted to know how good a match it was. Wendell sighed, complained he had a lot to do, but promised he would call back as soon as he could.

Background check phone calls be damned. Rigby decided there was no better time than now to make good on his promise to Smitty. He said he would take her to the Lincoln Memorial. He dialed her number and caught her at her desk at the Smithsonian. She was happy to hear from him; too giggly for the mood he was in, but he arranged to meet her at the steps of the Lincoln Memorial in an hour.

Smitty was punctual as usual. She hugged Rigby tightly, as if he had just returned from a year at the front. Her black-rimmed glasses twisted askew on her nose. She pulled away from him and readjusted them. He patted her on the head, but she took no offense.

"Are we still working the case? Is that why we're here?"

He nodded. "But we can't talk about it. Still secret."

"My lips are sealed and I threw away the key."

He wondered how long this ploy would keep her quiet. He noticed an extra detail of Park Rangers and police and knew the Monument Bomber was the reason for the added security.

He pointed up the stairs. "Well, I told you we'd see the Lincoln Memorial. Shall we?"

Smitty took his arm and led him along, climbing the marble steps and entering the temple between the huge columns. Thirty-six Doric columns, she informed him, one for each state at the time of Lincoln's death. He had no idea what Doric meant and didn't ask.

He was speechless walking into the temple. Instead of looking at the massive statue before them, Rigby wandered over to read the Gettysburg Address, inscribed on the south wall. He was moved by the words of the short speech, more so than he remembered when he was forced to memorize it in junior high school. One line caught his attention: *We have come to dedicate a portion of that field as a final resting place for those who here gave their lives that that nation might live.*

Abraham Lincoln also gave his life so our nation might live, but he didn't get a final resting place. At least, not one that anyone knew about. The body had been moved around so much and now it was gone.

Stepping back, Rigby looked at the mural above the engraved speech, which Smitty said depicted the angel of truth freeing a slave. As they walked between interior columns to a spot in front of the elegant statue, Rigby was aware of the silent men standing in the corner, not in uniform, but undoubtedly security. FBI? Homeland Security? DC Cops? U.S. Marshals? They probably were around all Lincoln sites tonight. Of course, Rigby knew from Crosby that the Judge didn't think a Lincoln monument was the real target and Duncan just confirmed it, but she couldn't be so certain as to deny a beefed up presence around Lincoln memorials.

Rigby wasn't so sure the Judge had it right.

His thoughts were distracted as he looked up into Lincoln's face. The statue spoke volumes just by silently standing there. The man's immense effect on history and humanity was so powerfully stated that, had Rigby worn a hat, he would have removed it out of respect.

On the back wall above the statue read the words: *In this temple as in the hearts of the people for whom he saved the union the memory of Abraham Lincoln is enshrined forever.*

He looked at the chiseled features of the president's worn face reflecting the immense burdens he carried. Smitty, Rigby's own personal tour guide, told him Daniel French Smith sculptured the statue out of Georgian marble. President Warren Harding dedicated the memorial in 1922.

That was the same year as the Springfield fire. He wondered if it was a coincidence or if the monument's dedication stirred Samuel McClavity's guilt and prompted him to set the fire.

Rigby looked at the hands sitting above the chair's armrests. They were quite distinctive and he pointed them out to Smitty.

"There's been discussion for years whether the hands were shaped on purpose to display finger spelling for the letters "A" and "L." From Lincoln's perspective the A is on the left and L on the right, although the L is slightly subdued. It should be like this."

She held up her hand with the index finger and the thumb, making the shape of the letter L, while her three other fingers folded down toward her palm.

He looked at the hand representing the letter A. The A shape was four fingers curled into the palm with the thumb against the index finger.

"So they spell out his initials. Clever."

"Well, maybe they do and maybe they don't," she said. "There's no certainty. The *Smithsonian* magazine had an article a few years back calling it wishful myth that his hands were letters. But we know that the sculptor, French, knew something about finger spelling. Years before doing the Lincoln statue he sculpted a statue up at Gallaudet."

"You mean the college for the deaf here in town?"

"Yes. French made a sculpture of Thomas Gallaudet teaching his pupil the letter 'A.' That was more than twenty-five years before French started the Lincoln statue. Some think he put his knowledge to work making the hands on Mr. Lincoln more expressive."

Rigby took a couple of steps closer to the statue and kept staring at Lincoln's hands. 'A' and 'L.' He thought he had seen those hand shapes before. Where?

"Are we finished here? It's dinnertime and I'm hungry. Take me to dinner, Z, and then we'll have dessert to end a perfect evening." She winked at him. He knew what she had in mind for dessert. That was not going to happen.

He led Smitty back to the top of the stairs and paused as he looked out over the Reflecting Pool, the World War II Memorial and the Washington Monument with its red lights blinking in the distance warning off low flying aircraft. Gorgeous, he thought.

"Beautiful, huh?" Smitty said, as if she could read his thoughts. No one needed to read hers, because she came right out and said what was on her mind. "And very romantic. Down by the pool. Or in the trees near the pool.

And, very private. There's a new moon tonight."

Rigby looked down at her.

"You like my suggestion?" she said hopefully.

"What did you say?"

"What? You weren't listening to me?" For the first time that evening sweetness drained from Smitty's voice.

"A new moon?"

"That's right," she said, hope and sweetness returning together. He *had* heard her.

"New moon," he repeated and looked up at the darkening sky. "A moonless night."

Chapter 33

Rigby had trouble sending Smitty on her way. She reminded him vociferously that he promised to spend time with her, and these few moments at the Lincoln Memorial were not sufficient.

"After all I did for you," she said and actually stamped her foot.

Rigby led her down the stairs, deciding to fall back on what he told her when she first arrived: that he was still working on the case. Although this time he told himself it was true.

"I need to spend some time here. Working this out. And I have to do it alone. But, you know once again, it's because of you. You led me in this new direction."

She seemed to calm a bit and said, "Me? What did I–"

He held up his hand. "You know I can't say. Not now. Later. I'll tell you everything when I can over that make-up dinner I now owe you."

Smitty still had a scowl on her lips, but she nodded. Rigby squeezed her shoulder, walked her to a taxi and sent her home.

Turning back to the Memorial, Rigby pulled out his cell phone and dialed FBI headquarters. A few transfers and he was talking to Associate Deputy Director Paul Duncan.

"I'm heading out the door, Rigby. I thought we were finished."

"Tonight's a new moon. That makes it a moonless night. The bomber is going to attack on a moonless night. I'm at the Lincoln Memorial. That has to be the number one target, but tonight all Lincoln sites should get special attention."

"We've been over this. We got protection out there, but we're not limiting it to Lincoln sites. It's another decoy–"

"No," Rigby cut him off. "I don't think so. He's changing his M.O. again."

"Stop meddling," Duncan demanded. "I understand you got a new assignment from upstairs. Do what you're told or I'll have you leading public tours of the building in the morning."

The phone clicked off. Rigby thought he might like to conduct a tour or two and point out the new team of asses who were running the Bureau.

All right. If he couldn't convince the brass, he would do a little protecting on his own. It very well could be a long and fruitless night, but he thought his reasoning was logical. The bomber had promised a shooting star on a moonless night. Rigby guessed no one could get close to the Memorial with a bomb. Perhaps the bomber could deliver one–a shooting star–from far away. Smitty had let him know this would be a moonless night.

The Judge thought the bomber was using Lincoln as a decoy just as he had used the Bunker Hill Monument to pull the FBI away from Old Ironsides. Rigby knew the bomber always changed his routine. There was no warning about the bomb placed in the Statue of Liberty. The letter came after the explosion, the bomber taking credit.

The hint of the next attack was an anonymous tip. Rigby now knew it was from the bomber himself, just to lead the FBI astray. That time the bomber had delivered his after-the-fact message in the backpack of the decoy. Then came the letter about Lincoln.

The routine would change again; Rigby was certain of it. Yet, the Judge was fighting the last war. Lincoln was the target. Lincoln was not a decoy. The Lincoln Memorial was on top of the list of Lincoln targets.

Rigby would make himself at home in the trees

alongside the Reflecting Pool.

Before he aroused suspicion from the security men on detail he identified himself as an FBI agent. He told them he was guarding the perimeter. With so many new people doing extraordinary things under the red alert issued after the bomber's letter arrived, none of the security personnel thought his assignment was strange.

Before settling in for the evening, Rigby went to a nearby souvenir stand and purchased a cheap sweatshirt with a picture of the capitol and big letters spelling out *Washington, D.C.* He anticipated a cool evening. He removed his jacket and his tie and shrugged on the sweatshirt, first shifting his gun from his shoulder holster to his pants pocket. He sat next to a tree that gave him a clear view from the edge of the Reflecting Pool all the way to the columns of the temple. He waited.

The last rays of the sun slipped away from behind the Memorial and the night brought along a breeze, sending the temperature tumbling. Rigby retrieved the suit jacket he had stashed behind the tree and slipped it over his new sweatshirt. A concession to age, he figured. He had noticed for some time, as he aged, that he grew colder more quickly.

As new visitors arrived at the Memorial, Rigby took notice. He was not sure what he was looking for, because he knew if the bomber were attacking that night he would doubtless take precautions to protect his identity. Rigby realized he could not even be sure the bomber was a male. Everyone was a suspect.

As the night progressed, the number of visitors to the Memorial declined. Some rowdy teenagers showed up around ten o'clock, but the D.C. cops stopped their partying before it began and shooed them away. When he couldn't sit by his tree any longer, Rigby rose and paced along the edge of the line of trees set a few yards from the Reflecting Pool. One time he walked around the entire pool, but decided that was not a good idea, because at the east end it took him too far away from the front of the Memorial.

Taking up his position next to the tree again, he huddled close to it to cut down on the breeze. Every ten minutes or so he stood and walked around, stirring the circulation in his legs.

His wristwatch became an adversary. He looked at it too often as the second hand swept by, mocking his effort. He had been on plenty of stakeouts as a private investigator and as an FBI agent, but he usually had more to go on than gut instinct.

As the second hand continued its lap around the face of the watch and the dark night shaded toward black, Rigby felt his eyelids droop. He fought to keep them open. He thought of those old cartoon characters that used to have toothpicks in their eyelids to prop them open. That image didn't help.

He felt himself falling. He moved with a start. His back had bumped against the tree behind him, leaving him in a sitting position. He looked at the watch. Fifteen minutes had passed. Nearly 11:30 p.m. He realized he had fallen asleep. Rigby cursed softly and yawned, his mouth wide open; eyes shut. As the yawn ended and his eyes opened, he saw the musician.

The man stood at the edge of the Reflecting Pool, a large musical instrument case, one that would likely house a cello, by his side. He wore an elegant overcoat with an upturned collar, an Englishman's flat cap on his head, and gloves. He looked like he was on his way home from a night at the symphony.

As Rigby struggled to his feet the man laid the case flat, dropped to one knee, and started manipulating the latch.

Rigby looked up at the Memorial. The agents and police on duty at the Memorial had noticed the musician as well. A couple of uniformed D.C. cops were jogging down the stairs of the monument.

The musician opened the top of the case, reached inside, and demonstratively began working over whatever lay in the case.

Rigby didn't think the man had a cello inside. He started to run.

The musician stood. He held a rocket grenade launcher, the missile already attached.

A shooting star! Rigby sprinted toward the man, but the Reflecting Pool prevented him from running in a straight line.

The musician–the Monument Bomber–hoisted the rocket launcher to his shoulder.

Rigby reached into his pants pocket, grabbed his gun and struggled to pull it clear. The hammer caught on the material. The bomber wrapped his finger around the launcher's trigger.

Rigby yanked the gun, heard a ripping sound of cloth as he got it clear of the pocket. He had no time to aim. He pulled the trigger.

The bomber fired just as Rigby's bullet hit the exhaust end of the launcher tube.

The rocket leapt skyward, a burst of flame exploding from the rear of the tube.

Rigby froze. He whipped his head around to watch the rocket. The approaching cops also turned to watch.

The rocket–the shooting star–streaked through the air, arcing toward the Memorial. Rigby could see the lighted figure of Lincoln sitting between the columns.

It was as if time stood still. The rocket soared toward the statue of the man, but in Rigby's eye it traveled in slow motion. Another projectile rushing to rip apart Lincoln's head. Another Lincoln assassination.

The rocket rose as it flew. Up, up–and over, clearing the roof of the Memorial, its course altered by Rigby's wild shot.

Rigby turned to the bomber. He saw a flash, heard a

small *pop* and felt a sharp sting on his right forearm. He dropped his gun, looked down at his arm, saw the blood.

Another shot exploded to Rigby's left. The bomber turned toward the advancing police officers and fired. The short cop on the left cried out and fell to his knees. The second cop got off a shot before he too was screaming in pain. Rigby saw a gush of blood erupt from the cop's knee.

The bomber turned back toward Rigby, his gun leveled.

The water in the Reflecting Pool splashed once, twice.

The bomber glanced back toward the Memorial. An officer with a rifle was firing from the steps as other security personnel rushed down.

The bomber started to run north, then turned toward Rigby and fired.

Rigby dove to the concrete and rolled into the Reflecting Pool. The cold water chilled him instantly. It didn't matter; he needed to get out of the line of fire. The water was only two feet deep. His feet found the bottom of the pool; he pushed off and hugged the edge of the concrete, staying low. Another shot clipped the concrete near his head. He moved sharply to duck the splinters, banged his head hard against the pool's edge.

Loud yelling now. More bullets fired, then, silence.

Rigby reached for the edge of the pool to pull himself out of the water, but only found air. A hand grabbed his, and he immediately pulled back, ready to fight.

"Easy, easy," came the reassuring voice of a woman. Rigby tried to focus, chase away the fog enveloping his brain. The woman wore a uniform of some kind. He stared at the red blur on her shoulder, which focused into a red cross on a patch. A paramedic.

"Easy, big fella," she cooed. "You're in good hands."

Rigby tried to push himself up, but the paramedic kept him on the concrete surface with a hand to his chest.

"The action's all over for now," she added.

"Let me be the first to say good job," came a deep voice from his right. He turned and saw a hefty cop, his pants dripping with water from the knees down.

"You pull me out? Thanks."

"Thanks, hell," said the cop. "Thank *you*. You stopped the bastard from destroying the monument and probably killin' me in the process. The whole place woulda fallen all over me, maybe. I was inside."

"Did you catch him?"

"Not yet," the cop said, "but we will. The place is swarmin' with my guys, and some of your guys, too."

Rigby nodded. He recoiled when the paramedic touched the wound on his arm.

"Hurt? Sorry. Not, too bad though. I'll clean it up and cover it. How's the head?"

"Partly cloudy," he said like his favorite weatherman on Channel 4. "How long was I out?"

"A couple of ticks," said the cop.

A man in a suit and tie joined the policeman. Associate Deputy Director Paul Duncan.

"Just got the call," Duncan said. "You okay?"

"He'll live," the paramedic told him. When she saw the stern look on Duncan's face she smiled and said, "Thought you wanted a professional opinion."

The paramedic helped Rigby sit up. The cop said, "You'll get a citation for this."

Duncan said. "What were you doing here?"

"Stopping the Monument Bomber," Rigby said firmly. "What happened to the rocket?"

"Fell harmlessly into the Potomac. We got lucky," the cop answered.

"Yeah," Rigby said. "Lucky. How are the officers he shot?"

"Heading for the hospital in a minute," the paramedic said.

"The Director will have a lot of questions for you,"

Duncan said.

The paramedic shook her head. "They'll have to wait. We need to bring this guy in for observation. Gunshot wound and knot on his noggin."

"I'll be okay," Rigby said.

"You did your job, John Wayne, now I gotta do mine," the paramedic said. "All goes well, you should be ready to meet the Director for breakfast. That isn't too long from now."

Duncan nodded. "Okay, gives us some time to get ready and maybe haul this bastard in. What can you tell us?"

"He was covered up. Maybe five-eight. Too dark to see his features under the hat. He had gloves on. You get the grenade launcher?"

"Got it," Duncan said. "Maybe some prints. When we see you later we'll have him. Shouldn't be too hard this time of night. Nothing much on the streets but a few taxis."

Chapter 34

It was well after nine a.m. when Rigby arrived at FBI headquarters. He wore a bandage around his forearm but had refused a sling. He was able to get his shirt and jacket over it so no one who wasn't aware of the wound would ask him about it. He went directly to the Director's office, but was stopped on numerous occasions to receive congratulations. The word had spread.

In the Director's outer office he received a pat on the back from the executive assistant. "The Director will see you immediately," she said, smiling.

Rigby's cell phone rang. He held up his finger to the assistant asking for a minute and answered the call.

"Rigby, this is Wendell Muboto."

"That was quick, Wendell, whatcha got?"

"Just a matter of running the computer. A DNA sample from the hand was extracted when it arrived here and the results are just in. I ran the findings against the results from President Lincoln's bone fragments. The hand doesn't match."

"*What?*"

"Those bone fragments we had at the museum matched the sample sent by Dr. Claire Orange earlier," Muboto explained. "But the DNA of the hand in the jar doesn't match up with the museum fragments."

Rigby didn't understand. "The hand is a fake?"

"It's real enough," Muboto responded. "Maybe a century-and-a-half old."

"But not Lincoln's?"

"Doesn't match the bone fragment we have from the

museum that's supposed to be President Lincoln's. Assuming the fragments weren't switched over the years," Muboto said, never willing to give an unqualified answer.

"You're saying the bone chip sent by Dr. Orange from Springfield didn't come from the hand?" Rigby needed to be certain what he was hearing.

"No, it did not come from the hand."

"But it does come from Lincoln?"

"That's what I'm reading, yes."

"Where did the bone chip come from, then?"

"From Springfield," Muboto said with a chuckle and hung up.

The hand wasn't Lincoln's. Yet, Lincoln's body was missing from his coffin and it was this hand that had led to uncovering that fact. Whose hand was it? What did this have to say about Claire, who'd discovered the hand? Claire, who was being questioned about a murder? Was Claire a phony, too, like the hand? Was he wrong about Claire– could she be a murderer? Where did the Springfield bone fragment, which matched the Lincoln fragment in the museum, come from?

Try as he might, he could not believe Claire was mixed up in any wrongdoing, let alone murder. Muboto's revelation turned his focus on a dime. He had to help Claire and discover the truth.

"Agent Rigby, the Director is waiting." The assistant had dropped her smile.

This time when Rigby entered the office the Judge rose from behind her desk, although she wore a stern expression. Paul Duncan sat across from her and did not stand. The Judge did not offer a handshake. As soon as Rigby reached the chair next to Duncan she sat down.

"We owe you congratulations for saving the Lincoln Memorial," she said. "Lucky stroll in the middle of the night, or did you have inside information."

Turning to Duncan, Rigby said, "I gave out all the

information I had."

Duncan squirmed in his seat and studied his hands.

"Well, we learned something," the Judge said. "He's always changing his M.O. and he's a man."

"As I suspected," Rigby said pointedly to Duncan. "And he can shoot straight."

"Yes, I heard. I'm sorry for that." Her voice softened a bit. "Is it painful?"

Rigby said, "Did we get him?"

Duncan looked up at Rigby and shook his head. "You remember anything else about him?"

"Just what I told you earlier. Face was impossible to see and he never said a word. How about prints?"

"Checking."

"Well, you're back on the task force," the Judge said, forcing a smile. "Immediately."

Back where he should be, he thought. A chance to run down the Monument Bomber.

However, he couldn't get the situation of the hand, and what it might mean for Claire, out of his mind.

"Did you hear the Director?" Duncan asked, astonished that Rigby did not respond.

"Yes. Thank you. Keep me informed," Rigby said.

"Informed?" It was the Judge's turn to be astonished.

Rigby stood.

The Judge said, "You're part of the Monument Bomber task force and the trail is hot."

He thought about the Judge's words, knew he wanted to be back chasing down the Monument Bomber and the time was now.

He also knew in his heart what he had to do.

Chapter 35

The tour group leader at the National Museum of Health and Medicine, on the grounds of Walter Reed Hospital, told the tourists the museum was founded as the Army Medical Museum in 1862 to study and improve medical conditions during the Civil War. She added, "The Museum houses a collection of over twenty-four million items including archival materials, anatomical and pathological specimens, medical instruments, and artifacts."

Rigby was interested in one particular artifact. He attached himself to the back of the group only because they were approaching the most interesting display at the museum, at least from his perspective: specimens and artifacts related to Abraham Lincoln's assassination.

As the tour guide pointed out the assassin's bullet that killed Lincoln, a bloodstained shirt cuff from a surgeon who attended the autopsy, and the thin probe used to detect the depth of the bullet in Lincoln's brain, Rigby concentrated on the small bits of white bone displayed in round protective casings–fragments of Lincoln's skull collected at the autopsy.

How could they extract DNA out of something so small? He thought that with the FBI lab's determination the hand did not belong to Lincoln, and with the body missing, these tiny pieces of bone and the similarly encased hair taken from Lincoln's head were the only known remains of the great man.

The tour moved on, but he lingered. What better spot to meet the person attached to the museum that sent the bone fragment to the lab?

"Agent Rigby?" a feminine voice, soft and sweet, came from behind him. Rigby turned to see her face, like her voice soft and sweet, and around his age. He had a strange sense he'd met the woman before. Had he seen her in a Washington restaurant or at a party? Sure, he noticed a lot of women, but as sweet as her features were, she didn't have the looks that would turn heads. She wore a white doctor's smock. Her nameplate read: Dr. Phyllis Canning.

"Thanks for seeing me, Dr. Canning."

"Of course. I hope I didn't keep you waiting. The message from the desk, that you arrived, only now reached me."

"That's okay. I wanted to see this display anyway."

"It's the most popular on the tour, as you can imagine. The probe there," she pointed to the thin metal rod, "was used by Dr. Barnes to find the ball lodged six inches inside the president's brain. Barnes was in charge of the Medical Museum at the time."

"Wonder what that bullet would get on eBay?"

She laughed easily and he gave her points for not being shocked by the question. In a conspiratorial whisper she said, "I've wondered the same thing. The expected answer is like they say in those credit card ads, 'priceless'. But there's a price for most anything."

Dr. Canning was a woman of the world, he decided.

"How difficult was it to release the bone fragments to our lab?"

"Procedurally, you mean. Yes, it was a unique request. But the FBI asked and we responded. We're all in the same family, you know."

That was true. He asked her what had been bugging him. "How do they get a DNA sample out of such small bone fragments?"

"Isn't science fantastic? Everyone in my family was taught about science and releasing its secrets. The museum actually didn't open the display case to get a piece of bone.

We have a number of bone fragments from Lincoln that were acquired at the autopsy. From his skull and his hand. Not many people know he put up his hand to attempt to block the bullet. An instinctive reaction when he sensed someone behind him. We had a slightly larger skull fragment in storage, which we sent to the FBI."

"Wouldn't it have been easier to send the hair?"

"Not this hair. No DNA. You need hair with follicles to get DNA."

"So there was no debate on whether to part with the skull fragment?"

"We're getting it back, aren't we?" She laughed again. No rattling this lady. "The request came in. I was here when it came. I split my time between the museum and doing some actual doctoring at Walter Reed. I volunteered to take care of securing the fragment and getting it to the lab. They didn't tell us why they wanted the fragment, of course, but I figured it was some important test and I wanted to be part of it, whatever it was. And now...." She cleared her throat and said, "Is there anything else you need from me, Agent Rigby?"

He noticed her hesitation and wondered if something was upsetting her.

"I hope my asking to see you didn't disrupt your day."

Again the good-natured doctor smiled and brushed all concern aside. "You call me if you figure out what you need. I have a small office in the building and I'm also over at the hospital."

He thought she sensed his uncertainty because instead of a handshake she patted his upper arm in a reassuring gesture and left him to ponder the Lincoln remains and artifacts.

When the second test indicated the hand was not Lincoln's, it became more important somehow. He just couldn't explain how.

Rigby wondered how this could help clear Claire from

the fix she was in. He tried to discover how she was doing, but no one would take his calls in Springfield: Claire, Sir Peter, Hunt, even Crease were 'unavailable'. Mrs. Huffington said flat out Crease didn't want to talk to him because he was bad luck for Claire *and* Mr. Lincoln. He learned from Mrs. Huffington that Claire had not been arrested but was still in jeopardy.

Staring at the bone chips, he thought about Dr. Canning asking if the FBI planned on returning the fragment. He wondered if other Lincoln bone chips had been circulated before for scientific investigation. Was the FBI request for a piece of bone the first time that happened? Had another chip been sent off and not returned, available to scam the FBI?

Rigby decided to ask Dr. Canning. He made his way to an information desk and followed instructions to reach the administrative offices. A couple of questions and his FBI credentials got him to the right place, an office along a short corridor. There was no name on the door. He knocked and waited for a response. Nothing. He knocked again and this time tried the knob. The door opened to a tiny office, clean and uncluttered. It looked like a way station for Dr. Canning, not her main office. A couple of books and reports sat on a shelf in a small bookcase; the other shelves were empty. The desktop had a pencil holder containing one pencil, a notepad and a small picture frame. He looked at the picture hoping to confirm that he was in the right office. The picture was of a black Labrador retriever holding a doll.

Then he looked up and saw a framed picture on the wall next to the office door. He recognized the photo immediately. He had seen it before. And, he knew he was in the right office. He also understood now why Dr. Canning looked so familiar. He instantly decided where he was going next…and he wasn't going to ask permission.

Chapter 36

He didn't bother making arrangements, or think about going home to pack a bag. He didn't call the office to tell them he wouldn't be around for a few days. Driving straight to Reagan National Airport, he parked in the most expensive nearby lot and headed for the ticket counter.

Fortunately, a flight to St. Louis was leaving in an hour and a commuter to Springfield was easily arranged. Knowing the FBI wouldn't cover the cost of this unauthorized expedition he used his personal credit card for the fare. He grabbed a newspaper and magazine to get him through the flight; once on the plane he didn't look at them. He just stared out the window and did some thinking.

There were a lot of pieces bouncing around in the evidence pouch he kept in the back of his head. All the loose ends, tidbits, and unconnected dots one came across while investigating a crime. Pieces of a strange puzzle, he called them. Not like a crossword with rules and definitions, not like a jigsaw with cut lines that fit together, but a puzzle just the same. One that could be tied together if he could just find the frayed ends of the strands that once matched.

Landing in Springfield in the evening, he knew he would have to wait until morning to see the person who had brought him back to town. He'd already checked for a home telephone number and did not find a listing. Work establishments were closed for the night and he couldn't use the FBI or police to help him find a home address. There was one place he wanted to go that remained open well into the night. He rented a car and drove to the Runaway Hotel.

As he neared the home for runaways his cell phone

rang and he answered it. "Rigby."

"Where are you?"

No hello, just the demanding question, and he recognized the Judge's voice right away.

"In a car," he said, trying to avoid an incriminating answer.

"Well, I don't need you here, I need you in Springfield."

Rigby didn't know what struck him as more fantastic–that the Judge wanted him to go to a town he'd already arrived in on his own, or the fact that she *needed* him twice in the same day. He wondered if the bomber had made contact.

"Why?"

"The damn press. My phone's been ringing off the hook. One of those workers at the grave opening squawked about the empty coffin. Word is out and reporters are hysterical, which means Congress is hysterical. I'm getting one call from a member of Congress for each two calls from reporters. I'm issuing a statement that we're involved and have been from the beginning. I need you on the ground saying you're looking into this."

"But I am."

"You are what?" the Judge replied, puzzled.

"I'm on the ground here in Springfield."

"You're in Springfield? Now?"

"This very moment."

She was dumbfounded and didn't hide it. After fumbling around for a moment she said, "You were here. You were back on the task force."

"I was. But a good agent anticipates."

She paused, not knowing what to say. Finally she said, "Just keep those reporters off my back. And, don't screw up again."

This time he hung up on her.

Reporters swarming around Springfield would make

things more difficult. He had to move quickly.

He parked in front of the Runaway and jogged up the stairs, entered the front door. Mrs. Rutherford was working the desk herself tonight.

"Don't you ever go home?"

"This *is* my home, Officer Rigby. I live here, too."

"That's Agent Rigby."

"Titles don't really matter, do they?"

He suspected Mrs. Rutherford had been a hippie for a long time, or whatever she was now. She probably had some run-in with cops in her younger years, but who didn't, including him.

"You seen a lot of cops lately," he said.

She nodded. "Poor, darling Flute. No one deserves that end."

"Did the connection to Claire Orange surprise you?"

"That Flute accepted a ride from her? That she had some opportunity to explore around midnight? These girls get desperate at times, Mr. Rigby. Little surprises me. Why shouldn't Flute accept a ride?"

"Did Claire ever come around here before that?"

"Never saw her."

"Flute was a friendly enough girl? Talked to strangers?"

"Friendly. Yes, I suppose she was. Had a number of friends among the girls. Always chatted with the postman when she worked the desk. The social workers that came by, some of the donors, the cleaning ladies. Friendly enough."

"Do you think any one of them could have been in on some business deal with Flute?"

"Not that I know. But I doubt it. Detective Hunt was here talking to the girls and one of them, Jaws 3, I think it was–"

"That's the girl's nickname?"

"Braces."

"What's the 3 for?"

"We're not judgmental here."

Against his instincts he was starting to like this old bird.

"Jaws 3 told Detective Hunt she saw Flute go out that last night and get into a fancy car."

"And she made a positive ID?"

"Apparently, Claire Orange's car. Yes."

He had a few more questions for Mrs. Rutherford. He left, feeling he'd accomplished little, but it all went into the evidence pouch. He planned not to stay at an upscale hotel downtown, choosing a roadside motel on the outskirts of the city, after first stopping at a Target store, before it closed, to pick up a change of clothes and toiletries.

The next morning he started early. Too early, he realized, to expect his prey to be in his lair. He wanted to visit Claire, see how she was doing, confront her with his new information, but he thought better of it and turned the car toward the Oak Ridge Cemetery. He entered the cemetery from David Jones Parkway, a more modern entrance, passed the Vietnam War Memorial, and wound his way toward Lincoln's Tomb in the older part of the cemetery.

The cemetery was a big place. Looking around at all the graves, he suddenly had a memory from his youth, and smiled. Electric Ed, everyone called him–an electrician from the old school. Cared for his customers, knew them all by name. Rigby worked for him one summer, sitting next to him in his beat-up panel truck, changing light bulbs and cleaning light fixtures for his clients. Ed taught him to respect the job he was doing while he was doing it. Got zapped a few times with electricity. That was a great teacher. He paid attention.

Why did he remember Electric Ed while driving through a cemetery? On the first day working for Ed he was just fifteen, still nervous with his first real job, they'd passed by a large cemetery and Ed asked how many people there were dead. Rigby guessed a big number. Ed supplied the answer: "All of them." Bad joke. Electric Ed laughed at that terrible joke all summer. Even right in the middle of some tough job, he'd look at Rigby and say, "All of them" and break out laughing. Yeah, bad joke, but Rigby remembered Electric Ed and his bad joke and the good times all these years. He always remembered to respect the job he was doing.

Rigby drove past the backside of the tomb and caught a glimpse of the place where he'd found Flute's body. Flute had brought him to Oak Ridge this morning, not Lincoln. He proceeded on to the Monument Avenue gate, hoping someone would be in the cemetery's administration office.

That someone was not what he expected. He thought Lurch would be manning the fort, tall, unsmiling, wearing an old-fashioned great morning coat like they wear at funerals and presidential inaugurations. A middle-aged woman greeted him with a warm smile. Dressed professionally, she showed the tight curves of a body exposed to hours of exercise. She asked him what she could do for him and he held his mouth closed, hoping that none of the improper thoughts pinging through his head would escape.

Finally he produced his badge. "I'm with the FBI. I have a question about the locks to the gates around the cemetery, and who has access to the keys."

"Office and maintenance staff. There are a number of copies."

"How often is that old side gate opened?"

"Not frequently. On occasion. Why do you ask? I've been getting questions about that gate all of a sudden."

"Who's been asking?"

She rattled off a few names, a couple he recognized.

"But no one wanted a key or got one. They just asked about the gate."

Rigby thought about this and remained silent.

"Tell me Agent. What do I do with all the reporters crawling around here asking about Mr. Lincoln? You must have experience with this."

Rigby shrugged, thanked her for the information and checked his watch. The time was right. He drove to the warehouse district containing the office of Dr. Bernard Rittinghouse. The doctor was in, and he was alone. Rigby walked in on him as he was typing some elaborate formula on a large computer screen.

Rittinghouse was not surprised to see him. "Ah, Mr. Rigby, one moment please." He finished typing, hit a button, and watched the computer calculate some answer, which he studied for a moment with a hand against his chin. The numbers and letters on the screen were as easy to understand as Egyptian hieroglyphics or, for Rigby, the recipe for a chocolate soufflé. Satisfied, Rittinghouse rolled the chair back and swiveled it so that he could face Rigby without getting up.

"So, I was hoping never to see you again," the doctor said evenly. "What brings you here?"

"Your sister."

He blinked. More than once.

"You know one of my sisters?"

"Passing acquaintance."

He eyed Rigby warily. "I seem to remember when you came in with Mrs. Orange and her boy, we established you as a cop of some kind."

"FBI."

"FBI? Here on official business?"

"I understand the administration at the med school asked you to leave."

"Why would the FBI be concerned with that? It's dead. Finished."

"Abraham Lincoln's dead, but we don't seem to be finished with him."

"You're confusing me, sir, and that's a rare thing."

Rittinghouse's ego wasn't hurting; he'd give him that. Rigby wasn't sure where he was going with his questions, but the picture he saw on Dr. Canning's wall was floating with those loose pieces in his head's evidence pouch. He now was looking at the exact same picture on the doctor's office wall, the picture Rittinghouse once told him was of all the doctors in the Rittinghouse family. The family resemblance is what he recognized in Dr. Canning.

"I was referring to your cloning experiments, Doctor. That's what scared the higher ups at the med school. Exactly what were you doing?"

"Exactly that, *experimenting*!" he said with a flash of anger. "Trying to move the frontiers of science. There are three things that stunt scientific progress–"

"And the last one's money," Rigby said, interrupting. "Yeah, we went down that road last time. Tell me about the cloning."

"If you're interested, you should take a course at the med school."

"But I couldn't take the class from you now, could I?"

Rittinghouse watched Rigby carefully. He leaned back in his chair and stuck his long legs out, interlocking his hands behind his head. "I think Craig Orange can walk again. Do you?"

"That would be nice."

"It won't happen unless people like me are given the support to try new ideas, push science down the road not traveled. My experiments were going down that road. I use cloning and stem cell research that I think will regenerate nerves, bring them back to full vitality."

"So what pissed off the administration?"

"There's a national debate on cloning, as you know. The debate includes many influential people, including your boss."

That caught Rigby by surprise. How could the Judge

246

be involved in this?

"The President of the United States," the doctor continued.

Oh, that boss.

"Everyone has an opinion on where the line should be drawn."

"And you crossed the line in the eyes of the school."

"Certainly not in the eyes of many other researchers, doctors and scientists," he said.

"Including family members."

"As professional people, they were on my side."

"One of those doctors was Phyllis Canning, nee Rittinghouse. Your sister."

Rittinghouse unlocked his fingers from behind his head and sat up straight. He sensed a shift in the conversation. Rigby guessed he wanted to be on his toes, both literally and figuratively. Rigby would not disappoint him.

"My file on the Abraham Lincoln case was very thin, so I remembered a couple of things. The DNA contained in a bone chip was shipped back to the FBI lab from Springfield. The hand wasn't sent, just a bone chip. The lab had a sample of Lincoln's DNA to compare it to. Pieces of bone from Lincoln saved at the time of the assassination are stored at the National Museum of Health and Medicine, located at the Walter Reed Army Medical Center in Washington. Guess who sent over the DNA sample from Walter Reed to the lab? You might want to bet it all, because it's Double Jeopardy."

Rittinghouse remained silent, but of course he knew the answer.

"Okay, I'll take on Final Jeopardy myself. Who sent the DNA sample from the discovered hand in Illinois to the FBI lab? Since Claire told me you're a wizard in many sciences, including DNA, and since she found the hand and she knew you because her son was your patient, you were the obvious choice.

"So the DNA came to the FBI lab from Springfield from the brother and the confirming DNA was sent from the museum by the sister. Following me so far? And when the hand finally gets to Washington my real boss, the Judge, wants to push this case aside so there's no second test on the hand right away. Instead, I win a company paid trip to Springfield."

"Is it a crime that a brother and sister work in the same profession?"

"The hand was finally tested. No match this time." Rigby watched Rittinghouse carefully, looking for signs of discomfort. He remained cool as the ice Rigby used to chip out of the old family freezer when he was a kid, and just as stubborn.

Rigby continued: "Here's what I think. The sister sent the brother a DNA sample in a bone chip from the museum and the brother submitted that to the lab saying it came from the mummified hand. When the sister sent another bone chip from the museum, then the DNA matched. Did I win the big bucks, Alex?"

"Bernard," he said, folding his arms across his chest. Rigby realized that he might be in the room with the only person in America who had never seen *Jeopardy*.

Rigby asked the question he needed confirmed, although he already knew the answer. "Was Claire part of this? Did she put you up to it?"

Rittinghouse refused to answer. He didn't have to.

Rigby pointed to the family picture. "Your sister has the same picture on her office wall."

Rittinghouse scowled. He seemed angrier that the FBI man was interfering with his experiment than he was upset about being caught at his subterfuge. "What is your point?"

"I think I know what you're up to."

"Really? What's that?"

Rigby decided to take the next logical step, pleased that there was no audience to hear him. "You're trying to clone Abraham Lincoln."

Rittinghouse jolted upright in the chair, seemingly in shock for a moment. Then he let out a roundhouse peal of laughter.

"You can't...can't..." More laughter. "You can't clone...human beings!"

"There have been attempts–"

He cut Rigby off. "You've been reading the tabloids, Rigby!" More laughter.

Rigby didn't know where he picked up the information, but sometimes those supermarket lines were really long. "You're saying human cloning has never been attempted?"

"Not what you're talking about. Somatic Cell Nuclear Transfer was used to clone Dolly, the sheep. Remember her?"

Rigby nodded.

"That same method, theoretically, could be used to make a duplicate genetic code copy of a human being. You'd have to implant a cloned embryo into a woman's womb for a live or reproductive birth. We're just not ready for that, scientifically or culturally or even morally. But most important of the three is *scientifically*. Just not ready. Your idea is foolish. Rational scientists will tell you that if you bothered to ask one."

"I asked you," Rigby said.

"Are you done asking? Because I have to get back to work."

Rigby felt he was on to something, but he needed to dig deeper. Rittinghouse wasn't giving him the time.

"All your experimenting must cost lots of money."

"Have you seen the price of gasoline lately? Everything costs money. Now if you'll please leave."

Rigby wasn't going to let him feel he won this confrontation. Reminding him that his sister and he were in real trouble for the stunt they pulled, Rigby was satisfied when Rittinghouse became sullen and ordered him out.

Rigby was the clear winner of this wrestling match. He decided to leave it at that for now. He was not satisfied, because he wasn't sure he was any closer to the answers about Lincoln or about Flute. That meant Claire was still in jeopardy. He needed to see her–if he could.

Chapter 37

Rigby's call to Claire's house went unanswered. He wondered if she was at the presidential library, or if the suspicion about her in Flute's death would keep her away. He decided that after the lunch hour, he would look for her there.

Rigby parked in a nearby lot and headed for the library's front entrance, where a crowd of people had gathered. He only wondered for a brief moment what was going on before he saw the cameras. The Springfield SAC, Crosby, frantically waved at him. He crossed the street and walked past the pack of reporters, camera operators and onlookers. Not knowing who he might be, no microphone was thrust in front of him. Rigby approached Crosby, who clapped him on the shoulder and hustled him inside.

"Am I glad to see you! What are we going to tell these guys? We got nothing but we have to say something. *You* have to say something."

"I don't talk to the press."

"What do you mean?"

"I tell the truth. The Judge wouldn't want me telling all these people that Lincoln's body is missing and we're not going to find it."

"Well yeah, we know that, but there are different ways of saying it."

"Why don't you use one of them?"

"Not me," Crosby said. "I was just holding the fort for you. Your job is Lincoln. Mine's McClavity."

"What about McClavity? What did you find out?"

"Splinters, like you said. Just got it confirmed. A

couple of minute ones in his neck that match the split rail. No prints on the rail."

"Since McClavity didn't fall down the stairs then get up and place the rail back in the governor's room, I'd say we have another murder to solve."

Crosby nodded. "Another murder. But solve one, you solve them both. The same killer murdered Mary Blair and McClavity. Same method. Death by bashing, I'd call it."

"Maybe," Rigby said. "But the connection between the two deaths is not apparent. Does Hunt still think Claire Orange is the murderer?"

"Top of the suspect list, but she's not under arrest. We're working closely with Hunt and the SPD because the two killings are linked."

"Maybe," Rigby said again and started to walk away.

"Hey, where you going? What about them?" Crosby pointed toward the reporters on the sidewalk.

"You talk to them. *No comment* works best."

Rigby proceeded to the administrative offices. Mrs. Huffington was not at her desk, so he continued on to Claire's office. She wasn't there either, just the poster on the wall of the Lincoln statue in Washington that he had recently seen in person. The statue he had saved. Lincoln stared at him as if trying to pass on a secret. He stared back for a long time. What was it? What had tickled his memory at the Memorial that he couldn't grasp? Something he had seen…something had been said…something in the Memorial triggered a blurred memory of an occurrence in Springfield.

Lincoln and Rigby stared at each other for a long time. *Tell me, Abe, what am I trying to remember?*

Finally, Rigby snapped his fingers. And appropriately so, for he remembered that it had to do with fingers…and hands. Lincoln's hands.

He headed to Huffington's desk. Mildred had returned and was reading a newspaper. He walked up to the desk, watching her carefully. When she sensed someone approaching, she looked up at him. Immediately, Rigby raised his left arm and, with his fingers, spelled the letter A.

Reactively, Huffington responded by raising her arm, her hand crafting the letter L.

He was right! In the cemetery on the day the coffin was opened, he saw Mildred exchanging a fist salute with Lenny Poler. He thought she was trying to be hip. He didn't get the significance of the shape of the hands at the time: first Poler's *A*, then Huffington's *L*.

Huffington turned red in her cheeks, like those Paris dancers with ample rouge, and buried her face back into her newspaper, as if the action just performed was as natural as saying 'good morning' to a passer-by.

Rigby smiled at her antic, thinking how as we get older we often act more like children. You know the trick. If you act like nothing happened, then no one will think it did happen.

"Gotcha," he said.

"Excuse me?" she responded, still red in the cheeks as she lowered the newspaper.

"My *A*. Your *L*."

"I don't understand you, Mr. Rigby. I really don't. You should improve your clarity of speech."

"You understand. Your hand signal is a symbol, like Mr. Spock's spread fingers. I could never do that." He showed her his inability to mimic Spock's greeting. "Your response to my letter A was the letter L." He duplicated the symbols. "The hand-spelled letters like the hands on the statue in the Lincoln Memorial."

"Hogwash, Mr. Rigby. You're seeing things."

"I'm seeing double, actually, because I saw you exchange the signal before with Lenny Poler in the cemetery." She did not reply. "You know what I think? I think the secret hand signal is flashed between members of the Lincoln Guard of Honor."

Huffington gasped. Her eyes widened and she folded her hands on her desk.

He said, "You're the Lincoln Guard of Honor. And, just maybe you know where the president's body is."

"No!" she exclaimed, paused and thought for a moment. "Come with me."

The elderly woman picked up her phone, pushed a series of buttons and said, "I have to leave the desk for a few minutes. It's a special emergency." She hung up, stood and waved for him to follow her.

He followed her down back stairs and into the rear warehouse area of the library. Mildred used her coded key card to give her access to the back rooms. Whatever information she wanted to share with him, she clearly did not want anyone else to hear.

She pointed to a door marked Custodial Services. "The janitor's room. We'll talk in there."

She pushed open the door and clicked on a switch. He followed her in. The room was bigger than he expected, with a table in the middle surrounded by a couple of folding chairs. A radio sat on the table next to an ashtray, which contained a number of cigarette butts and ashes. A smoky smell lingered in the windowless room. Portable metal shelves running along the walls were filled with light bulbs, toilet paper, paper towels and an assortment of backup goods a custodian needed to maintain a public building. As Mrs. Huffington closed the door, he noticed a bulletin board on the back with work schedules and state required postings on work safety. He also saw a calendar with the picture of a woman made up to be Abraham Lincoln with a top hat and false beard, wearing nothing above the waist. He didn't remember Abe looking like that.

"Sit down, Mr. Rigby."

He did so. Huffington did not take the other chair. She stood by the end of the table. He waited for her to tell him her story. When Rigby first met her, she'd said he should

Joel Fox

work on his story when he was trying to cover up his connection to the FBI. He expected now she was working over her story in her mind, which meant he was prepared not to believe what she had to say.

What surprised him was that she had nothing to say. She just stared at him, and Rigby stared back at her. The silence in the closed room felt like a tomb.

"Well?" he asked impatiently.

"In a moment," she said. "We're waiting for someone."

He wondered who it could be. They waited in silence.

Suddenly, the door to the room burst open and Lenny Poler rushed in. He looked like a defensive tackle blitzing the quarterback. Just now the quarterback was Rigby.

He jumped out of his chair, but his reaction time was no match for the younger man. Poler barreled into Rigby and they flew back over the chair, crashing into the metal shelving. Rigby could feel it sway with the impact. Toilet paper rolls rained on his head.

Striking the concrete floor, Poler lost his grip. Rigby rolled to his right and scrambled under the table, making it difficult for Poler to fall back on top of him. Rigby pushed himself off the floor in time to see Poler gain his footing as well. Mildred Huffington screamed something unintelligible in Rigby's ear. Out of the corner of his eye Rigby saw a portable fire extinguisher. He grabbed it, pulled the plug and aimed the hose as Poler charged him again.

The fire-retardant foam caught Poler squarely in the face, blinding him. He crashed into a chair and tumbled hard to the floor, his knee crunching against the concrete. It sounded like a melon being bopped by a hammer. He writhed in pain, grabbed his knee with one hand while trying to clean the foam off his face with the other.

Huffington wailed and ran to the young man's side. "Lenny, Lenny, you all right?" She fell to her knees, wrapped an arm around his shoulders, and helped him clean the foam off.

Rigby spotted a small sink in the corner. Grabbing a package of paper towels, he ripped it open, pulled off some of the towels and soaked them. He handed them to Huffington.

She wiped the spray from the young man's eyes. Poler relaxed and massaged his knee. Huffington repeated, "You okay, Lenny?"

"Okay," he replied. "Did he hurt you, Grandma?"

Didn't see that coming, Rigby thought, raising his eyebrows. Why should he be surprised? Mildred Huffington helped her grandson from the floor and guided him to a chair. Rigby did not lend a hand in case Poler wanted to use the opportunity to start fighting again.

"I'm okay, Lenny," she said. "At least I'm not hurt."

"Do you want to tell me what's going on?"

"I don't think I do, Mr. Rigby. Not after the way you treated my grandson."

Well that's a fine how-do-you-do, he thought. The kid comes in here preparing to rip his head off and somehow *he's* the aggressor. That would not stand. He spoke in the most grating, tough voice he could muster, like a gangster in a cheap B movie. "Assaulting a federal officer carries a long prison sentence."

"No!" Huffington cried, stroking her grandson's head. "He was just protecting me. Lenny's a good boy. He just gets rambunctious at times."

"Rambunctious? Is that what you call it? How about reckless and dangerous? He could kill somebody. Your prearranged signal on the phone was to bring your grandson down here like a bull in a China shop."

Huffington said, "It was a plan for emergencies. And, Mr. Rigby, ever since you came to Springfield you've been an emergency."

For his part Rigby was no closer to the solution of where Lincoln's body was than when he arrived in Springfield. He knew Mildred had a story to relate about the body, and he wanted to hear it. "Why don't you tell me what this is all about?"

"What's there to tell? It seems you already know it all."

"I don't know where President Lincoln's body is."

Mildred Huffington moved away from her grandson and sat wearily on the other chair. She looked at Lenny, as if wanting his approval for what she was about to do. "Mr. Rigby, we don't know where Mr. Lincoln's body is either."

"But you're the Lincoln Guard of Honor. You said you were researching the Lincoln Guard for Crease, but it was for you, too. The Guard was reconstituted. You're part of it."

"What's left of it. Us and a few others."

"Mrs. Huffington–"

"Come, come, Mr. Rigby," she said impatiently. "I don't know where the body is, but I did know it was not where it was supposed to be. The others didn't know what I knew. Only my grandson, once I told him. Would I like to know where it is? Yes, I would, but I don't."

"Why do I think you're doing your job as members of the Honor Guard by covering up where the body is?"

"I don't know where it is," she repeated. "Never knew."

It was Rigby's turn to weigh revealing the truth. He decided it would take a heavy burden off the woman's shoulders.

"I think I can tell you what might have happened to it."

Mildred Huffington and her grandson looked up at him with anticipation. He hated to disappoint them.

"Remember that research you and I did in the city library?"

She nodded.

"It comes back to Lenny's boss. The congressman. His grandfather, Samuel McClavity, may have taken possession of the body and became so guilt ridden that he destroyed the remains in the 1922 fire. Is that why Lenny took a position with McClavity? To get close to him and learn the truth?"

"That was his secret?" Lenny growled at Rigby, then looked at his grandmother in surprise.

Huffington sighed. "No. You're wrong."

"Circumstantial, I know, but there's some interesting things to consider."

"You're wrong," she said more firmly.

"How can you be so sure?"

"My daddy told me."

"And how would he know?"

"My daddy was one of the last true members of the Lincoln Guard of Honor. The Guard was formed to protect the president's body after the 1876 kidnapping attempt. Following the 1901 reburial the group's membership dwindled. The reason given publicly to those who knew the mission of the Guard was because the body was now safely buried under all that concrete. The real reason was that those in the Guard did not want anyone to find out that the body was not where everyone thought it was. The members of the Lincoln Guard of Honor didn't want to bring in new members. Occasionally, a family member was brought in, but that was it.

"By 1944 there were only three members left: my father, Willard Mandrake, and Mr. Herbert Sturbridge, a son of one of the original founding members of the Guard, and his son, Captain Walt Sturbridge. My father was dying and wanted someone to know the truth. He was extremely ill and had trouble speaking or even writing because of a stroke. He was quite elderly. I was the product of his second marriage to a younger woman. I was only ten, but I was his caretaker. There was just him and me. Mother skedaddled with another man. Never saw her again. But my father didn't abandon me. He never left me alone."

Rigby could hear in her voice that bitterness still remained toward her mother for leaving her, and admiration for her father for sticking around.

"Despite his condition, my father revealed what he

could to me. He swore me to secrecy about the empty coffin. Previously, he informed me about the Honor Guard and its sacred duty to protect Mr. Lincoln's body. He told me to see Old Man Sturbridge to learn the secret of the burial. He said so slowly and painfully, 'Have him show you the hand.'"

"Hold it," Rigby said. "The hand Claire found was phony."

"But when Dr. Orange found it, I thought it was the hand Daddy told me about, because Mr. Sturbridge never told me what it was. You see, I was too late. A week after I buried Daddy, I looked up Herbert Sturbridge but he was dead, too. Died of a heart attack on the news that his son, Walt, had been killed in the war in France. Herbert Sturbridge was only sixty-one years old, younger than I am now."

Rigby involuntarily found himself rubbing his chest over his heart, thinking that wasn't a whole hell of a lot older than him. Maybe all this excitement wasn't good for *his* health.

Huffington continued: "With the Sturbridges gone there were no survivors of the Lincoln Guard of Honor and the secret of the body was lost. However, I felt obligated to keep my daddy's mission alive. Not right away, mind you. When Dr. Orange uncovered the hand and the note, I was afraid the truth would be revealed. I revived the Guard of Honor. Recruited my grandson. Recruited the others, too, although I never shared the secrets I knew. I expected they would discourage the dig, but it didn't work out that way. Some of them decided it was a good idea to open the grave. Only Lenny here, my family, knew about the secret."

"Was Claire part of the Lincoln Guard of Honor?"

"Yes."

"Where is she now?"

"She went with Dr. Crease to claim some Lincoln artifacts from Chief Braddock's house on Lake Springfield.

The chief's wife comes from an old Springfield family. She found some papers about Lincoln."

Rigby looked at Poler, who was still rubbing his knee, and said matter-of-factly, "You wanted to keep the grave undisturbed. So you set off a dump truck bomb to scare everyone away."

Poler glared at him defiantly.

"What about Mary Blair? She get in your way?"

"No, no," Mildred said, standing in front of Poler to act as some sort of shield. "The bomb was my idea. I wanted him to mimic the Monument Bomber so maybe people would think twice about opening the grave."

"I didn't mean to hurt anybody," Poler said with an air of defiance. "The driver wasn't supposed to be there. And I never knew or saw that Blair woman."

"You're lucky the driver is recovering or you'd be facing manslaughter charges. You'll have to answer for the bomb."

"No! I told you, it's my fault," Huffington said. "Don't do this. His boss is dead, he'll lose his job. He was just doing what his grandma told him to do. Don't charge him with this. He's a good boy."

"He has to answer," Rigby said firmly. "You come with him."

"I'll just do that."

Exiting through a door by the loading dock to avoid reporters and Crosby, Rigby walked the few blocks to police headquarters with the old woman and her grandson. Detective Hunt was not in so he told the desk sergeant that Lenny Poler had set off the bomb at Lincoln's Monument. This time, Huffington did not claim responsibility for the bomb. The sergeant took custody of Poler and said he would keep him safe until Detective Hunt returned shortly. Rigby asked for directions to Chief Braddock's house.

The pieces of the puzzle were falling together. He was determined to see Claire and get to the bottom of this mess.

Chapter 38

Lake Springfield wrapped around the southeast corner of the city. Two smokestacks, sitting at the edge of the lake, spewed black clouds from the city power and light plant. The sergeant's directions took Rigby to the west side of the lake, where fingers of water reached out from the main body. Signs called this area Hazel Dell. An exotic name to describe a gentrified neighborhood containing big houses and emerald lawns sloping down to docks floating on the lake, with canoes and motorboats tied to them. Forests of trees covered the large lawns.

He drove down a narrow road until he found the correct street numbers attached to one of two columns marking the driveway entrance to one of the homes. A large Lincoln SUV stood in the driveway in front of the garage of a two-story red brick house with a widow's walk on top. Since Rigby felt sure that no sea captain lost his life to a marauding Moby Dick on Lake Springfield, the widow's walk must be a perfect place to keep an eye on youngsters canoeing in the lake, a bit different from its traditional use as a place to look for sailing ships off the coast that were overdue on their trip home. The SUV could have been the one he'd seen Abby Lamont driving in the cemetery the day he found Flute's body. He wouldn't be surprised if Lamont were accompanying Claire and Crease to pick up Lincoln memorabilia.

Behind the SUV was a second car equipped with high tech radio gear and sprouting antennae. The chief's car, he assumed.

Rigby parked behind the second car, quickly made his

way to the front door and knocked. The door opened, revealing a large lady both in height and girth. She wore a pinkish smock, her salt-and-pepper hair pulled up and covered with a net, and she held a pair of thin work gloves in one hand. He guessed she was a few years older than him, and a lot scarier.

"May I help you?"

He produced his credentials.

"You're looking for my husband." She turned to call him.

"Actually, I'm looking for Claire Orange."

The woman looked at Rigby and paused before saying cautiously, "Oh, I see. Well, she's here too."

Mrs. Braddock stepped aside and pulled the door open. He entered the house and could hear a stern voice lecturing in the living room.

"How do you think this will look? I'm the goddamned chief of police, for the love of–"

Chief Braddock stopped his harangue when he saw Rigby. Braddock was a broad-shouldered man in an ill-fitting suit with white, neatly combed hair.

"Who's this?" he asked his wife.

"You don't know?" Crease said in surprise.

Crease stood near the chief, who had his back to a fireplace. Abby Lamont stood a few feet from Crease. Claire sat crumpled up in a chair.

The house appeared to be in the middle of a transformation. Furniture moved about, boxes scattered throughout the entryway and the living room. The walls were devoid of any decoration. Apparently, Mrs. Braddock had been cleaning. The walls on either side of the fireplace were floor-to-ceiling windows looking out over the tree-covered lawn and the water below.

"This is Agent Rigby from the FBI," Crease told the chief.

"So you're Rigby." Braddock did not offer him a hand,

but made fists and placed one on each hip, like Superman in his most menacing pose. "I thought you were supposed to be taking care of the reporters. What're you doing here?"

"Looking for Dr. Orange." Rigby glanced at Claire and thought she looked awful. Bags puffed under her eyes, which were streaked with red. Her face was pale and drawn. Her posture was bent, her shoulders rounded, as if her spine was taking a break from carrying the heavy burden of suspicion. He asked her, "Everything all right?"

The chief said, "This woman is under suspicion by the department. She doesn't belong in the chief of police's house no matter how innocent the reason. How will this look if word gets out? That the chief condones favoritism? She's got no cause being here conducting business while she is a suspect in a murder."

"Innocent until proven guilty, Chief," Crease said, standing up for his suffering employee. "She's just doing her job collecting the letters *your* wife found and offered to the library."

Rigby was surprised at Crease's bold reaction. Good for him.

"I'll go," Claire said, holding back tears.

She stood and started to walk past Rigby toward the door, suddenly stopped, remembering she held some papers she should not be taking with her. She handed them to him; they looked like old letters.

"What are these?" He hoped to keep her from leaving.

"Letters between Phillip Sturbridge and Robert Lincoln," she said.

"You saw one in my office when you first arrived," Crease said. "These are the rest of the collection that Doris Braddock found while cleaning up her late mother's home here."

Mrs. Braddock added, "Phillip Sturbridge was my great-grandfather."

"That makes Herbert Sturbridge your grandfather and

Walt Sturbridge…what, your father?"

"Walt was my uncle," Doris said, surprised.

"How the hell did you know all that?" Chief Braddock demanded.

"Research on the Lincoln Guard of Honor," Rigby said.

"The *original* Honor Guard," Doris offered proudly, "not the new group that everyone here belongs to."

So the chief was part of the new Lincoln Guard of Honor. Rigby wondered how much he knew of what Mildred Huffington and her grandson were up to. He decided now was not the time to get into Mildred and Lenny and their misdeeds. He thought Claire needed protecting first, especially with the chief throwing the words *murder* and *suspect* around.

He looked at the letters again, seeing the distinct Robert Lincoln signature and the playing card symbols at the bottom from the on-going card game Phillip Sturbridge conducted with him. There were also copies of letters from Sturbridge to Lincoln, which must have been a chore in the days before copying machines. He could see Sturbridge's hearts and diamonds topped Lincoln's spades and clubs.

Claire started toward the door.

"Don't you go too far," the chief warned. "We want you where we can get our hands on you."

Claire's shoulders slumped still further and Rigby could hear her sniffing back tears. The suspicion that she had killed Mary Blair was crushing her.

There is never a perfect time where everything comes together when trying to solve a crime. Sometimes you have to take a shot, he thought. The pieces in his evidence pouch were still a jumble, but he could see how they might connect. He hated to see Claire suffer so he decided this might be the best time to lay out the pieces.

"Claire Orange is not guilty of murder," Rigby said. "She's only guilty of a scam."

Joel Fox

He let this revelation hang in the air. His statement stopped Claire in her tracks and she turned back.

Abigail Lamont said, "Who did she scam?"

"You."

"*What?* What do you mean?" she exclaimed.

"I mean she set up a scam to get lots of money out of you when she claimed to have discovered Lincoln's hand."

"Claimed?" Crease was incredulous.

Rigby studied Claire's face for a moment. Beyond the weariness and worry he could see fear. Yet, he felt he had to say more and relieve her of her greatest burden–the suspicion that she was a murderer.

"Claire Orange's son, Craig, is paralyzed from the waist down. He's been seeing a specialist in nerve regeneration hoping to crack the formula that will allow him to walk again. But not just any specialist: Dr. Bernard Rittinghouse is on the cutting edge of scientific experimentation and cloning and that sometimes creates enemies. He was fired from his position at the SIU Medical School, which meant it was tough getting grants for his work. He needed big dollars and Claire knew that. She was also aware of the obsession Abigail Lamont, a wealthy woman, had for her relative, Abraham Lincoln."

"Not obsession, *respect*," Lamont protested. "No more respect than the rest of the country has for the great man."

He ignored her. "Abigail Lamont wanted a Lincoln revival. She thought Abraham Lincoln could solve the current problems of the world with his wisdom." Looking at Crease, he continued: "I'm sure she's said that to you a number of times."

He nodded.

Rigby paused, all eyes on him. He was in control of the room now.

"I think Claire Orange and Bernard Rittinghouse convinced Mrs. Lamont that Rittinghouse could clone Abraham Lincoln."

Shouts exploded in the room.

"What?"

"You're nuts!"

Doris Braddock said, "You can't clone human beings. Dead human beings. I'm a biology professor at U of I here in Springfield."

"I didn't say you could. I said Rittinghouse and Claire convinced Mrs. Lamont it was possible. If she did a background check on Rittinghouse she would discover he experimented with cloning. That he was fired because he pushed the envelope, took risks. Why not believe he was on the edge of a great breakthrough? And she had every reason to believe in Claire, the historian of the library she gave so much money to. When Claire made the great discovery of Lincoln's hand, she *did* believe."

"No, no," Crease said. "I can't accept this."

Lamont stood stone-faced, which made Rigby think he had hit the target.

"She's rich, Crease," he said. "Your benefactor. The rich see the world differently than the rest of us. They're gamblers. They can afford it. The rich gamble on big payoffs all the time at a crap table or on a new Internet site. Claire and Rittinghouse probably said the only way they could get sufficient amounts of Lincoln's DNA was to dig up the body. That would take lots and lots of money. Rittinghouse's costs to complete his unique experiment would be enormous. The costs of the experiment were hidden in the costs of the dig, which Claire managed. She could siphon off funds for Rittinghouse."

Crease said, "There's a problem with your theory. Your own FBI lab said the hand was real. The DNA matched Lincoln's."

"Because the Lincoln DNA stored at the museum on the grounds of the Walter Reed Hospital was matched against a sample of DNA that also came from the same museum, but was shipped through Rittinghouse in

Springfield. Rittinghouse's sister is a doctor at the hospital, with access to the Lincoln DNA. She sent a bone chip to her brother. He sent it along to Washington and the match was good. The hand is phony. I had it re-checked."

Claire sagged toward the floor, her knees buckling.

"Unbelievable!" Crease said.

"Very believable." Rigby reached out to Claire and steadied her. "Claire's a loving mother. She wanted her boy to walk again. She believed the accident that crippled him was her fault. She would go to any lengths to help him walk." This had to be the truth. He couldn't believe she would carry out a fraud unless she had such an overpowering reason.

Claire did not fight back tears any longer. They poured down her cheeks.

Rigby looked around the room to see if his theory was gaining acceptance. The faces were attentive. He could tell no more. However, Abigail Lamont glared at him.

He pressed on: "My guess is Rittinghouse told Claire he was close to the solution to help Craig walk. Claire found the hand somewhere. It was the right age. She forged the blackmail note. Given all the effort to dig up Lincoln and what that took, Mrs. Lamont was convinced the cloning experiment was real. And Claire knew there was always this historical question: was Lincoln really in his grave? She made the most of that doubt."

"But Lincoln *wasn't* in the grave," Crease said.

"That surprised Claire, too. She believed he would be there. I saw her reaction to the empty coffin."

Lamont's scowl deepened the lines plastic surgery couldn't fix. She turned to the chief and demanded that Claire Orange be prosecuted for fraud to the full extent of the law.

The chief said, "This is interesting, but it doesn't change the fact that Dr. Orange may have killed Mary Blair out of jealousy."

Rigby said, "You're right. At least you're right to focus on Claire Orange. She's the centerpiece of what happened around Lincoln's Tomb."

Claire gasped and looked at him with pleading eyes.

"But Claire didn't kill Mary Blair."

"Then who did?" the chief demanded.

Rigby swallowed as imperceptibly as he could. He was about to be Indiana Jones taking that leap of faith, hoping the walkway across the chasm to the cave was there, although it was invisible.

He turned and pointed. "Abigail Lamont."

Lamont's severe expression washed away. Her face showed surprise, not shock, a surprise that came when a deep secret is exposed.

The police chief stepped forward, clearly trying to make sense of what he was hearing.

Rigby said, "Flute's friend at the Runaway Hotel–her nickname's Chicago–told me Flute was going to have a baby, that she was pregnant. Flute was going to be *carrying* a baby, be a surrogate mother. She had been given a down payment to do the job. That's the roll of money your officers found. She thought she was doing this for a couple that could not conceive, I imagine. Someone with a lot of money to spend had approached her. Someone she knew. Among Abigail Lamont's charities was The Home of Wandering Souls–the Runaway Hotel. A perfect place to find a collection of possible surrogate mothers who were the right age and in desperate need of money. I learned from Mrs. Rutherford, who runs the hotel, that Mrs. Lamont was one of the donors who dropped in to talk to the girls.

"The night of the murder Flute met the person who was going to introduce her to the prospective parents. It had to be a secret meeting because the father-to-be was a prominent figure and he didn't want to get the word out that he couldn't father this child with his wife in a natural way. Word from management of Oak Ridge Cemetery confirmed

Mrs. Lamont asked about the security at the east gate. Somehow she got a copy of the key."

He looked at Lamont, who had a blank expression on her face.

The chief said, "I still don't see how this comes together." His voice was not doubtful or cynical. He was interested in what Rigby had to say.

"After Claire dropped Flute at the Railroad Bar that night, Abigail Lamont picked her up and took Flute out to the cemetery to meet the baby's father. Unknown to Claire or Rittinghouse, Lamont took the next step in the cloning plan she believed to be real and found a surrogate mother on her own. It was in the cemetery that Flute was told the truth: she would be carrying the clone of Abraham Lincoln. Abigail Lamont would make the pronouncement as a great honor: *The world needs Abraham Lincoln now.* Flute would have a different reaction. She had a religious upbringing. She probably was sickened by what she was told. She likely said she would go to the authorities and expose the scheme. Lamont couldn't let that happen. She picked up a stone and hit Flute on the head, knocking her to the ground. Then she kept pounding the stone against Flute's head until she was dead."

All eyes turned to Abigail Lamont. The lady stiffened. She was silent as she stared at Rigby.

The chief said, "Well, Mrs. Lamont?"

The simple question broke her concentration. She looked around at the others in the room. Her eyes welled up. Softly, she said, "It…it was…a terrible mistake."

Tears came to Abby Lamont. She fell back into a chair like a puppet whose strings·had been cut and sat motionless for a moment.

"This was all about hope," she finally said. "That's what I'm about. Giving to the lost, homeless girls. To the library. Bringing back Mr. Lincoln. It was about hope. Really it was. Abraham Lincoln could save our country. He did it once. I didn't do this for me. I did it for us. *All of us.* The whole country."

She paused and turned to the chief. "But I made a mistake. A stupid mistake. My passion and temper took over. I'm so, so sorry. I'll pay for the damages. How much?"

The police chief got past his shock and said, "More than you got."

Chapter 39

Claire looked at Rigby through pleading eyes and tear-stained cheeks and whispered, "Is Mary's death my fault, too?"

He patted her shoulder and shook his head.

The chief told Abigail Lamont she was under arrest and ordered his wife to call for a patrol car. After Mrs. Braddock dialed the police, the chief took the phone and barked his own orders. Crease stood looking like a lost boy, not knowing which way to turn. His benefactor was a murderer; his trusted employee had manipulated a fraud.

Lamont remained in the chair crying softly. Although he didn't know how it fit in, he asked her, "Why McClavity?"

She responded, "What? What about him?"

Braddock told him to back off until Detective Hunt and the investigators arrived to ask their questions first.

Rigby comforted Claire for a while, and then decided she didn't need to be there while the police dealt with Lamont. They would have time to question Claire later. He moved her toward the door when the first patrol car with two uniformed officers arrived.

Outside, he led her to his car. He jumped behind the wheel, realizing he still held the Sturbridge-Lincoln letters. He reached behind him and gently floated them to the rear seat. Claire dabbed at her eyes with a handkerchief. When she had composed herself, she said, "Thank you, Zane."

He nodded, started the car, and set off down the driveway, not sure where he was going. He just wanted to get Claire away from this place. She was silent as he drove out of Hazel Dell, across the northern edge of the lake, and down its eastern shore. Near a golf course called Lincoln Greens–naturally–he pulled the car off the road.

Claire stared at the lake through the car's window. He hoped she could relax and waited for her to speak first. She did, after a long silence.

"I didn't want to hurt anyone. I wanted so much to protect Craig. To help him. If I could only turn back the clock...stop him from falling...or stop myself from scheming. But I can't turn back the clock. I have to live with it...all of it." She paused, sniffed. "I thought, maybe if...." She stopped again, sighed and turned toward him. "Zane, I love my family. I love my husband."

He took her hand in his, briefly. He wanted to ease her pain without sending the wrong message. Letting go of her hand he said, "I've learned something here–the past is the past. Abraham Lincoln would not be a savior for the nation today; our relationship is not what it was. I'm still in love with the memory of the Claire of thirty years ago. I hope I can be friends with the Claire of today. "

She gave him a weak smile. Mutually and silently they agreed not to kiss or even touch.

"The Claire of today thanks you for what you did for her, for setting her free of that awful suspicion hanging over her."

"Then let me buy you an early dinner. And, a couple of drinks. My doctor highly recommends straight whiskey at times like this."

"If he didn't, I imagine he wouldn't be your doctor for long."

Her broader smile brightened the mood considerably. Some guys are legmen, many are boob men; Rigby was a smile man. A beautiful smile could melt him faster than the Wicked Witch of the West.

Claire asked to borrow his cell phone to call her son and make sure he got home from school all right. She told

Craig she would be going out for dinner, but that his father would fix him dinner when he got home from work. When she was finished, Rigby started the car and followed Claire's directions toward downtown, where they shared a delicious steak dinner. Claire only had one whiskey; he had two. What could he say? Doctor's orders.

When they finished their leisurely meal, Rigby told Claire he'd drive her home. She said she had left her car in the library parking lot and asked if he could take her there. Rigby drove the short distance to the library. As he approached the parking ramp a vehicle sped by, cut in front of them and screeched to a stop, blocking the ramp.

The black pickup truck had dark tinted windows. In the bed of the truck, unfolded and standing on all four wheels was Craig Orange's streamer decorated wheelchair. The boy was nowhere in sight.

Chapter 40

Claire screamed and slammed her fist against the dashboard. She pushed the car door open. Rigby grabbed her shoulder and held her in place.

"Stay!" he demanded, as if commanding a dog not to chase a rabbit.

"Craig! What's he done...*my baby!*"

"Craig's okay. Close the door."

"No...my baby–"

"He wouldn't be standing there if Craig was hurting." He grabbed her wrist, struggling to keep her in place. The pickup stayed right where it had stopped, its engine idling. "He wants us to follow. Close the door. The sooner we go, the sooner we'll have answers."

She stopped fighting and pulled the car door closed.

"Bastard!" she cried and slammed the dash again. "That's the one who ran me off the road."

After a moment the pickup rolled forward slowly. He followed close behind. The vehicle traveled through the streets, never exceeding the posted speed limit.

"Where's he taking us?" Claire said, fighting tears.

Rigby couldn't answer that. He couldn't make sense of this mysterious attacker or his motivation.

What also didn't make sense was that Rigby wasn't able to concentrate exclusively on the problem at hand. He kept reaching back for some fleeting thought he'd had before the black pickup blocked their path. What was it that he was trying to remember, to figure out?

Claire slapped his arm. He followed her gaze to a police car parked at a mini mart, the cops standing by the vehicle sipping soft drinks.

He thought of the police chief, a member of the Lincoln Guard of Honor, and said, "No. We have to handle this. If the cops start to chase him, we may not learn where Craig is."

He watched her for a reaction. She gritted her teeth and stared straight ahead at the pickup.

Soon they were in the countryside. Expansive farmland separated the houses and barns. Dusk thickened toward darkness and he turned on the headlights. The pickup veered off onto a country road and traveled another couple of miles before turning onto an unmarked dirt road. The road cut through corn stalks and a grove of trees, finally emerging at the rear of a two-story farmhouse with a screened-in rear porch. There were no other houses in sight.

The pickup stopped and the driver turned the engine off. The door opened and Lenny Poler jumped out.

How the hell could that be? Rigby had left him under arrest at police headquarters. Then he remembered that Lisa Hunt was a member of the Lincoln Guard of Honor. He wondered how deep the conspiracy ran. Would Chief Braddock free Abigail Lamont when he had the chance?

No time to think of that now. Craig's safety was paramount and Lenny was pointing an automatic pistol at them. He limped slightly, maybe the result of their fight in the library. Rigby turned off the engine and they both got out, Claire meeting him in front of the car.

"This way," Poler said, motioning with his free hand.

"Is Craig here?" Claire demanded.

"He's OK," Poler said.

"Is he *here*?" she shouted.

"He's OK," Poler repeated. "If you ever want to see him again, you'll do what I say and shut up. Now move!"

As Claire walked past Poler he grabbed her by the arm and stuck his weapon in her back. "Your gun, Mr. FBI."

Rigby watched him carefully, wondering if he was the

kind to use a gun or just scare people with it. You never make a bet like that with anyone's life on the line and he certainly wouldn't now, but his bet was that Poler would use the thing.

Rigby pulled out his gun, dropped it to the ground and kicked it away. Poler let go of Claire, who ran straight to the screened-in porch; Rigby followed. Poler picked up the gun and put it in his pants pocket.

Mildred Huffington, dressed in billowy pants and blouse, waited for them on the porch, seated at a picnic table. She turned on a kerosene camp lantern to add light.

"Where's my son, Mildred?" Claire snapped, not making an effort to hide her anger.

"Safe," Mildred said. "But not so mobile."

"I demand to see him!"

"He's fine. Fine. Watching a movie, eh, Lenny?"

Poler, standing behind them, said, "*Goonies*. But without his chair and tied up, so I didn't leave him any popcorn."

"How dare you–"

Huffington cut her off in a louder voice. "Please, Dr. Orange. You're not the boss here."

"Does that make *you* the boss?" Rigby asked.

"*We're* the boss," Poler said, indicating his handgun.

"Okay, boss, tell us, what's this about?"

Mildred took off her glasses and said, "Lincoln's body."

"How much of that story in the janitor's room should I believe?"

"Why, all of it, Mr. Rigby. I don't fib."

"Then why are we here? Why put the screws to Claire?"

"I think you know why."

"This is crazy," Claire said. "What do you want? We'll give it to you so I can have Craig back."

"Exactly," Mildred said. "A fair trade. Craig for…"

"For *what*?" Claire's voice cracked.

"She told you, lady," Poler said, "Lincoln's body."

Claire looked at the punk with a stunned expression. "You think..." She now looked at Mildred. "You really think...that I know?"

"You know," Poler said. "We heard at police headquarters. They had us sitting there waiting for the detective. Word traveled fast after the chief called. You ran the scam on the rich broad knowing there was nothing to lose because you knew the body wasn't in the grave. 'Cause you knew where it was. Didn't come as a surprise to us. We always thought you knew. That's why I gave you that little scare on the highway. Shake you up. So when it came time to talk, you would. Now's the time."

"No! I don't know–"

"You better know if you want to see the boy." Poler tapped the barrel of the gun on his open palm.

"Don't be so crude," Mildred admonished him.

"If the sc...plan was to work..." Claire paused, composed herself. "...the body would have to be there. So Rittinghouse could pretend to extract DNA, pretend to continue the cloning. Don't you see? That's the only way Abby would continue funding him. Look. You saw Dr. Rittinghouse at the cemetery. He was carrying that black bag. He had some equipment to gather Lincoln's DNA. It was all part of the...the charade...to convince Abby."

Mildred said, "Dr. Orange, I don't believe you. I think with all that research I saw you do, you know what happened to President Lincoln's body. I do believe that you will do anything to get your son back in good health. I understand that kind of loyalty. I have the same loyalty to the pledge I gave my father to protect Mr. Lincoln's body. But I can't protect it if I don't know where it is. You must tell me."

"I don't know!"

"You do," Poler said and clubbed her shoulder with his

gun.

Rigby sprang at him, but Poler backpedaled, gripping the gun butt with two hands and leveling it at Rigby. At least he'd gotten him away from Claire. He went to her and rubbed her shoulder. She winced with pain.

Poler's voice was sharper now, uncontrolled. That scared him, because Poler would act without thinking. "Talk or I'll beat it out of you."

Mildred spoke calming words to Poler but he didn't listen. Rigby was afraid she could not control him, either.

Poler advanced on them, restrained some by his damaged knee. His anger was real and he came at them with intent to do damage. Rigby considered diving for his legs, hoping he'd surprise him before he got off a shot, but he might get one off, miss Rigby and hit Claire.

To get Claire out of danger Rigby had to tell him something. Suddenly, he knew what it was. Because abruptly his mind clicked on what had been bothering him.

Rigby said, "I know where the body is."

Poler froze in his tracks. Even Claire whipped around to look at him. "How?"

"Lincoln's hand."

Chapter 41

"Not that again!" Huffington snapped.

Rigby said, "Not the hand Claire found. The hand your father was referring to when he told you to call on Sturbridge. The answer to where Abraham Lincoln's body lies is with Lincoln's hand–*Robert* Lincoln's poker hand."

"On the bottom of the letters?" Claire exclaimed.

Poler scowled. "What the hell you talking about?"

"I think I know," Mildred said. "I saw a letter in Dr. Crease's office."

"We have others like it in the car," Rigby said. "Just picked them up from Phillip Sturbridge's descendent."

"You mean Doris? Go get them. We'll keep Dr. Orange here till you bring them in."

"He may have a gun in the car," Poler said, indicating he would accompany Rigby. He took the FBI agent's gun from his pocket and handed it to Mildred.

Outside, Poler warned Rigby to play it straight. "No need for you or your girlfriend to get hurt. You do the smart thing. Show us the body. I got plans."

"Your grandmother know about your plans?"

"Big plans," he said with a crooked smile.

Rigby had plans, too. To put this bastard in a small room with bars. *Hope he's not claustrophobic, like me.*

He retrieved the letters and returned to the porch. The sun had slipped below the horizon and they had to hunch over the picnic table, the kerosene lamp providing weak light.

Three curious faces stared at the letters while Rigby removed them from the file and spread them out. As he did

279

this he said, "It was something I've been thinking about since I looked at the letters. See here. In the card game between Lincoln and Sturbridge, Lincoln's hands were always black cards and Sturbridge's hands were always red cards."

"That's strange," Mildred said.

"I thought so too, then I focused on the number of cards in a deck."

"Fifty-two."

Claire added, "A half deck, all blacks is twenty-six cards."

"The same number of letters in the alphabet," he said. He took a pen from his jacket pocket and asked for a piece of paper. Poler pulled a calendar off the wall, ripped off the current month and turned it over to the blank side. Rigby made a symbol for spades and next to it he wrote A for ace, the numbers two through ten, then a J, Q, and K for the face cards. Below those symbols he started with the alphabet, a under the ace, b under the two, c under the three and so on. When he finished half the alphabet, he repeated the process using the cloverleaf symbol for clubs. Under the A for the ace of clubs he picked up the alphabet with the fourteenth letter, n, and proceeded to the letter z under the K for king of clubs. Next, he placed a heart next to the spade symbol to reflect that the first grouping would be hearts if using the Sturbridge letters and made a diamond next to the club in the second grouping of cards, figuring that hearts were the dominant suit over diamonds, so hearts represented the first half of the alphabet. Finished, he took the last letter from Sturbridge to Lincoln and looked at the card hand.

"This one puzzled me, but didn't register at first. He had two of the same cards, two five of hearts. It must repeat a letter. The cards make a pretty simple code. A lot of us used it as kids, but it was more original in Robert Lincoln's time. They probably figured they didn't need any extreme protections. Just something to keep a secret between the two of them when exchanging personal letters."

In the P.S. of Sturbridge's letter was the number ten followed by the diamond symbol; next came the eight of hearts, the five of hearts, the five of diamonds, and then the five of hearts again. He took the key that he had constructed and converted the cards to letters. Under his key, the cards spelled out the word: *where.*

"Amazing," Claire said.

"Hours of practice with my Captain Midnight decoder ring."

Mildred was excited. "Sturbridge was asking Lincoln where to put the body. What's the answer?"

"You have it," Rigby said.

"*I* have it? You don't know what you're talking about, sir."

"In your office. Or should I say Crease's office. The last letter of the correspondence is in his desk drawer. He showed it to me. Look at the date on the letters. This is Sturbridge's last letter from July 25, 1901. Lincoln's reply came in August."

"Yes, I've seen it," Mildred said. "Then we go to the library. I sit in the front seat with Mr. Rigby. Lenny, you're in the back with Dr. Orange."

She blew out the lamp and they all marched to the car. Driving to the library, Rigby tried to engage Mildred in conversation, but she advised it would be best if the drive were made in silence. He took the time to consider ways to get them free of the old lady and her grandson. He'd overpowered Poler once and he figured he could do it again. Or had he just been lucky? Poler had him by twenty-five pounds and twenty-five years. Okay, maybe not quite twenty-five pounds, and…yeah, more than twenty-five years, but did that really matter?

He also worried about the police. Where did those senior officers who were members of the reconstituted Lincoln Guard of Honor stand? Mildred and her grandson got away from the cops very quickly.

Rigby reasoned if Mildred and Poler discovered Lincoln's body was safe, their mission would be satisfied and they would leave them alone. Or would they? Something else he hadn't resolved yet bothered him. Poler might be the answer. Also, the way young Poler was twirling his gun around set the hairs on his neck on edge.

Mildred Huffington used her pass card and keys to get through the security devices protecting the library. A hello to a security guard well before the rest of the party reached him sent him on his way. They arrived at Crease's office. Mildred opened the door.

Turning on the lights, she went straight to Crease's desk and pulled open the desk drawer containing the letter in its plastic cover. She brought it over to a conference table and laid it out.

The row of cards in the P.S. read: six of clubs; three of clubs; two of clubs; seven of clubs; and two of spades.

Rigby quickly translated with the code he'd written on the back of the calendar and had brought with him. He came up with: *spotb*.

"So much for that theory," Mildred said, not bothering to hide her disappointment in either the conclusion or in Rigby.

He wouldn't give up. "They were communicating with the card game. It's the only thing that makes sense."

"Unless it really was a card game," Mildred said.

"With two five of hearts?"

Claire said, "Let's go back to the earlier letters."

Sturbridge's previous letter contained the card hand: three of diamonds; queen of hearts; ace of hearts; three of hearts; five of hearts. He spelled out the word *place*.

"He was asking Lincoln for the place," Claire said. "Let's see how Robert responded."

Robert Lincoln's follow-up letter contained the card hand: three of clubs; two of clubs; ten of clubs; five of spades; five of clubs: *power.*

When Rigby wrote the letters down, Poler howled, "For God's sake! This is getting us nowhere. What does *power* mean when it comes to Abraham Lincoln?"

Claire rushed to the bookshelf behind Crease's desk and pulled an old, thin volume off the lower shelf. Holding it up she said, "John Carroll Power, Custodian of the National Lincoln Monument and Secretary of the Lincoln Guard of Honor. His book, published in 1890, is the definitive history of the grave-robbing attempt. He was there that night and at the formation of the Guard of Honor."

Rigby remembered that Smitty had referred to the book in giving him some history of the grave robbing. She called it 'fascinating'.

Claire leafed through the book as she walked back to the desk, talking as she went. "Power told of hiding the coffin unburied near the obelisk's foundation for two years and then burying it in another location in the underground labyrinth below the terrace. He even drew a map of the tomb's ground plan. Marked the location where the coffin remained unburied but covered up, and the location where it was buried from 1878 to 1887. Then it was returned to the catacomb or burial chamber. Of course, his book came out a decade before the 1901 reburial.

"Here's the floor plan." She placed the book down on the table, opened to a map marked Ground Plan, Lincoln Monument. Pointing, she said, "This is where the coffin was placed, covered by planks."

The spot she indicated was marked with the letter A.

"And here is where the body was buried for nine years."

She pointed to a spot just north of the foundation of the obelisk under the terrace that today, after reconstruction of the tomb, would be just behind the crypts of Lincoln's wife and children. On the map, the spot was marked with the letter B.

"Spot B," Rigby said, pointing at the playing card symbols in the letter. "Robert Lincoln wanted to make sure his father's body was protected. So after designing an impregnable tomb he created a shell game and buried the coffin with the president's body where it had rested undisturbed for nearly a decade. Sturbridge must have had the coffins switched after the identification was made and the witnesses left the room."

"Then it must still be there," Mildred said excitedly.

Chapter 42

"One way to find out," Poler said. He pointed toward the door of Crease's office, indicating they should leave. "Let's go wake Mr. Lincoln."

Mildred scowled. "That language is unnecessary, Lenny."

"What do you need us for?" Rigby said, deciding it was not a good idea to be alone with Mildred and her grandson in the cemetery at night.

"To dig," Poler said.

"Where's Craig?" Claire pleaded. "Please, can't you take me to him? You got what you wanted."

"We'll see if we do," Mildred said. "Once we get to the cemetery."

"But we can't get in," Claire protested.

Mildred left Crease's office and went to her desk. She opened a drawer, removed a ring of keys and shook them. "Oh yes we can. I've been around a long time, built up quite a collection. I can get into most places in this town. Mrs. Lamont knew I had keys to the cemetery and the tomb." To Rigby she said, "Remember that day I couldn't find the keys? From what we heard at police headquarters about Mrs. Lamont and the murder, I think she borrowed the keys to take that poor girl into the cemetery that night then returned the keys the next day."

"You knew and said nothing?"

"I wouldn't do that, Agent Rigby. What do you take me for? I suspect it now, looking back over things. Come, let's get a move on."

Before leaving the library Mildred retrieved a narrow,

unmarked box maybe four feet in length from a storage closet. She also grabbed some flashlights from another room. She placed the box and flashlights in the trunk of the car, saying they would find other tools at the tomb and the site of the dig. They drove to the cemetery and parked in the small lot near Lincoln Park. Mildred's key opened the chain link fence lock, the same gate Flute and Abby Lamont had passed through days before.

They walked through the dark and silent cemetery. Claire clung to Rigby in a way he would have appreciated had the circumstances been different. He looked around, trying to see the silhouette of a guard or cop but could only make out stone columns and grave markers. They carried the flashlights Mildred had taken from the library. Poler told them to keep the lights off until they were inside the tomb. He carried the long box under one arm, his gun in his hand. Rigby's weapon was in Mildred's pocket.

They climbed the hill to the tomb. A temporary wall of plywood had been constructed to protect the burial chamber, wrenched open to bring out the empty coffin. They proceeded around the tomb to the gate and door protecting Memorial Hall. Mildred found the right keys to open the locks. Inside, she turned on a flashlight, walked to a door leading to the center of the tomb and opened it with another key, exposing a work area for the tour guides, in which wall brackets held brochures describing the statues and flags in the tomb, as well as its construction. Another door stood on the opposite side of the small room.

Mildred pointed her flashlight and gripped the door's handle. In a solemn voice she said, "If you're right, behind this door are the remains of Abraham Lincoln." She pulled it open.

The corridor behind the door was pitch black. The beams revealed a twisting empty passage.

"You first," Poler said to Rigby. "And be smart," he added, pointing his gun at Claire.

Rigby entered the corridor followed by Mildred, Claire, and Poler. The four flashlights cut through the darkness, revealing nothing but cobwebs and a healthy-looking cockroach scurrying across the floor. The corridor snaked around, exposing little nooks and crannies under the tomb's terrace. Rigby shone his light into one corner and saw shovels, picks, and a crowbar. In the next nook were more tools and a couple of sawhorses. One wide area contained a few stacked chairs, probably used during ceremonies.

The air felt stifling; a dank, musty smell filled his lungs. He remembered hearing from Smitty about the poor ventilation and wet stained walls at the time of the reburial. She said the air down here was described as 'villainous'. He took in that same villainous air and coughed.

"How the hell we supposed to find the right place?" Poler griped as they slowly moved around the circular foundation that held up one of the displays of military statues on the terrace above.

Spaces around the foundation widened. Their flashlights picked up old bricks scattered on the dirt floor, likely left over from the early construction or remodeling of the monument and tomb. Cobwebs were more plentiful here. Rigby used his flashlight to cut them down in front of his face. One web had a nasty-looking black spider hanging in the middle. The creature didn't seem so fearsome next to the kid with the gun behind him. Rigby ducked the spider's web and left it alone.

Mildred called a halt to the procession to get her bearings, a difficult thing to do with no markers. Even during a September night the place felt warm. Rigby's shirt, wet with perspiration, stuck to his back. He looked at Claire. She appeared to be holding up well.

Now that he had the lay of the underground, it was time to start thinking how to take Poler down. He knew this expedition would not end well for Claire and him if he did nothing. What could he do without endangering her? He also had to make them tell where Craig was. He had to be ready to take advantage of any opportunity.

Pointing her flashlight over Power's book, now opened to the page with the ground plan of the monument, Mildred said, "I place us somewhere between the statues on the east side of the terrace. We have to go on."

Rigby said, "Did it occur to you that you're working off a rough, not-to-scale drawing from 1890 before the tomb was remodeled a couple of times?"

"It occurs to me that I am finally about to fulfill the wishes of my daddy, so get a move on."

The flashlights cut through the dark. Dust kicked up from their feet. Claire and Poler coughed; Mildred sneezed. Rigby moved his hand back and forth in front of his nose like a fan to push away the floating dust and dirt, which was highlighted in their beams.

Something moved. All four beams cut to the same spot. A rat. It froze in the lights for a split second then was gone.

They moved around the foundation of another statue and walked in a different direction, going along the wall until they saw a split in the inner foundation wall.

Claire said, "This place looks like it hasn't changed in more than a hundred years. Even with the reconstruction. If Mr. Power returned he'd still recognize it."

"Wish he would return," Poler said, running the beam of his flashlight across the dirt floor and around the walls. "Then he'd tell us where to look. There's no signs of digging. Nothing to show where the coffin is, if it's even here."

"That's why I have this," Mildred said, tapping on the box under Poler's arm.

"What is it?" Claire asked.

"Something the archaeologists attached to the museum bought to dig around Lincoln sites."

Poler put the box down and opened one end then

turned the box upside down and let the contents slide out. Rigby recognized the instrument right away. "A metal detector."

It wasn't a heavy-duty model, more like one you could pick up in a hobby shop. The device had a search coil ring connected by an aluminum pole to a box with a lot of switches, a set of earphones plugged into the box, a handle and an armrest to keep the device steady.

Poler flipped some of the switches. A red light popped on, reflecting brightly in the dark chamber. He held the device out to Rigby and said, "Strap this on."

"I'm not doing your dirty work."

"I got to keep an eye on you," Poler said. "Come on, its not heavy, old man."

Right between the eyes, he thought. He grabbed the device and strapped the armrest to his right arm. As he lifted the earphones to slip over his head, Poler pulled the plug from the box and said, "We'll all listen for the signal."

Mildred said, "Run it over there. Midway between the walls, by that break in the inner wall."

Rigby followed her instructions, slowly passing the coil over the ground like a magician waving his wand. He did this robotically while thinking that by handing him the metal detector, Poler had made a mistake. He now had a weapon. He slowly shifted direction, moving to a spot where he would face the gunman. Poler was concentrating on the mesmerizing slow sweep of the coil, following Rigby's progress by keeping his flashlight on the coil. Rigby would move slowly at him. Force him back. Move Poler against the wall so that when he raised the detector as a club, Poler would have nowhere to run. He'd be pinned.

Rigby took another step toward the punk. Poler didn't move. The coil brushed against his pant legs just above his shoes. Rigby stopped and looked up at him. Poler took his eyes off the coil and stared at Rigby. He stepped back.

Rigby continued the sweep of the instrument. As the

coil moved toward Poler again he took another step back. He was now against the wall. Another step and Rigby would have him pinned. Rigby tightened the muscles in his arm, prepared to lift the detector with one hand and smash the coil against Poler's gun hand.

Rigby swept the detector wide to the side so he could hit him with force.

Beep-beep-beep.

The metal detector's alarm echoed sharply in the enclosed area.

Poler moved away from the wall as Claire closed in, preventing Rigby from swinging the instrument off the ground without hitting her.

"Come toward me," Mildred said, the excitement in her voice echoing in the chamber.

He moved the detector toward her, admitting to himself that the alarm had sparked his interest over what may be buried there. The alarm sounded louder and more rapid. Something other than a bottle cap was buried there.

"I'll get some of those shovels we saw," Mildred told Poler. "You watch them."

When she left, Rigby tried to catch Claire's eye, indicate to her he was thinking of overpowering Poler, but he could not get her attention. She stared at the ground, imagining the great find just below their feet. He turned off the metal detector. The shattering, sudden silence caused her to jerk. She looked at him. Too late. Mildred returned and pushed a shovel into Claire's hands.

Poler ordered Rigby to put the detector down and take a shovel. He handed the gun to his grandmother with instructions to keep it pointed at Claire and Rigby, and he picked up the last shovel.

They started to dig. Sweat collected on Rigby's neck, under his arms and dripped from his forehead. Poler positioned himself a few feet away. Claire threw herself into the dig, her professional curiosity apparently overcoming her fears for her son and herself.

Rigby looked at Mildred. She didn't seem sure of herself holding the gun. It would not be difficult wresting it away from her, but Poler would tackle him with an uncertain outcome. He continued to dig.

The air within the closed foundation grew heavier. All the diggers became soaked with perspiration. Even Mildred showed patches of sweat on her clothing. Each of the diggers took a few moments of rest but they kept digging, piling dirt up on the side of the new holes.

Two feet down, the spade clanked against metal. Glances were exchanged and the digging continued. Rigby's hole and Poler's were deeper than Claire's but she soon caught up, and all three banged the edges of their shovels against the metal with each stroke.

Anxious moments passed before they saw the lid of a long metal coffin.

Mildred moved toward the hole with her flashlight. Claire picked up another light and hopped out of the small hole. Poler and Rigby continued digging.

When finally cleared of dirt, the old coffin looked most un-presidential. It was long, made of iron and quite rusty from years of sitting in the ground below the leaky terrace.

Poler climbed out of the hole and retrieved a crowbar that Mildred had brought along.

"No!" Claire exclaimed. "Do you think we should? Exposing the body to the air with no scientific equipment–"

"It's probably all dust anyway," Poler said as he looked for a place to put the crowbar. "But we have to see."

"Open it, Lenny," Mildred ordered.

Poler wedged the crowbar below the lid. "It's loose."

He worked the bar in deeper and with a grunt pushed down on it. A loud creak screeched in their ears; the lid popped up and then banged down.

Poler looked up. "It's not locked."

Claire, Mildred and Rigby focused their flashlights on

the lid and waited for Poler to lift it again. This time he exerted less effort and strain. He gently worked the lid up with the bar, and then with one hand he grabbed the lip of the coffin and pushed the lid back.

The beams from their flashlights flooded the inside of the coffin.

Chapter 43

Empty.

The stunned silence lasted only a moment.

"No," Mildred said softly, a sob in her throat.

"A trick!" Poler yelled, creating an echo. He grabbed his gun from Mildred and turned it on Rigby. "You tricked us!"

"No. If this is a trick, its Robert Lincoln's doing. Something else to protect his father's remains."

"I don't believe you!"

"Please, Lenny, let me think." Mildred ran the beam of the flashlight into Rigby's face, looking for the truth that might be contained there.

"All this time and effort and all we got is an empty nothing. Nothing!" Poler moaned.

"Wrong again, Poler," Rigby said. "That's the trouble with youth. They see only one dimensionally. There *is* something here. A rusty iron coffin. It must be here for a reason. Why?"

"Who cares?"

Claire sank to a knee and touched the rusty surface. "Iron," she said. "And the coffin is so long." She looked up at Mildred. "Get me Power's book."

Mildred retrieved the book and handed it to Claire. Shuffling through the pages under her flashlight beam, she exclaimed, "Here! I remembered. Power came across a large iron coffin buried under the terrace and he didn't know what it was. He found out it once contained Lincoln's body but had to be replaced with a lead inner coffin because the iron one was too big to fit into the original sarcophagus."

"Big deal," Poler said. "So we know what it is. We still don't know where *he* is. This Robert Lincoln and his tricks. If I could get my hands on him–"

"That will be quite enough, Lenny," Mildred scolded. "Don't say anything nasty about Mr. Robert."

"It may not be a trick," Claire said. "Power complained about all the work to hide the body, dig the hole, move the heavy coffin, *fill* the hole. Using the iron coffin as a filler would eliminate some of the shoveling."

"One casket sitting on top of another," Rigby said.

"Right."

"Could be."

"That thing's too heavy to drag out of there," Poler said.

"We can dig a narrow hole down the side of the coffin, see if anything is under it."

"More digging."

"The only way to see if Claire's right," Rigby said.

"Dig, Lenny," his grandmother ordered.

They stood back and watched the kid do his stuff. Rigby glanced at Mildred. She had positioned herself on the other side of the pit, holding his gun at the ready.

A few shovelfuls of dirt and Poler asked for a flashlight. Rigby handed him one. Poler knelt on both knees and pushed the flashlight into the hole, his face close by the light, giving it an eerie glow. When he spoke his words were muffled, but distinct enough: "I'll be damned."

Poler stood and rubbed the dirt off the knees of his pants. "Another box under the coffin, just like she said."

"Let's get to it," Mildred said.

"That top one's too heavy to lift."

"Then we'll dig a hole next to it a little lower than the top coffin and shove it into the new hole." Mildred waved the gun at Rigby and Claire and said, "Come on, you two."

More digging, and more time doing it. Rigby looked at his watch. After ten. He wondered if guards made rounds of the cemetery and if they could hear them from outside.

Claire also checked her watch and said Craig was alone and scared and she had to see him. Mildred reassured her that someone was taking care of the boy. This raised more fear in her, Rigby knew. A stranger with her son. He wondered who else was working with Mildred and Poler. Another member of the Lincoln Guard of Honor?

"Who?" Claire demanded to know.

Mildred remained silent. Poler ignored the question and kept digging.

Claire threw down her shovel. "I'm not helping you until I know my son is all right."

Mildred thought a moment. "All right," she said. "We don't need the threat anymore. You're here and you're helping. Your son is fine, I'm sure. He's at home, in his own bed."

"With *who*? Who's with him?"

"His father."

"Peter?"

"It's late, you know, where else do you think your husband would be? To be sure that his father wouldn't work too late tonight, I made a phone call earlier with a handkerchief over the mouthpiece telling him his boy needed him."

Claire seemed confused for a moment, perhaps even faint. She put a hand to her forehead and sat on the ground. Rigby put a hand on her shoulder.

Gaining composure, she said, "Thank you, I guess. But I'm missing from the house. Peter will have the police out looking for me."

"And when they find you, you'll have made the greatest discovery in history. You'll tell them you had to be part of the discovery. So dig!"

Rigby didn't believe they'd give them the chance to tell anyone. They were probably digging their own graves. He helped Claire to her feet and they worked the new hole alongside Poler. Mildred continued to watch them. Their flashlights were at the edge of the pit, providing light.

Finally, they had created a hole a couple of inches deeper than the coffin.

Sweating heavily, Rigby joined Claire and Poler on the other side of the iron coffin. He and Poler put their hands on the coffin; Claire sat on the ground and placed the heels of her shoes on the coffin. On the count of three they all pushed and grunted and felt the coffin scrape against the wooden lid of the second coffin below.

They rested a moment, gathered their strength and again shoved against the damn iron. Rigby imagined it was like pushing a stubborn elephant determined to hold its turf. More sweat, more grunts and the coffin moved some more. Finally, they got more than half of it over the new hole. It teetered, and they gave it one more shove. The iron coffin fell into the open space. It still covered the edge of the wood box below, and it took more pushing and shoving before the box was clear.

Rigby decided right then he would not retire from the FBI and take up a new career as a stevedore. The three of them sat on the dirt, sweat rolling down their faces, musty air filling their lungs as they panted, dirt clinging to their clothes. All he could think of was Annie-May at The Railroad Bar and a row of beers lined up in front of her.

"Nicely done," Mildred said. "Now's not the time to stop. We have to see if he's in that box."

Rigby could have slugged her, but the others also seemed eager to learn the truth. Struggling to her feet, Claire grabbed a flashlight and handed it to him, then took up the other two and held them both. Poler grabbed the crowbar and began working on the lid of the cedar coffin.

The wood crumbled easily, becoming dust under Poler's assault. He pulled off planks of cedar, exposing a more ornate burial box inside. That too consisted of wood, and he made short work of it.

The lead lining of the coffin would be more of a problem, but the seal was weak from the number of times it had been cut open and re-soldered. The last time it had probably been done in a hurry so the coffin could be switched as part of the ruse. Poler banged the lid a few times with his crowbar, setting off a terrible echo in the enclosed space. Claire covered her ears, the beams from the flashlights shooting straight to the ceiling. The lead coffin's cut-away section moved. Rigby heard a hiss of escaping air. The section was loose.

"Now. Finally," Mildred said breathlessly.

They moved forward to see what was inside the lead coffin.

Poler cranked down on the crowbar, pushed up on the square and held the bar in place under the edge of the lead until it was a foot above the coffin.

Claire got to her knees and turned her two flashlights on the opening Poler had created. Mildred and Rigby angled their beams into the open space.

The light shone on the dark saddle-leather colored skin in the final stages of decomposition pressed to the skull like a thin sheet of onion paper. The features were unmistakably those of the sixteenth President of the United States.

"It's him!" Mildred cried. "Here all the time!"

Lincoln actually buried inside his tomb. Earlier, Rigby said that was the last place they should look for him. *So sue me.*

Mildred put Rigby's gun in her oversized pocket and placed the flashlight on the ground, so she could get down on her hands and knees for a closer look at the remarkable remains.

"Now what?" Rigby asked. "Bury him in the proper place?"

"Bury him?" Poler said. "After all this effort? No. We're gonna be like Boyd's men and sell the body back."

"Sell?" Mildred glared at Poler from her knees.

"That's right. Call it a reward or a finder's fee if you like. But it's the same idea. We get big money. They get the body back. Why do you think I agreed to help in the first place?"

Poler pulled the automatic from his waistband after wedging the crowbar in place under the metal plate, the other end of the bar dug in the dirt holding up the plate.

Mildred said, "I thought you wanted to help me. To fulfill the promise of the Lincoln Guard of Honor."

"I made no promise."

"But you have to follow your great grandfather's wishes. That's why we're here."

"You sound just like McClavity," he said. "'We have to find the body to preserve the legend, to honor the man.' That's all he talked about."

"Is that why you pushed McClavity down the stairs?" Rigby asked.

Poler whirled to glare at him. The expression on his face changed as a smile crept over him.

"He was crying about his grandfather. A congressman *crying!* He was drunk and crying over his grandfather and Lincoln."

"He told you his grandfather knew where the body was," Rigby said. It was not a question.

Poler stared at him a moment, then clapped a hand against the butt of the gun. "Very good, Mr. FBI man. He said his grandfather knew where the body was. Said he had to be near Lincoln and ordered me to take him to the old capitol. After parking the car, I found him in that front room and I couldn't stand it any longer. He knew where Lincoln's body was and I saw opportunity knocking, so many people caring about the body. I wanted to know what he knew."

"So you grabbed the rail to beat it out of him."

"To threaten him. He tried to run away but I caught him." Poler laughed at the memory.

Rigby guessed the rest. Poler had clubbed McClavity

with the wooden rail, sending the congressman down the stairs to his death. Poler had killed. The second time would be easier for him. Now he was really dangerous. They had to get away.

"You killed the congressman?" Mildred Huffington exclaimed.

"I hit him and he ended up dead," Poler said, justifying the death in his mind. "He could've helped us find the body. Or so I thought until I heard from the FBI man after our little encounter earlier that McClavity thought his grandfather destroyed it."

"To protect the body! That's *my* duty; *my* responsibility," Mildred said firmly.

"You will, Grandma. The body will be safe and we'll be rich."

"It will not be safe!" Mildred stamped a foot in the dirt for emphasis. "It will just be covered again. And could be stolen again. I must prevent that!"

She paused, looked at Rigby thoughtfully. Finally, she said, "There is only one way to make it impossible to steal the body."

Mildred reached into her pocket and removed a box of matches. "Burn it!"

Claire gasped. "You can't!"

"Your FBI agent friend here gave me the idea. With his suspicions of Samuel McClavity, the congressman's grandfather. Burn it and no one will trouble the body again. Burn it and the Lincoln Guard of Honor will fulfill its mission of keeping it out of the hands of thieves and outsiders."

"You can't do that," Claire said passionately.

"Look! Even my own grandson wants to sell the body. Mr. Lincoln's body will always be in danger. I see that now. Yes, I do. Burning is the only way. Then no one can take it. No one will move it ever again. Thank you for the idea, Mr. Rigby."

All Rigby could think of was the Judge. He was about to fail in his mission in the worst possible way: providing the idea for the destruction, not the safe return, of the president's body.

Turning to Poler, Mildred said, "Help me do this."

"*Help* you? Help you burn up a fortune you mean. I won't."

"You will. You must."

Mildred pulled out a match and drew it along the edge of the matchbox.

"Don't do it, Grandma. I'm warning you!" Poler leveled his gun at Mildred.

Rigby looked at Claire, still on her knees at Poler's feet. He wondered if he could bowl him over with a leap. Claire was in the way; she would take the blow.

Mildred said, "You won't hurt me, Lenny. I practically raised you. If it's money you want I'll give you all I have. Leave everything to you."

Poler blinked. He was uncertain but also agitated. He could explode at any moment.

Mildred picked up the empty carton that had contained the metal detector and held the match to a flap. The flame caught, the fire growing stronger, consuming more of the cardboard. She could easily thrust the flaming box into the opening Poler had created in the coffin.

Poler tensed for a moment. His hand shook as if he had a palsy. Rigby hoped the trigger finger would hold. Suddenly, Poler grabbed Claire by the back of her shirt and hauled her to her feet. He thrust the muzzle of his gun against her temple and shouted at his grandmother, "Don't do it. Don't burn up my fortune! I'll kill her right here."

Mildred calmly watched the flame burning down the length of the long box. "I advise you not to, Lenny. But it won't stop me. I'll do what I need to do. For my father."

Mildred stretched the burning box toward Lincoln's remains.

Rigby's mission was to protect the presidential remains. His *responsibility* was to protect Claire's life. He looked at Poler, whose gun hand trembled. He looked at Mildred. She inched the burning box closer to the corpse.

He would save Claire or die trying. He needed a weapon. Poler would shoot him if he lunged. Rigby slipped the flashlight into his pocket and in one step grabbed Mildred's wrists, her hands close together as she held the box. In one quick motion he re-directed the flaming box at Poler's face and banged his body against Mildred, loosening her grip on the torch. She staggered back, the matchbox fell to the ground.

Poler threw his gun hand over his eyes to protect his face from the flames. Rigby drove the burning cardboard into Poler's chest. The fire jumped onto his shirt. He screamed and knocked the flaming cardboard box from Rigby's hands. Poler fell to the ground, rolling over in the dirt, putting out the flame on his shirt and the box at the same time.

Rigby scooped the matchbox from the ground.

"Lights!" he hollered at Claire. He kicked at the flashlight on the ground and it went off. Claire doused her two flashlights as he clicked off the one in his pocket, putting the interior of the tomb into utter blackness. He grabbed her arm, pulling her toward him.

They ran. He hoped he guessed the correct number of strides to the far wall and the turn to the next corridor.

A shot exploded in the closed-in chamber, sounding like cannon fire. The bullet slapped the wall near him, concrete splinters stinging his hands. Claire cried out.

They made it around the corner and out of range before they heard the second shot. He put a hand over her mouth so she would not give their position away. She understood, and nodded.

Poler loudly swore that he was going to kill them. Rigby was sure he'd planned to do that all along. Rigby didn't intend to give him the chance.

They used the wall as their guide, making their way in the darkness down the hall, feeling their way past the nooks and crannies.

Damn! He stepped on one of those loose bricks. Stumbled. Pain shot through his ankle. Claire grabbed for him as he dropped to a knee. They could hear Poler swearing somewhere behind them. Rigby regained his footing despite the pain.

They continued working the wall. Another shot rang out. He felt the disturbance in the air like heat against his face as a bullet buzzed by his ear. Poler had gotten closer. Rigby's sore ankle was slowing them up.

Rigby pulled Claire behind him as he felt the wall, looking for the next indentation, a place to hide.

He found it, a narrow slit. He pulled Claire in with him. Immediately, he felt cobwebs adhere to his face. He cleaned them away. Claire pressed against him.

He tried to control his breathing, to be as silent as…well, as a grave. Claire took a gulp of air and he did the same. He couldn't outrun Poler, but hoped he could outsmart him.

Listening closely, Rigby heard Poler's footsteps coming fast. Poler then helped by shouting, "You won't get outta here alive!"

Cheap patter, Rigby thought as he raised his flashlight, prepared to swing in the direction of the voice.

An eerie glow appeared from the direction they had come. The light, though weak, pierced the blackness like the first rays of a morning sun still below the horizon. Mildred Huffington had found the flashlight they'd left on the ground.

"Lenny! Come back. Help me!"

"I'm going to kill them first. Then we'll make our peace about Lincoln. Take your gun and go down the other side of the tomb. Cut 'em off before they get through the door."

The ghostly light faded with Mildred's retreat. In the darkness Rigby strained to listen. He heard Poler's soft footfalls on the ground. One step, then a second.

He swung the flashlight as hard as he could and heard a dull thud and a groan as he made contact.

Rigby was all over Poler as he went down. He let fly a fist into the darkness and felt a solid connection to what he thought was a shoulder. Adjusting his aim a little higher, he swung again, this time connecting with the flesh and bone of a cheek. Poler groaned.

Rigby needed to know where the gun was. "Lights!" he yelled.

Claire clicked on both flashlights.

The gun had fallen only inches from Poler's hand, but he was dazed by Rigby's attack. Instead of sending another punch his way, Rigby rolled off him and grabbed for the gun. Holding it on Poler, Rigby offered some cheap patter of his own: "Move and I'll drill you." He frisked Poler, but knew the bastard had given Mildred the pistol. Where was she? Had she gone back to the coffin? Was she doing the unthinkable?

Rigby reached into his pocket and cupped the box of matches. Hopefully, she had no other matches, or a lighter.

Rigby directed Claire to send a beam of light down the corridor. Mildred was nowhere to be seen. She probably obeyed Poler's order, which meant she would be up ahead somewhere, waiting for them with his gun.

Telling Claire they needed to get out of there, Rigby pushed Poler in front of them and they soon reached the door that opened to the guide's room and Memorial Hall beyond.

No Mildred in sight.

Rigby ordered Poler to open the door. The guide's room was empty, the light still on, just as they left it. Rigby told Claire to turn off her flashlights as he switched off the room's light. He could see light streaming under the door that opened to Memorial Hall. They'd never put the light on in the hall.

Motioning Claire away from the door to the hall, he kept Poler an arm's length away, his gun on him. Bracing himself, he turned the latch and threw it open, crouching into a firing position.

Mildred Huffington and Detective Lisa Hunt stood in the center of the room. Hunt held a gun pointed at him.

"Drop it," she said.

Chapter 44

Rigby had no intention of dropping the gun. He wasn't going to be put at a disadvantage again. He stood up slowly.

Detective Hunt was part of the Lincoln Guard of Honor. She'd said so herself when he first met her. How else did Mildred and Lenny escape police headquarters after he left them there? He suspected membership in the Guard was their get-out-of-jail card. Still, he didn't know for sure.

Rigby grabbed Poler by the collar of his shirt. He pulled Poler to the door then pushed him onto the floor in the hall. Rigby could keep an eye on him there. His gun remained leveled at Hunt. Claire stepped up behind him.

Rigby said, "Mildred's the one you should be watching. She's got a gun."

"Already took it. I'll take yours and then you can tell me what's going on."

"I can talk while holding my gun." Rigby indicated Mildred. "What'd she tell you?"

Hunt was silent a moment. He could tell she was thinking whether she should be in a conversation with him. Finally, she replied, "Said she and her grandson were doing research for Dr. Crease in there and you went crazy with a gun."

"And, what did you say?"

Hunt stared at him for the longest moment. He tried to read her eyes, his finger tense on the trigger, ready to react to any move on her part.

Hunt said, "I asked her where she disappeared to from police headquarters. They put her and Poler in my office when you turned them in, to wait for me, but the cop assigned to guard them screwed his assignment. Left them unguarded for a moment. When I got there they were gone. We figured they escaped in the confusion after the chief called and said he solved Flute's murder. The place became a madhouse."

Oh, *he* solved the murder.

Mildred waved her arms in protest. "The nice young man told us to go–"

Rigby ignored her and said to Hunt, "So where does that put us?"

"I want you to put the gun down."

Rigby shook his head. "Your boss is part of this."

"The chief?"

He nodded.

"Part of what?" Hunt demanded.

"The Lincoln Guard of Honor."

"Yes, he is," Hunt said, as if it were no big deal. "When all this fuss began, Mildred recruited him and the mayor and me and others to restart the old Guard to make sure the dig went properly. She was in charge because of a relative or something."

Rigby looked at Mildred. She was using the chief and all the others. She needed their power to pull off her scheme, but she'd only included her grandson in on the secret. Rigby wondered if he could trust Hunt. He decided to gamble and slowly lowered his gun. Hunt watched him closely. She began lowering her gun and soon both weapons pointed at the floor.

Rigby stepped into the hall and Claire followed him. Hunt inquired about Claire's welfare. She nodded and said, "But, my son. Craig–"

"Fine," Hunt said with a grin.

"How did you find us?"

"Your husband called. Told us someone broke into your house, tied your boy up and stole his wheelchair. He didn't know where you were, but said you were missing. I went over to the Library and Museum. One of the guards reported seeing you with Rigby and Mildred at the library late. The three of you added up in my mind to Lincoln's Tomb so I took a drive out here. I'll take Lenny back into custody for the bombing and running out on us, but you'll all have to come along."

Rigby nodded in approval and said, "You can add the killing of Congressman McClavity to the charges on Lenny here."

Hunt's face showed surprise. She looked down at Poler lying in a heap on the floor then back to Rigby.

He smiled at her and said, "You're good. You're very, very good."

She offered up a smile usually reserved for ice cream on a hot day.

Rigby crashed to the floor. His gun fell from his hand and clattered onto the stone surface. Poler was on top of him. Stupid, he'd concentrated on Hunt and ignored the son-of-a bitch, who had pounced like a tiger.

Poler rolled off Rigby, grabbed the gun in one motion and jumped to his feet. An explosion boomed inside the hall, ringing in Rigby's ears. The acrid smell of gun smoke filled the air. Poler grunted and looked down at his midsection, at the red blotch that grew wider on his shirt. He staggered forward and the gun fell from his hand. Mildred screamed as her grandson toppled onto his face.

Rigby looked at Hunt, still holding the smoking gun. Claire had a hand over her mouth in shock.

Mildred was by his side in a moment, but she could do nothing for Lenny Poler.

Rigby pushed himself off the floor, nodded at Hunt and hugged Claire.

Mildred wailed, "This is not the way it's supposed to be!"

"Somehow I blame myself," Claire said, her voice quavering.

"Not your fault," Rigby reassured her for the second time that day. He broke the hug, maybe sooner than she would have liked, but felt it was enough. "It's over now. All over."

Hunt said, "Seems like nothing worked out like anyone planned. But you, Agent Rigby, managed to walk through a maze full of tricks and traps."

There was admiration in her voice. He shrugged. "Wasn't it Lincoln who said, 'You can't fool all of the people all of the time?'"

Chapter 45

After returning to Washington, Rigby headed to the Bureau. He had reported his success to the Judge from Springfield by e-mail, but had received no acknowledgment.

He went straight for the Judge's office. He wanted her to welcome him, personally, back to the Monument Bomber Task Force. As he reached the office door, the Judge's assistant emerged.

"There you are, Agent Rigby. Could you follow me, please?"

"I want to see the Director."

"Not right now. She's up on Capitol Hill reporting to Congress that the Bureau successfully discovered President Lincoln's remains and Congressman McClavity's killer."

The Bureau did, huh?

"This way, please. The Director has an assignment for you."

"I know where the task force is camping out."

"Please follow me," she insisted.

The assistant led him to an office door. On it was a plaque that read:

OFFICE FOR CASES OF
HISTORICAL SIGNIFICANCE

The assistant opened the door and indicated he should go inside. He walked past her into the office and saw the autographed baseball on the desk, along with some of the other items that decorated his old office.

"What's this?"

"The Director says we have to comply with Congress' dead presidents law and be involved with what it says on the door, cases of historical significance. And after what you did in Illinois, she says you're the best person for the job."

"She put me back on the task force."

"I believe that was before you ran off to Illinois to find Mr. Lincoln. She was very impressed."

"Please. I'm not a historian."

"Maybe not, but you use your years well," she said, smiling.

"I'll talk to the Judge about this."

The assistant shook her head in disapproval at the Director's nickname. "I'm sure the Director will talk to you, but she has to fill this post and her mind is made up."

He would talk to the Judge and get back on the task force. There was no sense in arguing with the Judge's assistant.

"Who's on my team?"

"You," she said, "are your whole team. The Director has her limits with all this. Your next case file is on the desk."

She walked out and closed the door behind her.

Rigby looked around the office. Small, but there was a window that looked out to the street. He walked over to the desk and picked up the folder.

The file's tab read: *FDR's Treasure.*

The first sheet of paper in the file was a summary with the word CONFIDENTIAL in big bold red letters stamped all over the page. It revealed that in October 1935 President Franklin D. Roosevelt was aboard the cruiser *USS Houston* off the Cocos Islands, a place purported to hide pirate treasure. Information recently received by the FBI indicated Roosevelt and his party may have discovered the pirate treasure, but left it there.

A second sheet of paper, also stamped CONFIDENTIAL, was from an aide to the Speaker of the House of Representatives, who vouched for the credibility of the source and said the Speaker wanted the story checked out.

Pirate treasure. They got to be kidding. Was the treasure still there? Why did the government care? Well, he guessed there was the national debt to consider. The Judge's signature on the bottom of the page indicated her assent to proceed.

Rigby's nose caught the unseemly odor of politics with this assignment. How do these things find him? The Monument Bomber was still out there somewhere. At least this job kept him in Washington close to the action. He'd find his way back on the task force.

Chapter 46

The taxi driver slowed his vehicle on 17th Street NW as it passed between the Washington Monument and the World War II Memorial. Past the latter he could see the Lincoln Memorial sparkling in the afternoon sun. He imagined a different scene. The Lincoln Memorial crumbled like an ancient Greek temple that had suffered the ravages of time. He had seen that image in his mind time and again. He thought it foretold the future. He was bitter that it did not.

A car horn blared behind him. The taxi driver pushed down on the accelerator and proceeded toward Independence Ave. A tourist at the World War II Memorial hailed his cab, but he ignored the man. He was not interested in picking up any customers just now. He was trying to decide what his next mission should be.

Should he pursue the image of a destroyed Lincoln temple? Or should he seek out a new target?

Another option he had been thinking about for days would not let go. Maybe he would announce his presence again by sending the agent who disrupted his last mission to hell. The thought made him smile. He accelerated the cab and began thinking about how to accomplish his goal.

Historical Note

On the night of November 7, 1876 an attempt was made to steal the body of Abraham Lincoln and hold it for both ransom money and the release of counterfeiter Ben Boyd from Joliet Penitentiary. The plan was to take the body to northern Indiana near the shores of Lake Michigan and bury it in a sand dune until the ransom demands were met.

The thieves were able to remove the lid from the Lincoln sarcophagus and remove the front marble plate, pulling the coffin partway out of the sarcophagus. Tipped by one of the men involved with the conspirators, Secret Service agents moved in and scared away the perpetrators, who temporarily escaped.

To prevent further attempts to steal the body, the coffin was moved out of the burial chamber to a place near the foundation of Lincoln's Tomb's obelisk, where it remained for two years, covered by wooden planks. The body was buried in another location within the foundation for another nine years before being returned to the catacomb and temporarily opened. The coffin was moved and opened again in later years, its journey not yet over.

 Joel Fox likes to say he has a long rap sheet in California politics. For three decades he has been a taxpayer and small business advocate, served on numerous state commissions, worked on many ballot issue campaigns, and advised numerous candidates, including Arnold Schwarzenegger in the historic gubernatorial recall election of 2003. He is an adjunct professor at the Graduate School of Public Policy at Pepperdine University.

Fox has authored hundreds of opinion pieces for many publications including the Wall Street Journal, USA Today, Los Angeles Times, and San Francisco Chronicle, as well as his well-respected blog on California business and politics, *Fox and Hounds Daily*.

His non-fiction works include a book, *The Legend of Proposition 13*, about California's most famous ballot measure, and a chapter in the book, *What Baseball Means to Me*, sanctioned by the Baseball Hall of Fame.

In 2008, Fox completed the Los Angeles FBI Citizens Academy program gaining a deeper understanding of the FBI and its mission.

Fox grew up in Massachusetts. He says he got his love for history breathing the air in the Boston area, daily driving past the homes of the presidents Adams and visiting many historical sites.